Love Trumps Logic

By

Lucy Balch

Beckoning Books
Published by Second Wind Publishing, LLC.
Kernersville

Beckoning Books
Second Wind Publishing, LLC
931-B South Main Street, Box 145
Kernersville, NC 27284

This book is a work of fiction. Names, characters, locations and events are either a product of the author's imagination, fictitious or used fictitiously. Any resemblance to any event, locale or person, living or dead, is purely coincidental.

Copyright © 2009 by Lucy Balch

All rights reserved, including the right of reproduction in whole or part in any format.

First Beckoning Books edition published August 2009. Beckoning Books, Running Angel, and all production design are trademarks of Second Wind Publishing, used under license.

For information regarding bulk purchases of this book, digital purchase and special discounts, please contact the publisher at *www.secondwindpublishing.com*

Cover design by Tracy Beltran

Manufactured in the United States of America

ISBN 978-1-935171-27-0

For David, Logan, and Zoe

Acknowledgement:

A big thank you to my sister, Karen, who guided my early attempts at writing and isn't shy about telling me exactly what she thinks. Thanks, too, to Joyce, Jeanette, Trina, Dianne, Stephanie, David, Marie and Mary—for their willingness to read early edits of my manuscript.

I'm also grateful to the Richmond Homeopathic Study group, for teaching me so much of what I know about homeopathy.

1.

"I'm done, Fergie," Lord Albert Beaumont said in his friend's ear, after the third matchmaking mama in one hour had introduced him to—this time—a freckle-faced girl with protruding front teeth. She had giggled so hard she hadn't been able to get one word out.

"Your reputation for liking redheads was the cause of that last introduction," Lord Ferguson said, trying to suppress a smile.

Beau took the last two glasses of champagne from a passing footman's tray and downed one of them in a single gulp. "No, it happened because I foolishly allowed your prattle about your cousin to lure me in here."

"It would all be worth it if we could find her. I don't lie when I say she's prettier than any chit here. Perhaps my aunt left early, since they're leaving for the country tomorrow."

"Let's go," Beau said, emptying the second glass as quickly as the first. He led the way toward the door, handing off the empty glasses to another footman on the way, and was ten feet away from freedom when a tall, silver-haired matron stepped in his way, grabbing the sleeve of his jacket.

Beau bit back a groan. "Good evening, Lady Pilchard."

"Good evening, indeed! What could possibly have brought you to the Stantons' party tonight?" the bony woman gushed, not letting him go. "Are you looking for a wife this season?"

Beau saw the greedy gleam of speculation in her eyes and repressed a shudder. Miss Priscilla Pilchard, the matron's daughter, was possibly the most shrill-voiced debutante to make an appearance in ten years, not to mention that she had paper-thin lips. "No. Lord Ferguson hoped to find his aunt here, and I accompanied him. His business is finished and we're leaving."

"Regardless, the gossip papers will say otherwise tomorrow. Perhaps you *should* be thinking of settling down. Aren't you nearly thirty?" she chided, tapping his captured arm with an ivory lace fan.

Beau smiled good-naturedly as he disengaged his sleeve from Lady Pilchard's impressive grip. "I've learned to ignore the gossip papers and I'm two years shy of thirty. Goodnight, Lady Pilchard."

Her eyes glazed over with delight at the sight of his smile, and Beau heard Fergie snort with laughter.

Beau eyed him sternly as they headed for the door. "Stop."

"Can't help myself when you titillate the matrons. That smile could soothe a colicky baby, I swear. Have you ever tried it on one?"

Beau ignored him and they finally escaped outside, into a night that was brightly lit by a full moon.

"Beau?" The sharp question came from a carriage that was stopped one block east of Lord and Lady Stantons' party.

Beau froze mid-step, causing Fergie to step on the heels of his boots. "Damn, this night cannot get any worse."

"Who is it?"

Beau didn't answer, instead stepping toward the carriage and bowing as the stunning Daphne Tarkington emerged. Her burgundy silk wrap perfectly framed her petite shoulders, and a carefully placed golden curl accentuated her décolletage. "Daphne, you look magnificent tonight."

He wasn't lying, but his admiration extended only as far as her face. She had turned out to be as ugly on the inside as she was beautiful on the outside. Within a month of *The Palaver* proclaiming gleefully that she was his new mistress, Beau was doing everything in his power to make her dismiss him. As much as he disliked her, he knew such an early dismissal initiated by him would be socially disastrous for her. He didn't want to ruin the woman, just disengage. He had made up an appointment at White's faro table this particular evening, and mentally kicked himself for not remembering that Lord and Lady Lovelace were throwing a much different sort of soiree next door to the Stantons' ball. One that Daphne had said she'd attend.

She was now giving Beau a smile that signaled neither happiness nor complaisance. "Did my eyes deceive me, or did I truly see you leaving the Stantons' ball for debutantes?"

"Your eyes did not deceive you," Beau said, squarely meeting her gaze. Her eyes sparkled with amusement at first, but grew ice-cold when it became obvious that he wasn't going to elaborate.

She waved a hand at the Lovelaces' entranceway. "Now that you're done playing with innocents, follow me."

"I have no intention of attending the Lovelaces' ball," Beau said, tired of games. Maybe it was a bit cruel, but he wanted to force her hand. He'd had enough.

Daphne's nostrils flared slightly, but that was the only indication of her fury. As insane as she was, she at least knew to keep her diatribes private. "I'll have Ridley send your things 'round," she finally said, and her slight shrug was for the benefit of the witnesses—Fergie, but also Lord and Lady Reddington, Mr. Bingham, and Lord Marshall—all of whom were happening by on their way to the Lovelaces' ball as well.

Beau wasn't fooled by the shrug; nonchalance was decidedly *not* the emotion this lady was feeling. He said a silent prayer of thanks for the onlookers. To Daphne he said, "As you wish," and inclined his head. He knew he'd never see his few items of clothing or his razor again. He'd bet good money that she'd use the razor to destroy the clothes, and throw his new phial of cedarwood oil into the dustbin. But that was a small price to pay for avoiding a nasty tête-à-tête. He was grateful to be done with her so easily.

Daphne gave him her dainty, cold hand with a look that might have made a weaker man quail in his Hessians. "Goodbye."

Beau mentally shuddered as he brushed a light kiss on it. He was glad those icy hands would never again touch his skin. "Goodbye."

Daphne turned away without another word or glance, her face a model of indifference. At the Lovelaces' door, she bent her head to hear Lord Marshall's comment, and her responsive laugh seemed genuine. Beau knew it wasn't but didn't care.

She disappeared inside, and Beau turned to find a gaping Fergie. "Come," he said, ignoring Lady Reddington's prying stare. He took his friend's arm and steered him across the street.

"You'd best watch your back, Beau. Her smile shot daggers at you."

"I'm not worried. What could she do? Besides, I'm going to avoid her as much as I can for a bit."

"Regardless, watch yourself. And stay away from my cousin. I thought her beauty might tempt you to change your heartless ways, but you can't turn a ground crawler into a clinging vine."

Beau laughed. "How much champagne did you drink? You're not making sense."

Fergie pretended to shiver. "You could have frozen fire with that exchange. Cold, my friend. Icy cold."

"If women were vegetables, Daphne Tarkington would be a pickle. And she breeds sour coldness wherever she goes."

"Are all women you've known given a vegetable equivalent?" Fergie asked, his gingery eyebrows twitching in amusement.

"Just the disappointing ones. Most are flowers."

"What flower was Miss Elliot?"

Beau stopped and took hold of his friend's arm, turning him so that they were facing one another. "I only told you of Daphne Tarkington's pickleness in self-defense, since you accused me of being heartless. I usually don't malign a woman in such a way. But enough is enough. And Miss Elliot's name should *never* be mentioned in the same conversation as Daphne Tarkington's."

"All right, all right! Sorry! And you're not heartless, but the whole thing gave me the shivers. You had not one spark of warmth between the two of you."

They continued walking as Beau explained. "Warmth dies in the presence of such bizarre malevolence. I don't think Daphne Tarkington has ever had a 'spark of warmth' in any situation. She favors control over love. Sadistic control—which is preferred by some, but not me."

"That's how it was, eh? Well, regardless, stay away from my cousin. She doesn't need your angry ex-mistresses wishing her dead. I foolishly planned this meeting because my aunt is about to try her hand at matchmaking. Apparently there's some mad scientist she wants Fiona to meet. It sounded strange, so I hoped to intervene on her behalf." They turned onto the Strand, heading for the hackney carriage stand where they hoped to find a carriage to take them to Gormier's.

"This evening makes me realize that I don't wish to involve myself with any debutantes at present—your cousin included. What I require now is a delectable new mistress who doesn't come close to resembling a vegetable. And one who has lovely warm hands."

Fergie grunted. "What have hands to do with anything? If you really must have perfect hands then it's good you didn't meet my cousin. They're her one flaw, I'm afraid. Rough. Short nails. Hideous, really."

"Why?" Beau asked, curious despite his decision to evade their meeting.

"She likes to dig in flower pots, and gloves—to paraphrase the excuse she gives her mother—don't allow her to feel the texture of the soil, or some such rot."

Beau eyed his friend doubtfully. "Perhaps *you* should refrain from matchmaking as well as your aunt."

"Hold on! Her intellect and beauty more than make up for her eccentricities. I doubt you've seen a more beautiful shade of red hair. It's as if the sun is continually shining on her head, even on the darkest of days. And her eye color is hazel without any of the mud, if you can envision it. Ah, here's one." Fergie hailed a hackney carriage and it pulled to a stop in front of them. "Gormier's," he said, stepping in and wrinkling his nose at the smell inside.

They continued their conversation inside the carriage.

"Tonight has made me realize that I'm still not ready for the hell called 'courtship.' Mamas breathing celery-tonic breath into my face, blushing young ladies barely able to converse, or, worse, attempting to flirt—" Beau shook his head as he pulled the dirty window flap aside, preferring London's stale air to the smell of vomit. "Your cousin—wonderful as she undoubtedly is—is destined to be snapped up by someone other than me this season."

"What about your talk of heirs last night?"

"I had a letter from my parents yesterday. My mother brought me up to speed on estate news, and my niece and nephews' latest exploits—Elizabeth and her family visited Castlewood recently—but in a postscript my father asked for news of an engagement. It was his way of saying that he wishes to see me married—soon, since his illness has progressed to the bedridden stage."

The ride became bumpier as the carriage turned off Fleet Street and onto a road that led toward Blackfriar Bridge.

Beau continued, his speech uneven because of the jolting, "I'd love to oblige him, but I can't stomach courtship at present. He'll have to understand."

"I sometimes wonder if you're not still pining after Miss Elliot."

Beau snorted. "Of course I'm not. I don't 'pine,' Fergie. That was six years ago, for God's sake, and she's been married to Lord Wolfrey for the last five of them."

"Didn't mean to offend ... I say, how's your mother holding up?"

"She writes that her anxiety about my father is showing in her hair, which is quickly turning white. She tries not to think too far ahead."

They continued on in silence, their mutual destination one of the seedier gaming hells because of its location near the docks. They liked it because newer money was allowed to mix with old, and merchants, they had discovered, frequently had deep pockets.

***

Miss Fiona Fairmont picked a nail file off her dressing table and impatiently went to work on a broken pinky nail. Her thorough scrubbing had gotten rid of the dirt, but now she had several jagged edges to contend with. The nightshade's repotting was the culprit this time.

Her younger sister, Felicity, shook her head as she watched. "Let me, or you won't have anything left!" After Fiona obligingly handed her the nail file, she added, "I thought Mother told you to wear gloves."

"She did."

Felicity finished the pinky nail and began to expertly file Fiona's thumbnail. "She might have a point, you know. If you ever *accept* a proposal, your future husband will surely think these are awful."

"My future husband will have to love nightshade, nettles and the poison nut as much as I do. Then he'll understand their need for repotting."

"Lord Vandermill thought you were a madwoman—or worse, a murderess—when you mentioned nightshade at tea last week. Did you see how big his eyes got? I thought for sure I'd choke; it was so funny. The fact that he still proposed the next day ... but then you refused him! I thought Mother would faint when she heard."

Fiona tapped impatiently with her free hand. She loathed having to spend so much time tidying her nails, all for the sake of a successful season. They only got dirty again when she tended her plants. "I wish Mother wouldn't take my season so seriously."

"Tell me again, *why* did you refuse him?"

"We have no common interests. I want, at the very least, to have an occasionally interesting conversation with the man I marry," Fiona said, pulling her hand away from her sister's filing and moving over to the comfy chaise longue that sat next to her fireplace. It was her favorite place to read.

"Common interests!" Felicity repeated, tossing the nail file down and laughing. "Poor Mother. If you don't have 'common interests' with this scientist you're meeting she'll probably collapse."

"Why must I marry by the end of my first season? Women often take two or three seasons to marry. I see no reason to rush." Fiona picked her book up off the floor where she'd left it, opening to the bookmark.

"A Witherspoon woman doesn't take more than one season to marry," Felicity said, imitating her mother's reedy voice. She continued, giggling now, "Mother *is* desperate, dragging us all to the country to see if this mad scientist will suit—Fergie's words, not mine," she added hastily, when she saw Fiona's frown. "Imagine this: you won't have to change your monograms if you marry Lord Featherstone, and he's rich enough to hire ten gardeners to tend your flower pots, if that's what they require."

Fiona shook her head and began to read, but Felicity wasn't put off. "Give him a chance, Fiona! Do you want to be an old spinster?" When she didn't get an answer she moved closer, shoving Fiona's feet to one side and plopping onto the end of the chaise longue. "Lord Diggerton let you talk about your books. He'd even bring them up. Why did you refuse his offer?"

Fiona sighed and put her book face down on her outstretched legs. "He was pretending, Felicity. He didn't *really* care about anything but horses. Besides, he had horrid breath."

Felicity gasped. "How—did you kiss him?" She was younger by two years and wouldn't experience a season in London until she, too, was eighteen, but she pushed Fiona for information whenever she could, rarely getting satisfactory answers.

"Almost."

"Tell me *everything*, Fiona. Where were you? What did

he say? What did *you* say?"

Fiona laughed. Her sister's eagerness about such matters was so different from the reticence that she felt.

"This isn't funny! Mother won't talk about kisses, so you *must*. She always gives me that pinched look, and tells me not to allow them until I've accepted a proposal, but I know that's nonsense."

"Yes, I know. Let's see." Fiona thought back, trying to pull the purposely buried memory back into focus. "He took me for a ride in Hyde Park and it started to rain. He opened an umbrella and asked if I'd grant him a kiss under it. I stupidly said 'yes' and he leaned toward me, but then he made the mistake of opening his mouth. The smell was quite bad. Do you remember when Grandfather Witherspoon passed gas last Christmas? I was reminded of that."

"Oh, that's nasty! Did you tell him?"

"What, that his breath reminded me of my grandfather's gas? Of course not! I couldn't bring myself to say anything, but I turned my face so that he kissed my cheek. The next day I noticed him smelling like parsley, but I avoided carriage rides and private walks with him despite that. No point in misleading a man, although he didn't take the hint. He proposed anyway, right in front of Mother."

"Poor Lord Diggerton. So smitten. Always so desperate to please."

"A man shouldn't be 'desperate to please.' If he has to struggle for it, then the match isn't right. Marriage partners should have an equal share in pleasing each other."

"Did Lord Vandermill kiss you?"

"Yes, and his kiss wasn't offensive, but—" Fiona paused, trying to remember exactly why she hadn't liked it. "It was as boring as he is," she said, shrugging.

"Mother would faint if she knew."

"Yes, I know. That's why I don't tell her. And you won't either."

"But how can you say he's boring? Caroline and Margaret think he's the catch of the season, if you aren't counting tenacious bachelors like Lord Albert Beaumont.

Speaking of him, oh, my goodness, did you see *The Palaver* this morning? He was at the Stantons' debutante party last night. He even danced with Harriet! *And* he's already done with Daphne Tarkington. They had a little scene right in the middle of the street, outside the Lovelaces.' Do you think he's looking for a wife?"

"Doubtful," Fiona responded vaguely, turning her book back over.

"I wish he'd wait two years. What I wouldn't give to dance with him. He'll be the catch of the century," Felicity sighed. She stood and began to waltz around Fiona, her hands poised in an imaginary dance with Lord Albert.

"Every woman feels that way about him, and as a consequence he's spoiled," Fiona said. "Take the number of mistresses he's had, if the gossip papers can be believed. Why so many? Does he grow bored? Is he so easily swayed by newness? If he's looking for a wife, I pity whomever he chooses. She'll be the woman *du jour* for about a month, and then she'll have to endure constant gossip as each new mistress is discussed at length."

Felicity's dance came to an abrupt halt. "He can fall in love too! I think he was engaged when he was younger," she protested.

"But, you see, it didn't last, did it? His type of love is shallow. It's easily shattered once a new beauty distracts him from one who's grown too familiar. I pity *him*, really."

"He doesn't need pity! He needs to find someone as beautiful as he is, and only you fit that description."

Fiona shook her head dismissively. "Being his wife would be a nightmare. For both of us really, since I wouldn't give him the daily dose of admiration that I'm sure he requires. He would find me quite lacking in comparison to what he's used to."

"He'd adore you. He wouldn't be able to help it," Felicity said, leaning over the back of the chaise longue to give her sister a quick kiss on the cheek.

"I don't want his adoration. Wouldn't it be interesting if debutantes were required to wear masquerade masks? Then we'd all know that proposals were based on something other than our pretty faces. I'd like that."

Felicity groaned. "You and Lord Albert would be perfect together ... two souls equally afflicted with the curse of beauty."

Fiona laughed, but said, "Lord Albert's vanity and selfishness aren't what I want in a husband. The man I marry will find gaming, horseracing, and all those types of things boring. He'll be a philanthropist, thinking of others' needs before his own."

Felicity made a face. "That's not a man you're looking for, that's a monk."

"Monks are men, Felicity. Now leave, please. I want to read." Fiona bent her head, looking determinedly at the page in front of her.

"You're hopeless. And your beauty is *totally* wasted. Why couldn't I have been given your looks? Instead I have the boring brown hair and the blue eyes. It just isn't fair!"

Fiona looked up again, exasperated but laughing, "You're beautiful, Felicity! Be *glad* you don't have red hair. It can be a curse."

"Why?" Felicity stopped at the door, her face glowing with interest.

"It's unusual, so it's often the topic of conversation with new acquaintances. I cannot count how many times I've been forced to recite the various redheads in our family tree."

"That *would* be boring. Fiona, do you really think I'm beautiful?" Felicity asked hopefully.

"Absolutely!"

"You're a dear. I almost don't want you to marry, since I'll miss you so much," Felicity said, her full lips curving into an infectious grin. "I'll leave you alone now."

Felicity scooted from the room, pulling the door shut with a bang. Fiona forgot about suitors, maternal expectations, and silly sisters as she got to the more interesting business of finishing her book.

2.

Beau cracked open one eye, the one that wasn't in the direct beam of sunlight streaming through bed curtains that had stupidly been left open. How in God's name had he forgotten to close them? Had he been that drunk? And why had reliable Smithers neglected to do it for him? He got his answer when he felt a hand touch his bare chest, ruffling the dark hairs over his left nipple.

He stifled a groan as memory flooded back. Smithers had not closed the curtains for him because Smithers wasn't here—here being Mrs. Beatrice Marsdon's house, more specifically Beatrice's bed. Yes, the frilly pink lace on those damned open curtains confirmed it.

After finding Gormier's tediously overcrowded with young bucks—the sort who ruined the gambling tables for the more seasoned players—he and Fergie had gone to one of Mrs. Marsdon's masquerade parties. Widowed at the age of thirty-five and determined not to be a stuffy dowager, Mrs. Marsdon spent a sizeable portion of her dead husband's money on entertainment. Besides the proper musicales and balls that she threw on a regular basis, she held a masquerade party on the first Saturday of every month, and they were notorious for being the beginning—and end—of many a naughty relationship. The virginal debutantes never even knew of these parties, except perhaps in whispered rumors.

Mrs. Marsdon had also played hostess to a private party in her bedroom on this particular Saturday, with Beau as her sole guest. She was teasing both his nipples now, watching in interest as his morning erection jerked in response. When he grabbed her wrist she gasped playfully and met his gaze. "Oh! Am I tickling you? That wasn't my intent, I can assure you!"

"No? Because I was about to take up the gauntlet, and I *never* lose a tickling contest," he warned, pulling her arm over her head and shifting his gaze to her armpit. Beatrice smelled good, her delicious natural odor mixing with traces of lavender water and fennel. She was giggling now, and daring him to carry out his threat by running her free hand lightly down his stomach.

Never one to shirk a dare, Beau reached his fingers into her armpit and tickled, causing a loud squeal of delight. But he quickly realized something. He wasn't in the mood to play this game and he wasn't in the mood for what typically would follow. His deflated erection told the tale better than words could have, but Beatrice hadn't noticed it. She had grabbed his tickling fingers and clutched them to the side of her breast to stop their motion.

Beau abruptly let go of her wrist and pulled his hand free. He sat on the edge of the bed, but couldn't stand because his head swam. Silently cursing last night's rum punch, he rubbed his temples. "I apologize, Beatrice, but I just remembered that I have a rather urgent appointment with my banker today. Do you have any idea what time it is?" he asked, squinting up at the light coming through the window. Was that a morning or afternoon sun?

In Beau's experience, a woman typically reacted with forced nonchalance when faced with such an excuse, but Beatrice wasn't playing that game. "On Sunday?" she asked, her voice disbelieving.

Beau glanced over his shoulder and gave her a smile that took most of the shadows from her eyes. "It does seem odd, doesn't it? We meet Sundays so we can play cards afterward. He's a stickler about keeping to his banking hours the rest of the week, never allowing for cards."

"But ... this early?" Beatrice said, trailing the line of Beau's spine with her finger, teasing where it ended. "Just when we're starting to have fun? Not that last night wasn't fun," she quickly corrected. "But the punch besotted us so thoroughly, I barely remember anything." She was pouting prettily now, but Beau's body remained disengaged—a fact that surprised him. Under normal circumstances he'd stay and frolic with this undeniably pretty woman all morning, especially since he barely remembered bedding her in the first place. But today he didn't want to. Maybe his experience with Daphne had made a deeper—more disturbing—impression than originally thought.

He stood and stretched hugely, yawning, and padded to the window. "I thought that looked like a morning sun," he said, closing the curtains for his pounding head's sake. He saw his breeches in an untidy ball on the floor and picked them up, shaking out as many wrinkles as he could.

"Don't go. Not yet," Beatrice said, interrupting his thoughts. He turned to look at her after plucking his shirt from her bedpost.

Her eyes pleaded, and against his better judgment he reached out to stroke her face, hating that he was hurting her. She leaned her face into his hand, closing her eyes, and he felt a puff of breath on his wrist as she gave a small, involuntary pant.

She put her hand over his, holding it against her face. He sat down on the bed again, watching her pouty bottom lip catch in her teeth. It must have been those lips that had captured his interest last night. They were indeed kissable, and her wondrously enticing scent was an asset she didn't even know she had.

He leaned over and kissed her lips because he wanted to make them smile one more time before he left. He remembered now that when they turned up at the corners they made a perfect cupid's bow and he wanted to see that again.

She rewarded him with a shaky smile but her eyes, when she opened them, glistened with tears.

"Why tears?" he whispered.

"I don't want you to leave yet. Please. It would absolutely ruin my day if you did," she said, worriedly wiping a tear as it rolled down her cheek.

Beau's resolve to leave wavered, not because he wanted

to stay—he still didn't—but he knew his reputation was such that to leave now would be a huge slap in her face, and she didn't deserve that. She was a surprisingly guileless woman, and far from the vegetable realm, so why didn't he wholeheartedly want to stay?

That was a question he'd examine later. For now, he'd grant Beatrice her wish. His body would oblige him if he focused on those lips long enough. Dropping his clothes back onto the floor, he leaned in to brush a lingering kiss on her plump lips.

"That appointment can wait then?" she whispered against his mouth.

"It can wait," he muttered, and his next kiss pushed her back onto her pillows.

***

"You *walked* from Mrs. Marsdon's abode? With your cravat crumpled in such a manner?" Smithers asked, his puckered lips signaling his displeasure.

"As I was obviously in evening wear, it shouldn't harm your reputation. *My* reputation is already in tatters, so no harm there," Beau said cynically, pulling the offending cravat off and handing it to Smithers.

He took it gingerly and assessed the damage. "Mrs. Marsdon's masquerade party must have run exceedingly late." In response to Beau's mind-your-own-business look, he added, "Will Mrs. Marsdon be filling Daphne Tarkington's shoes, my lord?"

"No, Smithers, she will not," Beau said, propping on the edge of his bed in order to get his boots pulled off. Smithers obliged, expertly removing one and reaching for the other one.

"Ah, I see," he said knowingly, frowning at the scuffmarks on the heel of one boot.

"No, you don't." Standing to stretch, Beau added, "Beatrice is perfection, especially her lips. But she made me realize something." He paused, sinking back onto his bed with a huge yawn.

"And you realized—?" Smithers prompted, rubbing at the scuff with his fingertip.

"I don't know, exactly. Maybe I need to be on my own for a bit. Last night I let Fergie talk me into going to a debutante ball, but that was dreadful. Then, later on—" Beau paused and shrugged.

"I think you're ready to find a bride, sir," Smithers said matter-of-factly, buffing the boot now with a soft cloth he'd pulled from his pocket.

Beau snorted. "You wouldn't say that if you'd seen me at the Stantons'. I was—"

Two footmen entered with the makings of his bath, and he was grateful for the interruption because he didn't quite know how to describe his feelings. Being "on the market," even unofficially, had felt contrived, without any real pleasure attached. Yes, he had done it as a younger man, but he didn't have the stomach for it anymore.

He stood and stripped off his clothes, then stepped into his waiting bath with a grateful sigh.

The footmen left and Smithers continued to buff the scuffed boot for another full minute without speaking. Finally satisfied with his result, he put the boot next to its mate and turned. "Pardon me, sir. But if you're not going to take a mistress, and you're not going to find a bride, what are you going to do?"

"Be alone for a bit, like I said," Beau murmured sleepily closing his eyes to better enjoy the steamy warmth.

Smithers made a soft noise of disagreement as he gathered the clothes that Beau had just abandoned. It was barely audible, but it made Beau open his eyes.

"What does that mean?" he asked.

"What does what mean?" Smithers responded, turning to face Beau with a puzzled expression.

"That noise you made. Like you don't think I can be alone."

"You said something similar after Miss Elliot broke your engagement. If memory serves me correctly you were going to ignore all women for at least a year. Isn't that what you said, sir? A year?" Smithers cocked an eyebrow doubtfully.

"You do me a disservice, Smithers. That was a broken heart talking, but this is different ... much less emotional." He closed his eyes again and deeply inhaled the steam.

"Do you want my opinion, sir?"

"You'll tell me regardless. What?"

Smithers folded the clothes over his arm, smoothing them as he spoke. "I think you're ready for marriage, and I think you'll find a bride this year."

Beau looked at him in tired amazement. "Did you hear one word I said earlier?"

"I did, but I'll wager you're wrong."

"Besides, I'm leaving for Castlewood tomorrow, so there will be no more debutante balls for this gentleman any time soon." He gave another huge yawn. Beatrice had truly worn him out, mentally and physically.

Smithers frowned. "A spontaneous decision, sir? You usually give me warning, so that I can notify your mother."

"She won't mind. And, Smithers, I'll make you that wager. If I'm not engaged by the end of this year, I win. If I am, you win. What do you say?" Beau asked, his eyes glinting mischievously.

"The details, sir?"

Beau thoughtfully soaped the foot balanced on his knee. "If I win, you have to reveal the name of your lady friend."

"And if I win?"

"A bonus of a thousand pounds," Beau threw out, overgenerous since he was sure that Smithers would lose.

"I accept your offer," Smithers said, without missing a beat.

"Finally, your secret will be mine!" Gleefully tossing his soap in the air, Beau missed it on the way down. It splashed back into the water, a few drops finding Smithers' clad leg.

"Don't be so sure, my lord," Smithers replied grimly. He put a towel warmed by the fire within Beau's reach, and left for a leisurely cup of tea and the morning newspaper.

***

Lady Winifred Fairmont poured herself another cup of tea. Her husband and her younger daughter, Felicity, had taken themselves off after one cup, and here was her opportunity to discuss the upcoming trip with Fiona—if she could tear her daughter away from her book, she thought bitterly. She watched Fiona turn another page, so absorbed that she hadn't noticed her mother's attention, her legs tucked under her skirt in a most unladylike fashion. She was sitting on the rose velvet window seat, her favorite place to read in the warmer months.

Lady Winifred daintily cleared her throat, but Fiona kept reading. With an exasperated sigh she said, "Fiona, dearest, I'd like to talk to you for a few moments. Will you please put your book down?"

"Yes, Mother, of course," Fiona responded. She read for another few seconds, chewing on her bottom lip, and then reluctantly closed her book on her finger as she looked up and gave her mother a questioning smile.

Lady Winifred sighed again, this time inwardly. She fervently wanted this conversation to end civilly, so she picked her words carefully. "I sent Lady Haresford a note this morning, telling her we cannot attend her ball. It's the first time I'll be missing her yearly event, but I'm willing to do so because of the importance of this introduction to Lord Featherstone. It's hard to imagine a man who wishes to stay in the country during the entire season, but he supposedly is that intrigued with his studies. He sounds perfectly suited to you, does he not?" How she wished her daughter was a more typical debutante, and how she wished she could use Fiona's books as kindling. They wouldn't have to buy coal for a year if she dared.

"I won't know if he's suited until I've met him, Mother. But if you want to attend Lady Haresford's ball, we can postpone this trip."

"Indeed not! And miss the Duchess of Kendal's ball next month? I'm hoping, dearest, that we'll be able to announce your engagement by then."

Fiona laughed in amazement. "Mother, you must lower your expectations regarding this meeting. If anything comes of it, it will be nothing short of a miracle."

"There! That's exactly the attitude that I cannot bear, Fiona," Lady Winifred exclaimed, clattering her half-empty cup into its saucer. The noise made her wince, and she remembered that it was only her eldest daughter who could provoke such lapses in her calm. "Why do you say that?" she demanded.

Fiona took a deep breath, and Lady Winifred said a silent prayer that her daughter would keep her temper. These types of conversations sometimes led to angry words, which inevitably made Lady Winifred cry. She hated being the one to cry, while Fiona remained dry-eyed, but her daughter could be sharp-tongued when annoyed.

"I think it's precipitous to plan engagement announcements when I haven't yet met Lord Featherstone. Can we not simply wait and see what happens? *He* may not be interested in marriage at present, especially since he isn't here in London this season," Fiona said. Her exaggerated patience irritated Lady Winifred more than a raised voice would have done.

But beyond simple irritation, she felt resentment. Her daughter seemed too willing to blame Lord Featherstone if the splendid match failed, rather than admitting any disinclination of her own to comply with the plan. Why was she even bothering with the trip, when Fiona was going to ruin everything? Was the famous Witherspoon record worth preserving in the face of such a headache? Maybe they should attend Lady Haresford's ball after all.

She smiled, not wanting Fiona to know how annoyed she was. "I've got the perfect solution," she said brightly. "I'll lower my expectations about this meeting if you'll agree to lower your expectations about what constitutes a good match. I think you're expecting your future husband to have a halo around his head, or some such nonsense, and I must tell you, Fiona: he won't."

"Not a halo. Just intelligence and an ability to look past my face and like who I really am."

Fiona's determination disconcerted her mother, who sometimes felt that she was the one getting the lecture, instead of the other way around. Nevertheless, she persisted.

"You'll be hard pressed to find a man who doesn't appreciate your beauty. You'll have to marry a blind man for that."

"Ah! I believe you may have the solution, Mother. Perhaps Lord Featherstone will let me blindfold him. What do you think?" Fiona asked, her deadpan face hiding a laugh.

Lady Winifred didn't understand Fiona's sense of humor and never would. "Please stop being ridiculous. Of course you can't blindfold him, and if he appears to be enamored of your looks do not hold it against him. You are one of the most beautiful young women to be presented in a long time. *Relish* the appreciation of others instead of dreading it."

"It's not the appreciation itself that I mind. But when a man appreciates me to the point of losing himself I find his company intolerable. As Lord Diggerton did when he took up the study of plants. He never would have bought *Herbs: Function and Growth* on his own. He did it to impress me, not realizing that his pretense had the opposite effect. Lord Vandermill went to the other extreme; I couldn't believe his pride in telling me that he'd never bought a book in his life. I'm sure he thought he'd 'cure' me of reading once I became his wife." Fiona shook her head in disbelief, putting a bookmark where her finger had been. Leaving her book on the window seat, she joined her mother by the tea tray.

"I'll be sure to tell Lord Featherstone to take care if he wishes to purchase books while wooing you. He must only purchase those that have nothing to do with your interests," Lady Winifred protested. "And perhaps I should tell him to avoid complimenting you as well."

"Who's being ridiculous now?" Fiona said, picking out a watercress and tomato sandwich. "And how do you know he'll want to 'woo' me? Be prepared, Mother. This trip will probably turn out to be a complete waste of time."

Lady Winifred bit the inside of her lip to quell her urge to cry. Were her plans for naught? But then she remembered something. "It might interest you to know that Lady Amelia told Lord Featherstone and his aunt, Lady Richland, about you—at my urging—and that your interest in plants and their medicinal qualities intrigued him. Believe me, I'd never pull you away from your season unless I had some assurance that—" she pursed her lips, not wanting to use the word "engagement" with her daughter's present mood.

Fiona's hand, holding her last bite of sandwich, paused halfway to her mouth. "Really? He actually wanted to meet me *because* of the plants, not in spite of them?"

"Yes, and I can see that I finally have your interest," Lady Winifred said, relief forcing a begrudging smile. "Fiona, dearest, please—I beg of you—be on your best behavior. Do not put Lord Featherstone off with talk about your love of reading novels and such. I suppose you must mention the plant books, but don't let him know that you read daily."

"I'm not going to lie to him, Mother," Fiona said, determination quickly replacing the sparkle of interest.

"I'm not asking you to lie," Lady Winifred responded quickly, clasping her hands nervously. "Simply do not bring up the subject of books. And if, by some unfortunate coincidence, *he* brings up the subject, then give noncommittal answers and change the subject as quickly as you can."

Fiona's chin bunched, a sign that she was getting angry. "To hear you talk, books are as bad a habit as laudanum. Yet Aunt Rose somehow managed to snare Uncle Roddy, despite the fact that she stays sauced all day." She tossed her uneaten last bite onto her plate with too much force.

Lady Winifred closed her eyes. "Please refrain from crude language, and do not throw food about."

"I didn't throw it," Fiona objected.

"Your aunt was worth twenty thousand pounds. You are not so fortunate. Books are for bluestockings, Fiona, and as a general rule, men do not care for bluestockings. Perhaps Lord Featherstone will be different, but one never knows. That's why I suggest that you change the subject if books are mentioned."

"I'm not going to lie to him," Fiona repeated through clenched teeth, and her mother knew that further conversation would be a mistake.

She stood and put her teacup on the tray with careful deliberation. "I'll leave you now. I need to verify that my new suede gloves are packed." She walked to the door, feeling her daughter's angry eyes following her as she went. Taking a calming breath, she turned and faced Fiona in the doorway. "Fiona, dear, I love you and only want what's best for you."

Her words relaxed Fiona's tense face. "I love you too, Mother." But the tiredness in Fiona's voice made her mother sad. She gave her daughter a bittersweet smile and left, wondering why she had bothered to have the conversation at all. Such exchanges never accomplished what she hoped they would.

***

Fiona stared at the empty doorway, wishing that those endearing words could feel real instead of forced. She and her mother said them too often, as if they were trying to convince themselves of it.

She returned to the window seat and picked up the book of Shakespeare sonnets she'd been reading, absentmindedly rubbing its soft leather binding.

Once again, her mother had shown a complete disregard for everything she cherished. Worse, she had shown an utter dislike for the woman Fiona had turned out to be. Her mother loved her, she knew that, but she neither understood nor liked her, and the sting of that fact never ceased to hurt.

Fiona blinked away a tear and allowed Shakespeare to soothe away her troubled thoughts.

3.

Lord and Lady Hasselton's house party was smaller than Fiona expected. Other than herself, her sister, her parents, and Lord Featherstone, it included Lord and Lady Skeffington, who were Lady Amelia Hasselton's ancient grandparents from Cornwall; the Earl and Countess of Richland, who were Lord Featherstone's aunt and uncle; and Lady Amelia's niece, Emily—invited so that Felicity would have a companion for the duration of the party.

Introductions took place during an extended tea in the Hasseltons' comfortable drawing room. Travel-weary guests were encouraged to partake of sandwiches and tea before getting a tour of the house, to see Lady Amelia's impressive art collection.

Lady Winifred chose to take tea in her bedroom, but the rest of the Fairmonts were introduced to the Richlands and the Skeffingtons, who had arrived ahead of them and were already midway through their tea. Lord Featherstone was conspicuously absent.

"Our nephew is busy, as usual, in his laboratory," Lady Richland explained. "You'll meet him at dinner tonight."

The bluntness of it rendered Fiona almost speechless. "Oh? Yes?"

Lord Richland shyly ducked his head in agreement, and Fiona was struck by his mousiness—in his personality and expression, but also in his finely textured, gray-brown hair. Strangely, the Countess' round face, watchful eyes and almost nonexistent lips reminded Fiona of a cat.

Lord Skeffington took Fiona's hand next, his cloudy eyes brightening with admiration. "You're beautiful, my dear! Just the thing to get Lord Featherstone out of his books."

"I ... Thank you, sir."

Felicity stifled a giggle and Fiona turned to give her a chilly glance. She sat stiffly next to her father, wishing herself back in London, and accepted a cup of tea from Lady Hasselton with a nod of thanks. While Felicity and her father were carefully sipping their steaming cups of tea, Fiona added extra milk to hers so that she could gulp it. Finishing quickly, she excused herself from the art tour by pleading travel fatigue and left, not caring if she was perceived as rude.

She went in search of her mother, asking the housekeeper to show her the way, and barged into her mother's room without knocking. Lady Winifred was lying down and half asleep, obviously trying to counteract a real case of travel fatigue.

"Mother, you didn't tell me this was to be such a blatant matchmaking. No other unmarried adults present except Lord Featherstone and myself? It's humiliating," she said, sitting at the dressing table and picking up her mother's bottle of lavender water. She splashed herself liberally, hoping that the calming scent would serve its purpose.

Lady Winifred sat up to place another pillow behind her back, plumping them both carefully before answering. "Dearest, why pretend? Lord Featherstone won't tear himself away from his hobby long enough to look for a wife, and your criteria for a husband is highly specific. Every indication points to your suiting one another very well. Why bother inviting more people to confuse the matter?"

"It's embarrassing, that's why. How do you expect me to converse normally with someone who's been told—even if it's not true—that I'm his one chance at marriage, and he, mine?" Fiona complained.

"Trust me. Lord Featherstone won't think twice about it. He's too absorbed in his studies."

And for once her mother was right.

***

"Meeting Samuel Hahnemann was the *highlight* of your

trip?" Fiona asked, putting down her fork. "Who is he?" She had taken a bite of the salmon, but didn't care for it since it was smothered in a sickly sweet sauce.

Lord Henry Featherstone smiled. He had a nice smile, with even teeth and a wide mouth. His lips might be a tad thin, but they went well with his thin nose and close-set, gray eyes. He was not a handsome man, but his smile made him attractive. And—fortunately for him—he didn't resemble his uncle at all.

"You've not heard of him?" he asked, surprise etched on his face. "I thought—well—that you might have." He shook his head, taking another bite of salmon, oblivious to the syrupy ruination of it.

"If you tell me who Samuel Hahnemann is, then perhaps I can explain why you made the mistake," Fiona said, pleasantly surprised. Lord Featherstone had yet to take on the glazed look that signaled unadulterated admiration, and he had not once looked at her cleavage. Nor had he asked her to name the source of her red hair.

"He's a man who'll be talked about—and read about—for years to come. A man who devotes his life to the worthy cause of homeopathy. I plan to follow his lead wherever I can, but my contributions will seem paltry in comparison."

"I read an article in *The Times* about homeopathy last summer. It's been deemed poppycock, although I felt skepticism because of the vehement tone used. Herbal remedies are often maligned in the same way."

"I'm glad to hear that you don't believe everything you read in *The Times*. Homeopathy is certainly not poppycock. What's poppycock is that its detractors cannot agree as to whether it's an unprecedented danger or a simple placebo, but I can easily refute both. It isn't a placebo if it helps babies as well as adults, is it? And it is no more dangerous than the treatments used by the prominent 'physicians' of today, who use undiluted mercury and bloodletting. Hahnemann has discovered that mercury minimized to its molecular form is infinitely safer—and more effective—than the crude substance. Mark my words, Miss Fairmont, the potentized remedies that Hahnemann is developing threaten to discredit those very men, and that is why they are desperate to discredit homeopathy—before it ruins them."

"But, what exactly is it? The article in *The Times* said it's no more than mesmerization specific to medicine. That people are given nothing but sugar pills and told they will be cured—placebo effect, as you said. You also said that mercury is changed into a molecular form, but what does that mean exactly?" Fiona asked, so fascinated she hadn't picked her fork back up to try the turnips.

Across the table and two seats down, Fiona's mother watched her daughter and Lord Featherstone and allowed herself to hope. Finally, a man was winning smiles and lively conversation from Fiona instead of suppressed yawns and a puckered brow.

"A substance is diluted with distilled water and grain alcohol," Lord Featherstone explained. "And then it is shaken—succussed—like this." He clumsily clattered his fork onto his plate and closed his fingers around an imaginary bottle, pretending to hit the bottom of it firmly against the palm of his other hand. Lady Skeffington—on his other side—started and turned in her chair to stare at him down her thin nose.

Lord Featherstone continued, heedless of her disapproval. "How many times it is diluted and shaken determines the strength of it. Amazingly, the more dilute, the stronger. It's as if the shaking somehow wakes the substance up, and the more it's shaken, the more awake—powerful—it becomes. The water acts as the medium in which it can express itself. The alcohol preserves it." Lord Featherstone paused because Fiona looked puzzled, but then he said, "I could chatter away all night about it, and you still mightn't understand. I can show you my laboratory, if you're interested."

Fiona noticed Lady Skeffington's disapprobation, and it perversely served to increase her interest. Here was a man whose actions weren't dictated by society's rules. He made his own rules. "I'd love to see your laboratory," she gushed, immediately realizing that she'd sounded like an overeager schoolgirl. She added, more sedately, "So homeopathy is different from herbal medicine because the amount of plant used to treat is much smaller?"

Lord Featherstone explained further, not bothered in the least by Fiona's childish exuberance—if he even noticed it. "Yes and no. Amounts used are certainly smaller, but they're infinitely more powerful as well. Also, Hahnemann does not limit himself to vegetation. At the talk I heard in Germany, sulphur was the topic."

"Sulphur? I've heard of sulphuric water being curative in spas, but only in the form of a bath."

"Imagine getting a curative effect from drinking a sip of water that had such a diluted amount of sulphur in it that you couldn't smell it anymore."

"Oh, my. Go on," Fiona said.

"It's so diluted that it is now energy. Molecules. You therefore cannot smell it, but its essence remains, able to cure if the disease has a similar energy. Like cures like, in homeopathy. Hahnemann has proven sulphur, which means that he gave it to healthy individuals until a pattern of symptoms emerged to define it. And think of all the substances in the world—animal, vegetable, and mineral. Homeopaths have their work cut out for them in all the provings that lie ahead, and that is where I hope to contribute most. Once homeopathic remedies have exceeded herbal remedies in terms of number and efficiency, I predict that herbal medicine will be a thing of the past. It could happen as soon as next century," Lord Featherstone said, not realizing that in so saying he had shocked Fiona thoroughly.

"How so?"

"As I said, I could chatter about it all night—all week in fact. But you really need to see it in action. I didn't quite believe the truth of it either, until I experienced it firsthand."

He took a sip of wine, apparently finished, so Fiona prompted, "What happened?"

Lord Featherstone frowned, remembering. "I burned myself rather badly during my travels. A scalding cup of chocolate found its way into my lap whilst I was in Germany. Several of Hahnemann's followers were staying at the same inn as I was, for he was going to be lecturing again the next day, and one of them gave me potentized Spanish fly. The hideous pain diminished miraculously. I couldn't believe it at first. Thought it was mere coincidence. But then the pain returned after a few hours, and I was given a second dose. Well, the pain disappeared in the same way and this time stayed away. I haven't questioned homeopathy's validity since. I stayed on in Germany to learn as much as I could about it."

"That's incredible," Fiona said. Not wanting this truly interesting man to think her trite, she added, "I look forward to seeing it in action, and maybe I can tell you about some of the herbs you'll be diluting."

She was rewarded by Lord Featherstone's warm smile. "I can give you and your family a tour of my laboratory—tomorrow, if you'd like. It's close by, on my uncle's property. I haven't bothered to set up a laboratory on my own property yet. Not when I have a perfectly good one here." Lord Featherstone paused to clear his throat. He gave Fiona a smile tinged with embarrassment. "The truth of the matter is that my aunt and uncle dote on me and don't wish me to leave. I'm like a son to them." He dabbed his mouth with his napkin. "I'll enjoy your company. I rarely get a chance to discuss my passion. People usually change the subject rather quickly. My aunt and uncle try to listen, but cannot hide their boredom for long."

Fiona knew exactly how he felt. "I would like very much to tour your laboratory tomorrow." My God, had her mother really been responsible for putting this fascinating man in her way? She never would have believed it possible.

***

"Before I die, I wish to see you married," the Marquess wheezed, giving his son a baleful glance. "Your mother and I married for love, but perhaps you need to look for a bride whom you could grow to love. Many successful marriages begin just that way." He pulled his covers higher with shaking hands. His head, lifted to give emphasis, fell back onto his pillows and he closed eyes that were deep hollows in a yellowish, gaunt face. "If not a wedding, at least an engagement," he said, adding in a whisper, "I'm running out of time."

"Father, I'll try. For you, I'll try," Beau said, his heart breaking with the knowledge that even his best efforts would probably come to nothing. As much as he loved his father he couldn't resign himself to a lifetime of discontent.

Beau squeezed his father's frail hand gently. What he wanted to do was give him an enormous hug, but those days were long gone. His father was too fragile now.

"I'll let you rest," Beau said. He was halfway to the door when he heard his father's weak voice again.

"Beau, whether you marry for love or convenience, choose someone who will get along well with your mother. She'll be lonely after I'm gone."

"I will, sir," Beau said, his heart wrenching.

Choosing a bride based on this new criterion was probably the best idea he'd heard so far, since he didn't believe in his ability to fall in love anymore. He'd thought he had been in love with Miss Lucinda Elliot—now Lady Wolfrey. After their "friendly" break up six years ago—when the precocious Miss Elliot insisted that their mutual feelings were nothing but childish infatuation—he had put a guard on his heart. The love affairs he had filled his life with since the break had been largely forgettable.

He closed his father's bedroom door softly and went in search of his mother, finding her in the east rose garden. The morning newspaper had fallen onto the grass, and her head dipped every few seconds as she dozed. Her fatigue told the story of late-night caretaking, and Beau turned away, determined not to disturb her rest. But the sound of the gravel crunching under his boots pulled her out of her light sleep.

"Where are you going? Come sit with me, Beau," Lady

Margaret said, patting the space next to her.

"You look tired, Mother. Can't you let someone else—Nana, perhaps—take a turn with Father overnight?"

Lady Margaret shook her head, despite the fact that her children's ancient nurse would have been perfectly capable. "I wouldn't be able to sleep, even if I arranged it."

"Father wouldn't want you to tire yourself," Beau responded gently. "He loves you so much. He's told me that my wife must also be your friend."

"Really?" Lady Margaret murmured, her eyes brimming with tears.

Beau sat next to his mother, putting an arm around her slim shoulders. "It's not a bad plan. At least now I have a guideline on which to base my choice."

"Promise me you won't," she scolded, sitting up straighter and frowning at him.

"I can't make such a promise. I think it's a brilliant plan, since love eludes me." The words were spoken nonchalantly, but Beau's tense fingers, tapping the back of the bench, told a different story.

Lady Margaret pushed a loose strand of white hair back into her bun, eyeing her son thoughtfully. "I sense a cynicism in you that I cannot like. You've been in love."

"I was told it wasn't love, but infatuation, and—"

"And what?" Lady Margaret prompted when he didn't continue.

"Most women are too determined to please. They lose themselves in the pleasing somehow."

"Oh, dear. I've always known your looks would be both a blessing and a curse."

"Perhaps seeing you and Father so happily in love raised my expectations. You must know that what you had together—have—is not ordinary."

"There hasn't been a single day when I've taken it for granted," Lady Margaret acknowledged.

"And my reputation isn't particularly marriage-worthy. Perhaps I should find a foreign wife, so she won't have heard of my reputation."

"Don't be ridiculous!" Lady Margaret chided through a laugh. She reached into the pocket of her morning gown and pulled out a letter. "Lady Aldwinkle already knows you're here. I received this letter from her earlier today, inviting us to a party this weekend. She wishes to celebrate her new gardens, and it promises to be quite an event. I certainly cannot go but you should, Beau. Who knows? Perhaps some young woman, who has not yet heard of your so-called 'reputation,' will be there."

"Young women are tedious. They either stutter and blush or subject me to their amateurish flirting."

Lady Margaret ignored her son's grumpiness. "May I write to say that you will go?"

"I suppose," Beau conceded, remembering the promise he had just made to his father. It was his duty to try. He added, his smile mirthless, "Are there any unattached women in the vicinity that you particularly like?"

"If there were, I wouldn't tell you!" Lady Margaret exclaimed. She stood and bent to gather the newspapers, but Beau beat her to it, handing them to her.

"Of course not. I see now that finding a bride will be a tedious ordeal that I must face alone. Sort of like getting leeched," he said, following her through the garden. She made a noise of exasperation so Beau changed the subject.

"I'm off to the stables, Mother. Matthews will have discovered what's ailing Merlin by now."

"Is he lame?"

"No, just out of sorts. He gallops with only half a heart these days." Perhaps he was just mirroring his master's present mood.

"Matthews will set him straight." Lady Margaret turned to face Beau, reaching up to give him a peck on his cheek.

"Your bed would be a better place for a nap, Mother," Beau said gently.

"That little nap in the garden was all I needed. I'm going to see if your father needs anything now. We can talk more at dinner."

Beau watched his mother walk away, wishing he hadn't

agreed to the cursed party. Hadn't he come to the country to escape such dreary entertainments? He almost called out to tell her he'd changed his mind, but he didn't.

"I need to bloody try, don't I?" he muttered, slamming the garden gate so hard that it bounced open again, hanging crookedly.

He found a better mood at the stables, where Merlin was a changed horse, thanks to Matthews' elderflower tonic. His twelve-year-old brother, Michael, was there too.

"Beau, you have to take me for a ride in your new curricle," Michael insisted.

Beau watched as his brother jumped from the loft into a pile of hay below it. "I do?"

"If you don't I'll bother you until you do," Michael said, brushing straw off his trousers.

"No, you won't. But I'll oblige you," Beau said, ruffling his brother's hair affectionately.

"'E's been lookin' in tha' new buggy all day, wonderin' when you'd show up 'ere. Lucky for ye both tha' Merlin is feelin' better," Matthews said, leading the horse out of his box.

They made quick work of hitching Merlin to the curricle and Beau spent a glorious afternoon driving his brother over Castlewood's extensive grounds.

4.

"I couldn't care less. Truly! If you want me to go with you, I will. But I'm perfectly happy not going."

"But don't you wish to experience Lord Featherstone's company in a variety of settings? We've visited his laboratory four times—"

"Only twice, Mother. This makes three," Fiona said, laughing. They were on their way to the laboratory again, having borrowed Lord Hasselton's open carriage. Lord Featherstone was already there, as he typically awoke at dawn, rode over, and didn't appear at the Hasseltons' house again until dinnertime. "Did Lord Featherstone accept the invitation?"

"I have no idea. But if you're going, surely he will."

"Not necessarily. He only comes to dinner because food is a necessity. Dancing and chit-chat are avoided, since they don't satisfy a basic need or add anything to his studies," Fiona said, smiling.

Lady Winifred adjusted her bonnet to block the morning sun from her face. "But that's—well, too serious! I cannot believe that I'm complaining, and I hope I don't regret saying this, but Lord Featherstone seems too consumed with—what is it again?"

"Homeopathy. And he's consumed because he's passionate about it. Do you know how lovely it is to meet a man who has a life goal? A passion? I've never met such a man. Read of them certainly, but never met one. It's utterly refreshing to be around him."

"But does he appreciate you as a suitor should?"

"Who cares?" Fiona retorted.

"I care. The whole point of this trip—" Lady Winifred

paused, her brow furrowing. "Fiona, is there no chance that a proposal will come from this?"

"I don't know, Mother. We do make a good pair, since I've been able to teach him a thing or two about how to raise plants. He wasn't giving his marigolds enough sun, and his chamomile plant was near death, with its roots rotting."

"Yes, that's all very well. But do his interests extend to gaining a wife?"

Fiona gave the question due consideration before answering. "They might."

"By the way, if you're wondering why he is still living with his aunt and uncle at age five and twenty, when he has vast properties of his own to ramble about on, it's because of them, not him. Lady Richland, in any event. She and Lord Richland became his guardians when he was orphaned at age seven. She dotes on him and cannot bear to have him leave, especially since her daughter's marriage to an American took her so far away."

"Poor thing ... an orphan!"

"An eccentric, *rich* orphan at that. Fiona, I find it ironic that the one man who does not appreciate your beauty is the one man you would consider marrying," Lady Winifred reflected.

"What's ironic about it? I loathe the other option, of marrying a man who only cares for my face, who only tolerates my love of books and plants because he must, or worse, tries to bully me away from them."

"Can you not have both?"

"I don't think such a thing is possible."

At the laboratory, which was really a converted greenhouse, Lord Featherstone answered their knock himself, a heavy brown apron covering his linen shirt and breeches.

"Come in," he said hurriedly, turning away to rush back to his worktable. On it was a crate that he had obviously been in the process of opening, since he had answered the door with a claw hammer in his hand.

"What's in the crate?" Fiona asked, following him.

"Good morning, Lord Featherstone," Lady Winifred said stiffly. She stepped into the laboratory, a place she had come to loathe bare minutes into the first visit. It smelled of outdoors—earthy smells she couldn't quite place—and it housed a dangerous beehive that was attached to one window where a pane should have been. The thing had a wooden box separating it from the inside of the laboratory, but Lady Winifred had seen a bee or two slipping between two broken slats, and the constant buzzing made her nervous.

Lady Winifred picked her way around a large, open-backed bookshelf that was overstuffed with jars and books and dried plants. When she reached the worktable, Fiona and Lord Featherstone were already there, exclaiming over a crateful of mushrooms—ugly things with scaly, yellow caps that smelled like almonds and dirt. Everything in the place smelled somewhat of dirt, in fact. After yesterday's visit, Lady Winifred had asked her husband to smell her sleeve. His puzzled eyes had widened in dismay after smelling it, confirming her worst fears.

"Lord Featherstone, will you be attending the Aldwinkles' party?" Lady Winifred asked, trying for Fiona's sake to sound as friendly as possible. Too bad that he ignored her, making the effort pointless.

When Lord Featherstone didn't respond, Fiona nudged his arm and drew his attention to her mother.

"So sorry. What was that, Lady Fairmont?" he said, half turning, a pucker between his brows.

"I asked if you plan to attend the Aldwinkles' party this Saturday. Fiona and I plan to go, and we'd like you to accompany us."

He considered Lady Fairmont, assessing her as he might a new plant specimen whose slender thorns had proven surprisingly painful. Finally he said, "I've already declined. I dislike that sort of—"

"Lord Featherstone, diligent work is to be applauded, but surely you can tear yourself away for one small party?" Lady Winifred said in exasperation.

Fiona intervened, before Lord Featherstone could completely disgrace himself. "Why don't you come, just this once? It might be fun," she coaxed.

Lord Featherstone winced, but after scrutinizing Lady Winifred's face said, "I suppose I could be convinced."

"Wonderful," Fiona said, giving him a warm smile as she turned toward the table again. "What type of mushrooms are these? Mother, do you care to see them?"

Lady Winifred suspected that it was the question about his mushrooms, not Fiona's pretty smile, that made Lord Featherstone lose the frown that mention of the party had caused.

She shook her head and sighed, moving away to sit gingerly between an ugly plant with long, black thorns and a wall of windows that looked as if they hadn't been washed in years. She pulled out needlework and said a silent prayer that the torture she was suffering would not be in vain.

***

Saturday morning, the day of the Aldwinkles' garden party, turned out to be a gorgeous day. A delicious warm breeze kept insects at bay, and the fluffy clouds were just numerous enough to keep the sun from being scorching.

The atmosphere in the Hasseltons' drawing room was not so nice.

"He probably lost track of the time. Scientific types are like that, aren't they? Should we give him another fifteen minutes?" Fiona's father asked.

The vehemence of his wife's answer took him by surprise. "Science is not an excuse for unforgivable rudeness," she snapped, the jut of her chin signaling fury.

"Let's go without him. He knows where it is if he decides to come later. We won't wait any longer," Lady Amelia soothed, tucking her friend's arm in hers and leading the way to the front drive. Fiona, her father, and Lord Hasselton gratefully followed.

A carriage stood waiting, two horses stamping

impatiently, anxious to be off. A footman opened the barouche door and handed the ladies into the dark green velvet interior, and the gentlemen followed. It was a bit of a squeeze, but less than if Lord Featherstone had been with them, and they weren't going far.

The elderly Skeffingtons and Lord Featherstone's aunt and uncle had left for the Aldwinkles' party thirty minutes beforehand. Perhaps Lord and Lady Richland had intentionally left their nephew to the Hasseltons' barouche, knowing that he'd probably not show up. Whatever the reason, they conveniently hadn't been on hand to make excuses—or not—for his absence.

"It would only take us five minutes out of our way to stop by the laboratory. I'm sure that he just forgot," Fiona offered. She would have liked Henry to come, but wasn't taking his absence personally, as her mother was.

"We will not!" Lady Winifred fumed, her eyes flashing with anger. "I'll develop a migraine if I have to see his ridiculous brown apron one more time. In fact, Fiona dear, I will be asking Anna to accompany you to the laboratory from now on. That is, if you can stand to go again, after he's been so rude. Imagine! Not even a note of explanation!"

"He didn't remember, Mother. I know Henry. He isn't being intentionally rude. Please don't be offended," Fiona said, giving her mother's arm a reassuring squeeze.

"It's 'Henry' now? I suppose I should be grateful that you seem unaffected by this—this fiasco! But let me tell you, Fiona, Lord Featherstone's behavior today forces me to question—" Lady Winifred paused to lean toward her daughter and whisper, "Has he proposed, since we last spoke about it?"

Fiona shook her head. A thought occurred to her, one that brought with it a cloud of sadness: *It can be no other way. Mother will never like a man that I find interesting. It isn't possible.* To change the subject, she said, "Your new gloves are lovely, Mother."

"Thank you, Fiona." Her mother seemed unaware that she had dampened her daughter's mood. "Lady Skeffington told me that these gardens are quite the thing. The Aldwinkles are hoping to set a trend with them."

Lady Amelia agreed. "They're rumored to be gorgeous. Lord Aldwinkle started the project over a year ago in honor of his daughter, who died giving birth to her third child two and a half years ago."

And the rest of the ten-minute ride was spent listening to Lord Hasselton give a history of the Aldwinkles' old gardens. To hear him talk, they were as unruly as forests.

***

The new gardens were every bit as lovely as promised. Elaborately carved trellises supporting ivy and climbing roses separated the gardens into intimate sections with different themes. There was also a hothouse that had exotic bird of paradise and anthurium plants flowering around a lavishly tiled goldfish pond. One of the outdoor gardens felt wintry, with its sweet peas and Queen Anne's lace covering the ground like a blanket of snow. White stone pathways and whitewashed wrought-iron benches bordered by white hydrangea bushes completed the picture. Another large section was devoted to sunflowers that were on the verge of bursting forth their large yellow petals. A gravel pathway circled through them, taking a visitor to the woods and back.

Lord and Lady Aldwinkle led three formal tours throughout the day, but several partygoers preferred to wander without direction, discovering the gardens haphazardly. Fiona's group took the Aldwinkles' last tour and the sun was just beginning to set when it ended. The numerous guests were shifting indoors now, hopeful of more robust sustenance than the cucumber sandwiches, lemon tarts and almond-truffle mushrooms that had been offered at midday.

The Aldwinkles didn't disappoint. Not only was there a huge buffet of assorted meats and everything that one could wish to go with them, but guests were supplied with champagne or a delightful punch made of crushed cranberries, grapes and apples, spiced with innocent cinnamon and ginger and laced with sherry. And while guests filled their plates and glasses, a string quartet in the corner opposite from the buffet struck up Haydn's last Opus with a nod from Lord Aldwinkle.

Fiona couldn't remember ever being in better spirits at a party. Perhaps it was the innumerable, beautiful plants she had just seen, but she suspected that it also had to do with the fact that she had shed her official role as debutante. At this party she was just another guest, not out to impress anybody. And there was no dance card given out at this informal gathering. If she wanted to dance she could, but there was no expectation that she should.

***

Beau put off leaving as long as he could. Since it was a garden party, he supposed he should make an appearance during daylight hours, but he didn't. He waited until the sun was a large, orange ball on the horizon before tearing himself away from Michael's archery lesson.

"Damn me, you're good. Who taught you?" he said, watching as his brother let fly another perfectly aimed shot.

Michael grinned. "I taught myself."

"You're eerily expert for your age, but I'll have one more go at besting you. Tomorrow. I promised Mother—and Father—I'd go to that cursed party," Beau said, nodding toward the faint sounds of laughter and music drifting across the meadow. "Father wants me married," he explained. "And the perfect bride is supposedly just over that fence."

Michael fit another arrow. "I was able to see one of the gardens from the apple tree."

"And?"

He took careful aim before answering. "It was all white, like snow. There were crowds of people in it." His arrow hit the bullseye again.

"Crowds? Lovely," Beau replied, his sarcasm wasted on Michael, who was busy retrieving arrows.

After tucking the arrows into his quiver, Michael swung easily into the giant apple tree that had the bullseye propped against it. It had a natural seat at the juncture of three branches, and it had been one of Beau's favorite spots, too, when he was Michael's age. Peering up through the branches, Beau saw that Michael was looking toward the party. "What do you see?"

"Not much, since it's getting dark. You're going to miss it if you don't hurry."

"That possibility doesn't bother me in the least. I'd send *you* in my place if I could, since you seem interested."

Michael looked down, grinning at this brother. "But I'm not the one looking for a bride."

Beau snorted. "So, same time tomorrow? You do the same shooting tomorrow and I'll be truly astounded."

In the dimming light, Michael shrugged. "Hey, maybe you'll hit bullseye tomorrow."

"Don't hold your breath." Beau gave his brother a final wave before heading indoors to find Smithers and his evening clothes.

Fifteen minutes later, Beau was on Merlin, galloping north toward the Aldwinkles' party. He had shocked Smithers by making haste with his evening toilette, refusing the shave and accepting the first tie of his cravat. But he really hadn't cared what he looked like. Despite his earlier good intentions, the prospect of this tame party had worn down his resolve to oblige his parents' wishes. His plan now was to down a glass of champagne, find his hostess and give her his compliments on her lovely gardens—hadn't Michael said they looked nice?—and leave. In the morning he could truthfully tell his father that he had attended, thereby sparing him any unhealthy disappointment.

Beau pulled to a stop in front of the Aldwinkles' well-lit mansion, dismounting and handing the reins to a waiting footman. He laughed to himself when a servant bearing champagne crossed his path just as he stepped through the doorway. Aha! His plan was manifesting nicely! Now he just had to find his hostess.

But as he glanced around the room, his attention was captured by a cascade of red hair, shimmering in the glow of a nearby wall sconce. Auburn sprinkled with gold and copper swam together in the candlelight.

Beau took a sip of champagne, in no hurry to find his hostess now. He watched as the owner of the hair laughed and gave a small shake of her head, making her highlights dance even more. She was wearing a gown of sea-green silk that showed off a petite and well-proportioned figure, and Beau willed her to turn around. Could her face possibly match the perfection of her hair and figure? If so, a goddess was gracing the earth.

***

Lady Amelia saw Beau approaching and gave him a bright smile and a wave.

"I didn't know Beau was in town! He's such a dear; I don't care what the gossips say. He and my sons are the best of friends. They were inseparable as boys," she said to Fiona.

"Who?"

Fiona turned and saw an astonishingly beautiful man. Beautiful was an unusual word to describe a man, but it was the only one that fit. His lips, nose, and chin reminded her of the drawings in her book on Greek statues, and his intelligent, dark eyes were framed by eyelashes that rivaled hers in length. Black hair, shiny as silk, tumbled across his brow. But there was something else: a warmth behind his eyes that made her want to step closer to him.

"Beau, so good to see you! If I'd known you could be torn from London, I would have invited you to my house party," Lady Amelia said, extending her hand. "This is one of my house guests. Miss Fairmont, meet Lord Albert Beaumont. Beau, Miss Fairmont." Lady Amelia nodded expectantly at them.

"I'm pleased to make your acquaintance," Fiona said, her mind roiling behind a polite smile. So this was the infamous Lord Albert? He, of the selfish vanity she had so maligned only five days ago? For the space of a few seconds his beauty made her want to forgive him all his transgressions. She fully understood how the many women in his life forgave him his sins, if only to have a small share in his alluring aura.

When he took her gloved hand and touched it to his lips, her body's unbidden thrill was horrifying and fascinating all at once. "The pleasure is mine," he was saying, but she barely heard him. And when he released her hand, she experienced disappointment.

This wouldn't do! This spell he was casting over her was dangerous. And it brought with it the exact sort of mindless adoration that she had despised in her previous suitors. She now understood how they'd felt, and her former impatience was replaced by pity.

But since she recognized the spell for what it was, she would overcome it.

"May I have the next dance, Miss Fairmont?"

Fiona's mind steeled itself against his magic. *Dancing will only serve to strengthen his pull on me.*

"Lord Hasselton hoped to be home by nine o'clock, and it's already after eight. I'm afraid—"

"You have time, Fiona! It will take me at least fifteen minutes to find Hassie in this crowd," Lady Amelia said, oblivious to Fiona's hesitations. "Go ahead," she urged, as the strains of music slowed and faded, signaling that a new dance was about to begin.

Beau held out a gloved hand. "May I persuade you?"

Fiona hesitated, thinking that perhaps she should feign a sore ankle, but she had never been a good liar.

Besides! Just one dance. What could it hurt? Her heart urged.

Fine! Dance with him, but think about his flaws. His many mistresses, to be exact, her mind argued.

She took his hand and he led her onto the dance floor, deftly twirling her to face him when they reached an open spot. He bowed and she curtsied as the first strains of music began.

"If I remember correctly, Lord Hasselton is not likely to leave a card game early. A garden party, maybe, but not a card game," he said, indicating with a tilt of his head that Fiona should look over her shoulder into the room set up for card players. She did, and saw her host happier than she'd seen him all day, throwing down a card as he laughed uproariously at something the player to his right had just said.

"I see what you mean. In that case, we may be the last to leave."

Beau circled around Fiona as specified by the dance, saying as he faced her again, "I'm acquainted with your cousin, Lord Ferguson."

"Fergie. We adore him for his good-natured silliness," Fiona said, taking her turn to circle.

"That describes him perfectly. Did he tell you that we looked for you at the Stantons' ball? You were nowhere to be found, although Fergie swore you'd be there."

Fiona hid the surprise she felt that this notorious and stunningly handsome man—whom she hadn't met before tonight—included himself in the act of looking for her at the Stantons'. "I had a better offer—to see a play at Vauxhall that evening. Opening night of 'The Tempest.' Have you seen it?"

He smiled. "No, I haven't. Should I?"

It was an intoxicating smile that made Fiona feel the way she had after having brandy at her cousin Sylvia's wedding—warm all over and slightly wobbly. And it made her miss his question, since her eyes had dropped to his lips, trying to work out how a smile could be so alluring. It was almost sinful that one person should contain such a lion's share of beauty. "Why were you and Fergie looking for me?" she asked, forcing her eyes upward. Her heart lurched when she saw his amused gaze.

Wonderful! Now he thinks I'm one of his thousands of smitten admirers.

He gave the barest shrug. "Fergie wanted me to meet

you."

"Why?" Fiona pressed.

"He wanted us to fall madly in love with one another so that you'd be saved from a fate worse than death—marriage to a mad scientist. Which, I'm just realizing, must be Lord Featherstone. The Richlands are neighbors of ours, so I know of his reputation."

"Oh!" Beau lived nearby? And knew Henry? As for Fergie, he definitely had a lecture due him, next time she saw him.

"Is *that* why you're attending a country house party in the middle of the season, Miss Fairmont? To meet Lord Featherstone?"

Fiona appreciated that he had dropped the "mad scientist" moniker, but she didn't like this line of questioning at all. "More or less," she responded vaguely.

Beau raised a gloved hand. "Which is it? More, or less?"

Fiona gracefully raised her hand to meet his and they circled. "It's too long a story to bore you with."

"I won't be bored. Tell me," he coaxed, and Fiona was sure that, apart from his looks, it was his ability to appear truly fascinated—captivated—that had succeeded in melting many hearts. Not hers, though, she thought, forcing herself to consult her very good logic: *He's a rake who excels in the art of flirting. Do not fall for such a ploy.*

"If you insist," she said, laughing. "I'll try to shorten it a bit. Let's see ... my mother is afraid I won't get married this season since I've turned down two proposals—two that she thought were perfectly good ones. She and Lady Amelia schemed for me to meet Lord Featherstone, a supposed 'perfect match.' Thus the house party, since Lord Featherstone avoids London during the season."

She stopped, congratulating herself on her succinct summary, but Beau shook his head. "No, no, no. You can't stop there. Is he the perfect match they'd hoped for?"

"Since I met Lord Featherstone less than one week ago, I can hardly judge the outcome," Fiona said, wishing that her skin hadn't turned all tingly. What was it about his gaze? If she didn't have such good sense at her command, she'd be as quick to fall in love with him as every other woman in London. His attraction was uncanny.

"First impression?"

"First impressions are exactly what I hope to avoid, Lord Albert. They are based on superficial attraction rather than true knowledge of a person. The word 'love' is thrown about far too loosely, since it is so often based on initial attraction to physical traits. While I don't deny that some level of attraction is necessary, true love always takes time to grow." Fiona hoped she didn't sound as breathless as she felt. His dark eyes—seeming to look right through her—had completely winded her.

"You're either wiser than your years normally allow or you're scarred. Which?"

"Certainly not scarred," Fiona said, amused. "My parents' marriage of convenience is one of the happier ones, thanks in part to their mutual determination to remain respectful and kind to one another."

"And the refused proposals?"

"Neither gentleman was a good match, albeit for very different reasons. But in both cases we remain cordial," Fiona said, dipping her head in a graceful curtsy as the dance came to an end.

Beau bowed in response. Straightening, he said, "Then you hold wisdom far beyond your meager years. Lemonade, Miss Fairmont?"

"It's too sweet and I'm not thirsty," she replied. Even if she'd been as dry as the desert she'd have refused because she was acutely aware that, somewhere in the last few minutes, this *magician's* formula had wormed its way into her heart. Her heart told her to stay, drink lemonade with him and talk to him until Lord Hasselton finished his card game hours hence.

But she wouldn't allow it! He was a rake, and his accomplishments in the realm of wooing and winning were legendary. It was a given that she felt intrigued, but that didn't mean she had to indulge the feeling. "I'd best find

Lady Hasselton. I don't want to delay their departure."

He took her gloved hand and expertly dropped a kiss on it. "Thank you for the dance, for it turned an otherwise dreary evening into a memorable one."

Fiona turned and walked away, acutely aware that Beau was watching her. Just before she entered the card room, she glanced back. He stood where she had left him, and when their eyes met he gave her a smile whose intimacy made her heart jump. Her lips responded fleetingly, but the shock of an unexpected blush made them serious again. She turned into the card room, determined to look at him no more. *He's a menace*, she thought, scanning the room for Lady Amelia.

***

Fiona's blush made Beau's heart leap. He watched her lithe body disappear into the card room, and turned toward the refreshment table, hoping to find a glass of champagne. Lady Aldwinkle was there too, making sure that her household staff had properly replenished it.

"So good of you to come, Beau," she chirped. "Did you like the gardens?"

He took the glass of champagne she offered him. "What I saw here today is beyond comparison, Lady Aldwinkle. Truly exquisite."

"Oh, my! Which did you like best?" she said, opening her fan. Its slight breeze was no match for the beads of sweat that covered her brow.

Beau considered a moment, then gave a slow smile. "Perfection cannot be pared up, like the lowly apple."

Lady Aldwinkle gave a nervous laugh. "What's that, dear? Which garden?"

She'd known him since he'd been a lad in knee pants, so he didn't mind the familiar endearment. "It's all beautiful, Lady Aldwinkle. Thank you for inviting me."

"Yes, of course! Well, I'm so glad you came. Please give my best to your parents." And with a puzzled smile she scooted off to make sure the young ladies sitting on the settee next to the dance floor were partnerless by choice.

Beau downed a glass of champagne and sought out Lady Amelia. He remembered her partial invitation and wished her to make good on it, despite the fact that his relationship with Featherstone and the Richlands was cool, at best. But that was old history, hopefully forgotten, and not enough to keep him away. He wished to see for himself how the matched pair were faring.

Not finding Lady Amelia, he turned into the card room, hoping to catch sight of Fiona again. Only ten minutes had elapsed since she had been at the door, her lovely flushed face filled with confused curiosity.

With a pang of disappointment, Beau saw Lord Hasselton by himself, no wife or lovely redhead hovering nearby. He turned to leave, but—

"Beau! Good to see you! What brings you to the country?" Lord Hasselton called out, raising a hand in greeting. He excused himself from the table since he was the dummy in this particular round, and motioned Beau to wait for him.

Beau retraced his steps back to the refreshment table, in Lord Hasselton's wake. "I'm here because of my parents, mostly."

"How are your parents faring?"

Beau gave his usual reply, "Well enough." Then, so as not to get into a long explanation of his father's health, he added, "Your wife told me you're hosting a house party."

"Yes, a small affair, and mostly for the sake of matching a skittish filly to a foal that doesn't have the sense to get his head out of the grass. We all thought it was working until he went and stood her up today. He was supposed to be here but he hasn't shown his face."

Beau made a noise of commiseration, while taking great pleasure in this bit of information. So, Lord Featherstone wasn't yet smitten. The "skittish filly" was not yet claimed. Not that it would matter if she were because—to be honest—he was supremely confident in his abilities to woo and win hearts, even ones that were already taken.

"Are the cards treating you well tonight?" Beau asked, in complete good humor with this bearer of happy news.

"Yes, indeed! My wife tried to pull me away when I was up by twenty points! I sent her off, by God!" Lord Hasselton exclaimed, his large blue eyes bugging out in indignation at the injustice. He picked up a glass of punch to take back to the card game.

Beau bid him farewell, impatient to find Fiona so that he could ask her to dance again. He searched the crowd inside for a few minutes, and was about to exit onto the terrace when Lady Amelia called his name. Beau turned, and saw that she was accompanied by an attractive matron of about forty, whose catlike green eyes told Beau that she must be Fiona's mother. Age difference aside, a worried, pinched look prevented Lady Fairmont from being as stunningly beautiful as her daughter.

Lady Amelia introduced them, adding, "Beau's mother is a dear friend of mine. She's the only person I know who truly enjoys discussing art with me." She placed a hand on Beau's sleeve, continuing earnestly, "How *is* your mother? I confess, I haven't seen her in too long!"

"As well as can be expected. My father's illness has taken its toll, but she remains in good spirits."

"I've meant to pay her a call these many weeks now, but never know what time is best. Are mornings good?" Lady Amelia asked.

"I haven't been home enough to know. I can ask her—" Beau was momentarily distracted by a sea-green gown, but it wasn't Fiona. He turned back to Lady Amelia with an apologetic grin.

She raised her eyebrows questioningly, but said, "Do, and come to dinner tomorrow with the answer."

Beau bowed. "I will, thank you. It was a pleasure to meet you, Lady Fairmont." He took his leave, once again determined to find Fiona.

Lady Winifred stared after him a moment. "Goodness," she murmured to herself. To Lady Amelia she said, "I'd forgotten Lord Albert is your neighbor. He *seems* nice enough, but his reputation—"

"He's made a reputation for himself, certainly, but I've known him since he was little, and it's the good-natured boy that I remember. He and Rupert were the same age, but he always allowed my youngest son, Gordie, to tag along with them—swimming and such. He has a heart of gold, my dear, despite all the gossip you hear."

"And he's coming to dinner tomorrow. I wonder if he'd ever consider courting Fiona. He'd be the catch of the decade, never mind the season! He might be just the one to attract Fiona's attention away from odious Lord Featherstone—and yes, I'm being fair, Amelia," Lady Winifred insisted, when Lady Amelia demurred. "But I know I shouldn't have any such expectation. If anything, Lord Albert will be taken down a peg or two by my daughter's supreme lack of interest. She may have granted him a dance, but if I know my Fiona, she won't give much more."

"I agree with you. If any young woman is immune to his charms it will be your Fiona."

But Fiona wouldn't have agreed with their analysis. She was on her way home, squished between the elderly Skeffingtons, who were once again riding with the Richlands. As luck would have it, she had run into them as they were leaving and had begged admission to their landau in order to avoid further contact with a man who threatened to overturn her good sense.

Lady Skeffington had read her a lecture. "You can't possibly be tired! When I was your age, I didn't leave a party until dawn, and here it is not even nine thirty. What a waste of good looks, young lady."

Fiona stifled a sigh. "Yes, ma'am. I suppose so."

"And with Lord Beaumont's son there tonight! Now there's a fine-looking man, if ever there was one," Lady Skeffington effused.

"Fine looks are a waste, if they accompany a character such as his," Lady Richland huffed. Her husband cleared his throat and she patted his arm, adding, "He's a fickle rake, and don't let anyone tell you otherwise."

"Fickle to whom? If you're referring to Miss Elliot, *she* broke their engagement, and everyone knows that no relationship has meant a thing to him since," Lady Skeffington argued.

"I'm referring to his engagement to my daughter. It's a little known fact that *she* was engaged to Lord Albert, long before he met Miss Elliot, and he broke it off without a word of explanation."

Lady Skeffington looked skeptical, but held her tongue—much to Fiona's chagrin. What was this about another engagement? For the first time in her life, Fiona wished that she paid as much attention to the gossip papers as Felicity did.

But a moment later, Lady Skeffington's reminiscing continued. "That boy's attraction is famous, you can't deny that! His every word—his every smile—is as alluring to the women as cream is to a cat. Lady Amelia sends me wonderfully interesting letters that help to stave off the boredom of Cornwall. In one, she told me quite a tale about Beau: He was getting ready to go to Oxford—I believe it was the summer of '03—and his parents hosted a farewell party for him. This was before the Marquess got sick, of course. Well, some poor neighborhood girl became emboldened by too much champagne and almost ruined her reputation by climbing a trellis into his bedroom. He got her quietly back home—chaperoned by his Nana—but the girl was heartbroken. She was married off to an American and left the country."

If Lady Skeffington's eyesight had been sharper she might have noticed that Lady Richland was scowling at her. Her sight being what it was, she continued.

"Do you remember that story, Lady Richland? Now that so much time has passed, the girl's name could be told. Lady Amelia withheld it from her letter, but I'm curious. What was that silly girl's name? Did we meet her parents tonight?"

The Countess' spine stiffened. She glared at Lady

Skeffington before answering. "That is none of your business, ma'am, regardless of the time lapsed."

Lady Skeffington puckered her lips thoughtfully. "Tell me, did that incident happen before or after Beau broke the engagement?"

"I'll have you know that you have been misinformed, and I can only hope that Lady Amelia did not spread lies maliciously. My daughter *never* would have thought to climb that trellis if Lord Albert hadn't put the idea into her head. Fortunately for the skin on his back, the Beaumonts' nursemaid happened to witness my daughter's disgraceful behavior and put a stop to it. And this happened *after* Lord Albert had broken off their engagement! Not only did he crush her tender sensibilities, he tried to ruin her into the bargain. I should have had my lord whip him anyway. I regret that oversight to this day!"

Lady Skeffington looked skeptical. "But why have I no recollection of this engagement? Wouldn't it have been in the papers?"

"It was between our families. An *understanding*."

Light dawned in Lady Skeffington's nearsighted eyes. "Ah! I see."

"What do you 'see'?" Lady Richland asked angrily.

"Between the families, was it? Then it was doomed from the start. From what I know of Beau, an arranged marriage isn't something he'd tolerate."

Lady Richland looked haughtily down her nose. "He 'tolerated' it for many years, then broke it off unexpectedly, just when my daughter was of an age to begin planning their nuptials."

As if on cue, Lord Skeffington's loud snores inhibited further conversation. But Fiona had been given plenty to think about, regardless.

5.

"You're going where?" Lady Margaret asked, putting her slice of freshly buttered toast back on her plate without taking a bite. Not only had her son joined her for breakfast, something he almost never did, but he was also being chatty—something remarkable for morning time.

"The Hasseltons', for dinner," Beau said, heaping his plate full of eggs, then putting three fat slices of bacon on top.

He took the seat across from his mother, smiling as she eyed him suspiciously.

"Why are you—? Beau! Did you meet—? What happened at the party last night?" Lady Margaret knew that Beau's childhood friend, Rupert Hasselton, was traveling the continent with his new bride. The younger son, Gordon, was with his regiment. Beau's happiness about dining with the Hasseltons' must mean he had met a young woman. She hoped so.

Beau took a bite of bacon, swallowing before he answered. "I'll tell you what happened: I met Miss Fiona Fairmont."

"Miss Fiona Fairmont," Lady Margaret repeated. "Isn't she one of this season's debutantes? Quite beautiful, if I'm remembering the gossips correctly."

"I'm glad to see you aren't solely immersed in father's care. Yes, she's quite beautiful, but also intelligent. And she's one of the few women I've ever met who didn't—" Beau shrugged, and avoided finishing the sentence by polishing off his eggs.

"Didn't what?" Lady Margaret prompted. She wasn't going to let him off that easily.

"Who didn't—I don't know—didn't seem unreasonably smitten," Beau said, pushing back his plate and taking a final sip of tea. "If you'll excuse me, Mother, I'm off for another round of humiliation by Michael; another archery contest."

"Wait a moment! That's all you have to say? She's not smitten, but you're going to pursue her? Please don't tell me that you require that sort of challenge to fall in love, Beau," Lady Margaret chided.

"No, it's not like that. I find her fascinating, challenging or not. Lady Amelia invited me, so—" Beau shrugged again.

"So you're going to further your acquaintance at dinner tonight. That's wonderful news, Beau! I cannot wait to tell your father. By the way, when you see Michael, tell him that his father loved the charcoal drawing. That child is quite the artist! Have you seen any of his drawings?"

"Yes, and I can say in all honesty that he's almost as good at drawing as he is at archery. How I came to have such a talented brother, I'll never know," Beau said, dropping a kiss on her cheek before leaving.

Lady Margaret poured herself another cup of tea. She reopened her newspaper, this time scanning it for any word of Miss Fiona Fairmont. There was only: *The delectable Miss Fairmont remains buried in the country. When will she return to grace our London ballrooms?*

Lady Margaret closed the paper, wondering what would take a debutante to the country midway through the season. Could she be so calculating that she disappeared to make London wonder and gossip about her? Perhaps it was time to invite Amelia to tea. She hadn't seen her old friend in weeks, and it was time to hear firsthand what Beau was up to.

Lady Margaret closed the paper and went to tell her husband the good news that, at last, their son might be getting engaged.

***

The morning after the party, Fiona and Anna walked to the laboratory. Henry wore a sheepish expression when he turned from his table to greet them.

"Let's hear it, then. What distracted you?" Fiona asked good-naturedly.

"Please accept my apology," he said, looking so contrite that Fiona had to laugh. "Onions woke me at four in the morning. Have you ever had a flash of insight knock sleep away as readily as a clap of thunder? I did night before last. You know how onions make a person's eyes smart? I had the idea that potentized onion might be just the thing for allergy attacks that affect the eyes, so I got up and extracted onion juice and made a remedy from it."

So that was why he smelled of onions today, Fiona thought. "It took you all day?" she asked, but not coldly, as her mother might have.

Henry grimaced apologetically. "No, I finished early, at eight. But then I took a sorely needed nap. I intended to sleep for only thirty minutes, but didn't wake up until three in the afternoon. At that point, I thought it was too late to bother with the party."

Fiona wondered what had prompted him to agree to the party in the first place. Had he agreed to it to stop her and her mother's insistent pushing, and, if so, why had he not simply told them that he wasn't going? Or, had he really intended to accompany them? His excuse seemed plausible enough. "Don't say another word about it. Apology accepted."

Henry was visibly relieved. "Thank you for not being angry. I'll go next time."

Fiona put her sunbonnet on a hook next to a hanging planter that had one scraggly twig growing out of it. She had decided to wash the huge greenhouse windows today, so that sunlight could better reach the hundreds of little, neglected plants that adorned the shelves and tables in forlorn pots. It would be quite a project, but it would transform the place and be so good for the plants.

Henry gestured toward his workbench, distracting her from starting her self-imposed task. "Can I tell you how I made the onion remedy?"

"Of course." Fiona listened as Henry explained the

process of extracting onion juice. He had her sniff the original extraction, which of course smelled strongly of onions. Then he opened his bottle of potentized onion, all the while explaining how he had mixed it with a few drops of alcohol, then distilled water. He didn't show her the shaking process because his potion was already at its optimal strength. She sniffed it, amazed again that this supposedly potent onion potion—that didn't smell of onion at all—could cure anything.

"But how will you test it, to see what it cures?"

Henry held up a thick, well-worn journal. "I test it on myself, and record my symptoms in this." He opened the book, and Fiona saw a page covered in neat, blocky print. "As you can see, I've already experimented a bit. I have almost a dozen remedies' symptoms recorded in here. The horse chestnut was probably the worst one to test, since it eventually caused an extremely uncomfortable case of hemorrhoids, but after taking peppermint tea baths they went away. You see, whatever symptom the remedy causes is what it will cure. I now know that the horse chestnut cures piles. Brilliant, eh?"

"You make yourself sick?" Fiona asked, clearly surprised.

"Never deathly sick. The symptoms go away in time, once I stop taking a remedy, and I've found that peppermint helps to take the symptoms away even faster. What I have in return for a little discomfort is information I'll be able to share with Hahnemann himself."

"So, with the onion, do you expect your eyes to start smarting? Which might mean that onion remedy could cure a cold or allergy that involved burning eyes?" Fiona asked, fascinated.

"Exactly! I'm particularly interested to see which symptoms come in *last*, for those have the highest value."

"Why?"

"The more a person takes, the clearer the picture of the remedy."

Fiona nodded slowly. "I see." But she was still trying to

absorb the fact that Henry experimented on himself. His selfless devotion to his passion was something she had never encountered before. It amazed and humbled her.

"It's not easy to grasp," Henry continued, unaware of her awe. "I explained it to our local surgeon until I went hoarse, but he couldn't break free from the prejudice that one must be able to visualize a thing to believe in it. He called it hocus-pocus. I suppose I should feel lucky to live in a time when people aren't persecuted for witchcraft. I would surely have been burned at the stake by now."

"It's not hocus-pocus. And you—" Fiona placed a hand on Henry's arm and smiled up at him, "—are one of the most selfless people I've ever met. It's people like you who change this world for the better. Do you know that I admire you very much?"

Henry stared at her, as if seeing her for the first time. He blinked rapidly and opened his mouth, but no sound came out. Finally, he said, "You're the first person who has ever said such a thing to me. Thank you."

Fiona smiled inwardly at his befuddlement. The poor man had never had any encouragement, it seemed. "You're welcome. What are you working on today?"

And then he was back in his element, telling her about a moss he had gathered the day before. She watched as he crushed the moss into a fine powder and put a few grains of it into a jar, adding alcohol. As he continued with it, Fiona busied herself with the windows, completing almost an entire side before Anna reminded her that her mother wanted her back in time for tea.

"It feels like we just got here," she mused, her hair curling around her face from the humidity.

"You've been busy," Anna acknowledged. She had offered to help, but Fiona had refused her, hating that Anna had to take time out of her already busy day to play chaperone. Anna had spent her time in the greenhouse mending the Fairmont family's stockings, and certainly hadn't had time to clean windows.

Fiona removed her apron and traded it for her

sunbonnet. "You'll be at dinner as usual tonight?" she asked Henry. "I hope to get an update on how the onion remedy is treating you."

"I'll be there," he said, giving her a warm smile before he shut the door behind them.

Yesterday's beautiful weather had continued, and Fiona's mother was sitting in the shade of a majestic elm tree when they walked up. Fiona joined her.

Lady Winifred waited until Anna was out of earshot before sharing her news. "Lady Amelia invited Lord Albert to dine with us tonight."

Fiona hated that her heart skipped a beat at mention of his name. "Really? I'm surprised—since Lady Richland despises him so."

"She does? His other neighbors—Amelia, Hassie, the Aldwinkles—all seem to adore him, despite his bad reputation. I suppose I shouldn't say 'bad'; it's not as if he has ever been accused of ruining a maiden, but his number of mistresses is truly astonishing. Perhaps that's typical, I don't know, and maybe we only hear of his conquests because his looks and charm make him prime gossip material. He certainly is charismatic, don't you agree? I saw you dancing with him. What was your impression?"

"I understand his attraction. His eyes say so much, without being offensive in the least. He looked at me as if I was a treasure, just discovered, and yet—logically—it must be the very same gaze he uses to make all women adore him. He certainly has a gift there."

"Did he seem interested in you?" Lady Winifred asked eagerly. "Do you think he accepted the dinner invitation because he wishes to know you better?"

Fiona shook her head in amusement. "Doubtful, Mother. The Beaumonts are old friends of the Hasseltons. If he's coming to dinner, that's why."

"My darling child! Don't tell me you've been around Lord Featherstone so long that you've forgotten that you are one of the most beautiful women to ever grace this earth. All his talk of plants and bugs would be enough to make a queen forget her due! It's not right! But I've said too much," she said, taking note of Fiona's disapproving face. "It's what you want, I realize that, but I will go to my grave wondering why."

"I'm thrilled that he doesn't abandon his passion while courting me to the point of suffocation. I hated knowing that I could be utterly beastly to Lord Diggerton and he took it without a fight. Do you know I once told him he was boring me to tears—I admit I was in a particularly foul mood from a week-long rain that looked as if it meant to go on for another week—and all he could say was, 'So sorry,' and look pained. If he'd been a dog he would have had his tail between his legs. The sad thing is that if he'd given me what I deserved and shunned me for the rest of the evening, he might have had a chance at winning me."

"There is middle ground between abject groveling and an insulting lack of appreciation."

"With whom, someone like Lord Albert? He doesn't seem the kind to grovel, and he could never be accused of ignoring a woman, but would one want a marriage in which, as you said, each new mistress is the main gossip item of the day?"

Lady Winifred sighed. "I suppose not," she acknowledged grudgingly.

They went in to tea a few minutes later, but Fiona wasn't hungry. After a quick cup of tea, she excused herself and retired to her room to read. She put herself to sleep reading the book that Henry had lent her about the various remedies that were already proven. Not that it wasn't interesting, but she was going to have to get him to explain the part about symptoms disappearing in one of four directions again.

***

"Fiona, wake up! We need your help."

Fiona sat up, blinking the sleep out of her eyes, and Henry's book slid off her chest and onto the floor with a thud.

Felicity retrieved the book, giving it a doubtful look as she handed it back to Fiona. "We want to spy on Lord Albert tonight, and Emily's governess will never allow it. But I guess we can call him Beau; after all, he's a friend of the family now. Anyway, do you have any ideas for something to put in her tea? So she'll go to sleep early?"

"I mostly adore her, but she always wants to read to us after supper, and tonight we want to spy on Lord Al—Beau—instead," Emily added. "We know just the place to do it, too: The terrace outside the dining room, behind the boxwoods. Nobody will see us after dark."

The prospect of such an adventure made Felicity's eyes gleam. "It'll be perfect!"

Fiona looked from one to the other and couldn't help laughing. They both looked so eager, like children on Christmas morning.

"Instead of giving poor Miss Johnson something without her knowledge, why don't you both feign tiredness and turn in early? Or, to make it more believable, one of you be tired and leave, giving the other one an excuse to feign boredom ten minutes later. Reconvene when Miss Johnson has retired to bed."

"Didn't I tell you she'd help us?" Felicity said.

"And if you're caught?" Fiona asked.

Felicity made a face. "Oh, we won't be. And even if we are, it'll only be embarrassing for a moment. Beau will be flattered, not angry, and Mother's lectures are never too bad. You're so lucky, Fiona, that you get to eat in the same room with him."

"I'd give up my place to you, if Mother would allow it. After I danced with him, I—"

"You danced with him?" Emily breathed, and for a fleeting moment Fiona wondered if the poor girl would topple. Felicity must have thought so, too, because she grabbed her friend's arm and herded her to the door. She stopped short of exiting, with a parting shot:

"Forget about Lord Featherstone, Fiona. He's nice enough, but Fate has intervened on your behalf and put Lord

Albert Beaumont in your way. If you set your sights on him, I bet you could catch him."

"I don't want to catch him. His notoriety negates his appeal," Fiona said, thinking how easy it was to make such a statement when the man wasn't present.

"But he's ready to settle down, I tell you! His notoriety could be laid to rest—with the right person," Felicity insisted.

"Right. And pigs fly," Fiona said, moving to her dressing table. "Felicity, dearest, you've been reading too many romance novels, in which the hero is always handsome, dashing, and a little bit naughty. That's not realistic. Now, someone like Lord Featherstone, who has common interests with me and who demands respect—he's real."

"Have you kissed him yet?" Felicity asked, shushing Emily's gasp at the question.

"No, not yet," Fiona admitted, beginning to brush her hair. It wasn't that she didn't *want* to kiss him. Their relationship had thus far not precipitated such a thing.

"But is it because you don't want to or because he hasn't tried yet?" Felicity prodded.

"He's different, Felicity. He has more important things to think about than courting and kissing and marriage. That doesn't mean that his kiss won't be lovely, if—when—it happens."

Felicity gave a disbelieving grunt and left, hauling Emily behind her, and leaving Fiona alone with her thoughts.

Truthfully, she had a hard time imagining Henry even trying to kiss her. He had simply not shown that sort of leaning, which wasn't to say he never would.

Fiona stopped brushing. She fingered the soft bristles of her ivory-handled hairbrush absent-mindedly, remembering her mother's complaints about Henry. His indifference was a refreshing change, and yet …

She remembered the way her skin had come alive with Beau's touch, and she gave an anticipatory shiver—would he be seated next to her at dinner? But the next minute she brought the hairbrush down hard on her thigh, deeply disturbed by this unusual path her thoughts had taken.

"Not you, too?" she moaned, appalled at the notion. "Do not let your head be turned by his flattery and fleeting interest. Henry could provoke the very same response if wooing was his focus, but it's not. And be glad of it!"

She tossed the hairbrush onto the table, disgusted, and forced herself to read another chapter of Henry's borrowed book as penance.

***

Fiona and her parents entered the drawing room together.

"Fiona, that dress is perfection," Lady Amelia exclaimed. "Oh, sometimes I wish I had had a daughter!"

Henry seemed to agree about the dress. Fiona recognized his rapidly blinking eyes from earlier in the day, when she had given him the compliment.

"Introductions are in order," Lady Amelia said, taking Fiona by the hand and turning toward a woman who was pretty in a curvaceous way, with dark curls, deep dimples, deep cleavage, and plump lips that naturally pouted. She proceeded to introduce them to Lady Clarissa Cowper, a family friend from the next county over.

"I've hunted with your father," Lord Fairmont said conversationally, as he stared into the well of cleavage before him. Fiona saw him give a jump and knew that her mother's fingers, demurely curled into his elbow, had pinched him. He pulled his eyes away, guiltily clearing his throat. "Fine buck I bagged on that trip."

"Father would hunt year round if it was allowed," Lady Clarissa replied. Her soft, high-pitched voice was annoyingly kittenish, although it didn't seem to be bothering the male listeners, Fiona thought wryly.

"I don't remember seeing you in London this season," Fiona said.

"Not this year, no! My mourning year won't be finished

until the fall, but I've recently started accepting dinner invitations from close friends."

"I'm so sorry! Was it unexpected?" Fiona asked.

But the question wasn't heard, because it coincided with Beau's arrival. At sight of him, Lady Clarissa looked liked a dieter grown weary of lettuce and carrots, who has just been offered a large dish of iced cream with chocolate shavings.

He looked magnificent, Fiona conceded. God had taken no shortcuts with this male specimen. From his glossy black hair, to his straight, white teeth, to his well-formed hands, one of which was now taking Lady Clarissa's hand in greeting—he was perfection.

He next greeted Lord Featherstone, and Fiona was surprised to see usually cordial Henry turn coldly superior, barely tilting his head in response to Beau's warm greeting. The only other time she'd seen his nostrils flare like that was when he'd talked about the physicians who claimed homeopathy was nonsense.

Lady Amelia noticed the change in temperature too. Visibly flustered, she said, "Beau, you know Lord and Lady Richland, of course."

Beau's bow was a shade too formal, and Lady Richland's response was barely civil, with the Earl following suit under the duress of his wife's watchful stare.

It was quite an interesting scene, and Fiona couldn't wait to get Henry's side of things. Would he, too, blame Beau for his cousin's near disgrace? And what was his opinion about the engagement that had never made the papers?

Beau interrupted her thoughts. "I'm delighted to see you again, Miss Fairmont." He took her gloved hand and bowed gracefully over it.

"The pleasure is mine." She gave him a dazzling smile, in part because she wanted to make up for the cold reception he had received from Henry and the Richlands, but mostly because it sprung up naturally in response to his smile. She was acutely aware that this man—who had taken in everything from the gold and pearl comb in her hair to the shimmering gold cloth of her dress—this man found her attractive. But his appreciation didn't annoy her at all. Rather, it threatened to make her face flush again.

Lady Clarissa chose that moment to break in, asking, "Lord Albert, how are your parents?"

"Call me Beau, please. They're as well as can be expected."

Lady Clarissa bit her lip sympathetically. "Your mother stays rather secluded these days, does she not? I completely understand her situation. Lord Cowper took months and months to ... well, it was dreadfully drawn out."

His gaze slid to Fiona, and she could have sworn that his eyes held amusement, as if he were sharing a joke with her, but the next moment he was saying, "You've been through a trying time," and he remained thoroughly engrossed in Lady Clarissa's explanation of it.

Dinner was announced. Lady Amelia, apparently still flustered by the Richland family's cold reaction to Beau, busied herself pairing the couples for the walk to the dining room, something she had never bothered with before. Fiona, on Henry's arm, found herself directly behind Beau and Lady Clarissa. She searched Henry's face for any sign of continued dislike, but his thoughts were already elsewhere.

"Lobster is on the menu tonight, one of the as-yet-unproven species. It will take hundreds of years to create remedies from the ocean creatures alone," Henry commented, oblivious to the interesting scene in front of him.

"Yes, indeed," Fiona murmured, only half listening. She was watching in interest as Lady Clarissa batted her eyes to emphasize something she was saying quietly, for Beau's ears alone. He responded by dipping his head closer to her ear and giving his own quiet response, at which Lady Clarissa giggled. The sight of them—along with the bruise she now sported on her thigh from the hairbrush—strengthened her resolve to withstand his charms.

"In fact, I think the cuttlefish is the only oceanic proving so far," Henry continued.

Fiona forced her gaze back to him. "What does it cure?"

"It's mostly a woman's remedy, if you follow my meaning."

"Yes. Like fenugreek and black cohosh in my world of herbs. Henry, how is the onion treating you?"

"The official name is Allium Cepa, and what I've noticed so far is that my nose feels as if I've eaten a bit of horseradish, without actually having done so."

"So nothing too uncomfortable, hopefully."

"Not at all, not at all." Henry held out Fiona's chair and seated her before taking his own seat next to her.

Fiona gasped inwardly when Beau sat on her other side. Her father usually took that seat, but Lady Amelia had obviously seen fit to make changes. She looked toward her father, who caught her eye and winked, which only served to increase her discomfort.

A pair of footmen ladled delicious-smelling squash soup into everyone's bowls, and Fiona took a spoonful. She dipped her spoon in for a second taste, self-conscious in her knowledge that Felicity and Emily might, at that very moment, be spying. They ate much earlier than the adults and had had plenty of time to put their plan into effect.

"What do you find most tedious about the country, Miss Fairmont?" Beau asked her, closing the gap between them by a good three inches. He even smelled perfect—sandalwood mixed with something utterly enticing—and Fiona put down her spoon, her stomach's needs suddenly overtaken by nerves.

"I'm not finding it tedious in the least," she replied, meeting his gaze earnestly.

He took a spoonful of soup and made an appreciative face. "Do you prefer the country to London then?"

"Yes. London's air is bad for my plants, I've discovered."

"Fergie mentioned that you liked plants. What is it about them that fascinates so much?"

"The question should be, 'what doesn't fascinate?'"

"Enlighten me."

Fiona wished he'd go back to making Lady Clarissa

giggle, but perhaps she could force the issue by waxing philosophical. Men generally hated it when she did that. "I love what plants represent. They mirror our own life cycle—life and death, certainly—but more. They thrive with love and attention, but it has to be the right kind. They, too, can become victims of good intentions gone awry, if one gives them too much water or too much light, thinking that more is better. They, too, are wonderfully varied, with some being delicate, some hardy, some beautiful, some ugly, some cruel, like the nettle; some soothing, like lavender. They are a world in and of themselves."

"You're wearing lavender tonight, I noticed." Without waiting for a response Beau continued, "And if you were a plant, how would you describe yourself? I see you as a newly unfurled rose, yellow with dark pink edging and a high center. The kind that grow one per stem ... that stand alone in a bud vase without any need for background greenery."

"I'm hardier than a rose," Fiona insisted, thrown that his eyes hadn't glazed over from her previous speech, yet delighted by his comparison. But now it was time to offer details of her medical history. That would certainly put him off. "When my sister and I got the measles, *I* was the one who recovered in six days while my sister took ten. I was the one who did *not* faint at sight of the leeches."

Henry, who had been listening to their exchange from Fiona's right chimed in with, "Ah! I'm always looking for hardy subjects. It's slow going proving only one remedy at a time."

Fiona felt a bit shocked by his suggestion. "I think I want to see how the onion treats you before I agree to be an experimental subject." Was that all she was to him? A tester for his remedies? Was that the price she would have to pay to remain in the company of genius?

"What experiments are you conducting?" Beau asked.

"Have you heard of homeopathy?" was the clipped reply.

Beau shrugged. "Some type of healing thing is all I

know."

Fiona laughed, wishing that Henry could get over his affront and laugh as well. But it didn't prevent him from talking about his favorite topic when given the chance.

"Like cures like. A bee sting that causes redness, heat and swelling can be cured by infinitesimal amounts of the bee's poison. But the science is new and it will take time to test each plant, animal and mineral on the earth. I was teasing, Fiona, when I said you should test them with me." He gave her a rueful half-smile.

Lady Clarissa cleared her throat and placed her hand on Beau's sleeve. Fiona saw a tightening in his jaw, just before he acknowledged the widow. She pouted prettily, once she had his attention. "I feel ignored."

"That won't do, Lady Clarissa. May I make amends by reading you my favorite poem after dinner?"

He has a favorite poem? Fiona thought with interest.

"A poem? I don't know, I was thinking of something a little more … unless you care to read the poem at Knollton? I would welcome an escort home," Lady Clarissa replied, looking at him through lowered eyelashes.

"Tempting, my lady, but I must decline. Nursing duties stand in the way, and since my mother rarely accepts such offers of help I cannot be late. She agreed to it tonight only because I swore I'd wake her at any sign of change … and she knows she's no help to my father exhausted."

"Oh, you poor dears!" Lady Clarissa exclaimed, almost—but not quite—hiding her disappointment. "I heard your father had gotten worse recently."

"He's following the natural course of his disease, which means he doesn't get better, only worse."

Lady Clarissa squeezed his arm, her large brown eyes imploring him. "I'm so sorry. If you ever need someone to confide in, I'd be happy to listen."

"Thank you. You're very kind." Beau turned his attention to the servant who now stood behind him holding a plate heaped with various kinds of meat. He pointed, saying, "I'd like that lobster tail, and one of those filets. They look delicious."

Fiona picked out a small quail breast and a lobster tail. Determined to stop eavesdropping on the pair to her left, she turned to Henry and asked, "Henry, you're coming to the picnic tomorrow, aren't you?"

"Er, what picnic?"

"Lady Amelia has tentatively planned one. We could look for new plant specimens together." Fiona popped a bite of lobster in her mouth and sensed rather than saw Beau leaning toward her again, bringing with him another intoxicating cloud of his delicious scent. Henry's eyes shifted to Beau and his expression changed from disinclined to disgruntled.

"Did I hear you mention a picnic?" Beau asked, his breath tickling Fiona's shoulder.

"The possibility of one," Fiona replied. Now who was eavesdropping?

"And I heard you say you wanted to explore plants. Well, Castlewood is the place to come, then. Our chef, André, has the best herb garden in these parts. Lord and Lady Hasselton would agree with me."

"What's that, dear?" said Lady Amelia from across the table.

"Lady Amelia, I'd like to offer Castlewood as the destination of the picnic tomorrow. Miss Fairmont wishes to see plant specimens, and I think you'll agree that André's garden is one of the most extensive in these parts."

Lady Amelia cast an uneasy glance at Lady Richland. "That sounds lovely, Beau, but won't your mother mind?"

"Not at all, as long as you don't expect her to play hostess. She may attend briefly, but only if my father isn't needing her."

"I haven't experienced André's food in a long while. My mouth waters just thinking about it," Lord Hasselton chimed in, unaware of Lady Richland's glares.

Beau had taken in her disapproval—her loud sniff and the glance that shot daggers at him—but he continued anyway. "It's settled then. Bring nothing. André will make us a feast and we'll see scores of plant specimens, both in the gardens and along the edge of the forest." He turned toward Fiona with a smile, but she ignored it, focusing on her lobster tail.

"Thank you, Beau. It sounds lovely," Lady Amelia murmured, perhaps not willing to give a stronger commitment in the face of the Richlands' ire.

"I wonder if André remembers how much I love his crème brûlée. Is that even possible at a picnic?" Lord Hasselton asked.

"No challenge is too great for him, even crème brûlée at a picnic. He'll appreciate the opportunity to show off," Beau said. "It's settled, then?"

"I—" Lady Richland began.

Lord Hasselton, his mind on the delicious crème brûlée awaiting him, cut her off. "Of course! What a treat."

Lady Richland's mouth pursed into a thin line of frustration, her argument—whatever it might have been—effectively squelched.

"Are you positive your mother won't be put out, dear?" Lady Amelia urged. "I hate to think what she's going through right now, and our convergence on Castlewood might prove tedious."

"You might not even see her, and please do not think her rude if that's the case."

It seemed settled. Fiona wondered if the Richlands would conveniently come down with migraines tomorrow.

But the mention of Beau's mother reminded her of something. Turning to Beau, she asked, "Have your parents consulted an herbalist? If not, I'd be happy to talk with them. There might be something that could make your father more comfortable, that he's not yet receiving."

Beau gave her a long, considering look before answering. "That's very kind of you, Miss Fairmont. I'll certainly ask them. Thank you." The emotion in his voice surprised her.

"You're welcome. It's nothing, really," she insisted, but his expression clearly showed that he disagreed.

***

Beau was true to his word and left after one glass of port. Fiona noticed with amusement that Lady Clarissa said her goodbyes shortly after realizing that Beau was gone, but she had to agree—he really had taken a large part of the gathering's joie de vivre with him.

She took the opportunity to satisfy her curiosity. "Henry, you don't seem overly fond of Beau," she said, discarding the seven of diamonds. They were playing gin, Henry's favorite game, and she was losing badly since her mind wasn't on it.

Henry frowned. "He's a rake," he said, as if that explained everything.

"But I understand from your aunt that he was engaged to your cousin? That was surprising to discover, since only the one engagement to Miss Elliot made the gossip papers."

"It wasn't widely known; something between our families."

"Why did he break it off?"

Henry closed his fan of cards and tapped them impatiently on the table. "Because he's a complete scoundrel. He and his family strung poor Olivia along for years, but shortly before he started at Oxford, just when my aunt approached Lady Margaret about an engagement announcement, he decided to break it off. No explanation given. Perhaps he had already met Miss Elliot, but all I know for sure is that my cousin was devastated. She ended up marrying a man who carried her overseas to America. We hardly ever see her, and the whole affair broke my aunt's heart. Now, can we play cards or must we gossip all night?"

"Just one more question: Did Beau make your cousin *think* he loved her?"

Henry shook his head in exasperation. "How should I know that? I was never privy to their private conversations."

"Well, but—"

"Fiona, are we going to play? If not, I need to retire. My

eyes are stinging a bit from the remedy."

Fiona reluctantly let the subject drop. "Let's finish our game."

6.

As his father lay in an uneasy sleep, Beau listened patiently as his mother reviewed his father's various medicines for the third time. When she finished, he said, "Mother, I'm confident I can remember this now. Please go get some rest."

"Yes, of course you can. And I'm right upstairs if you should need me."

But she continued to hover, so Beau brought up something he'd been meaning to tell her. "At dinner tonight, I invited the Hasseltons and their party guests to a picnic tomorrow. I let them know that you may or may not make an appearance. In any case, I would like for you and Father to meet Miss Fairmont. She's an amateur herbalist and very kindly offered to consult about Father's condition."

"That's very kind of her. I take it the dinner went well?"

Beau snorted. "Not as well as you're thinking. Miss Fairmont seemed quite taken with Featherstone."

"Oh, dear! And the Richlands were there as well?"

"Yes, and as angry as ever. I hadn't thought about that ridiculous engagement in years, but apparently they hold longstanding grudges—not that the arrangement was seriously meant by us. It *was* simply a thought tossed out at our joint christening, wasn't it?" Beau asked, picking up one of his father's medicine bottles to read its label.

"Truly! But Lady Olivia fell in love with you, and her mother cannot forgive you for driving her daughter across the ocean."

"What's this one for?" Beau asked, indicating the bottle he held. It was one his mother hadn't mentioned.

"You can give it to me, and I'll dispose of it. It was something to aid his joints when he was still walking."

"I'm sorry, Mother," Beau said, handing the bottle over. "Try to get a good night's rest."

***

With the sun still hours away from rising, Lord Beaumont opened his eyes to the sight of his eldest son standing by the window, gazing out at a starlit sky.

"What're you thinking about?" he asked, clearing his throat when the last word came out raspy.

Beau started and was beside his father in two long strides. He reached for the tall, brown bottle. "Do you need more laudanum, Father?"

"No, not yet. It makes me too groggy to think straight, and I've wished for a chance to talk with you."

"Are you in pain?"

"Nothing I can't tolerate. Beau, your mother told me about Miss Fairmont. Now you tell me about her."

"You can meet her yourself, Father—tomorrow, since she kindly offered to prescribe herbs to you. She's coming here for a picnic luncheon."

"Herbs? What does she know about herbs?" Lord Beaumont asked. Because of his pain it came out grumpier than he would have liked.

Beau pulled up a chair for himself. "It's her hobby." After a pause he added ruefully, "I'm in love; her offering of this herbal consultation clinched it. But I'm not at all certain that I'll win her. She may have gotten it into her head that she prefers Featherstone."

"Featherstone, eh? I hope for both our sakes you're wrong, because it's my dearest wish to see you married. But what poetic justice, eh?"

"I suppose," Beau acknowledged grudgingly. "That thought crossed my mind as well."

"Why do you think she prefers him?"

"He has medicinal interests. Not herbs, but—I don't know. The name eludes me."

"Maybe he can look at me too. Is he coming tomorrow?"

"He's invited."

His father heard Beau's irritation, and bit back a smile. "But perhaps just one consultation at a time, eh? I shouldn't mix prescriptions."

"I hope he doesn't come at all, truthfully. Perhaps he and the Richlands *won't* come, since—you know."

"Of course. The broken 'promise.' One careless statement made at a christening, and the Richlands treated it as a signed covenant. They wove it into their daughter's head from the time she could talk." Lord Beaumont remembered homely Olivia, who frequently played with Beau's twin, Elizabeth, when they were children.

"I always assumed she was playacting when she said we were to be married. I'd pretend with her sometimes, with Elizabeth standing in as our quite obnoxious daughter—whenever they caught me in a good enough mood for such nonsense. But when her mother brought up engagement announcements—!"

"Yes, poor Olivia. And to have such a mother. I'll never forget the tirade that harridan fed us after you destroyed her tidy plan."

Beau ran a hand through his hair, exhaling loudly. "It's old news, and not worth dusting off. In the here and now, Miss Fairmont deserves a much happier in-law situation."

Lord Beaumont's laugh came out more as a cough. "I agree! Your mother would be the perfect choice, so get moving. I haven't too much time."

"I'd propose today if I thought she'd accept," Beau admitted.

Lord Beaumont winced and closed his eyes. "I wish you the best." After a wheezy inhalation, he added, "I'll take that laudanum now."

***

Miles away, the lady being discussed also was awake in the wee hours of the morning, her mind in a turmoil over the events of the evening. Once again, Beau had impressed her.

Once again, she had had to force herself to remember his reputation, to focus on the way he had made Lady Clarissa giggle, to remind herself that her feelings for him mirrored every other English woman—and girl's—feelings. She was angry—at herself, for having such a boringly predicable reaction to him, but also at Beau for being so appealing in the first place. After he had left, it was as if a beautiful fire had been doused too early.

Fiona heaved a huge sigh and rolled onto her side, tucking her hand under her face and forcing her thoughts onto Henry. Here was a near genius whose preoccupation with his science had won her immediate admiration. He didn't waste time flattering her and flirting with her, but she had every reason to think that—eventually—he would propose. Her certainty had to do with the way his aunt's face became almost predatory whenever she focused her attention on Fiona.

You don't deserve him, though, Fiona said to herself, thinking that the way she craved Beau's attention was weak and pathetic, and unworthy of Henry's single-minded greatness. She remembered their parting conversation after the card game.

"You've decided to go to the picnic?" she had asked him.

"You want me to, don't you?" he had replied, meeting her gaze with resignation.

"I do! Plant gathering could be fun, and if you wish to avoid Beau I'm sure his grounds are large enough to accomplish that."

Henry considered her with a knitted brow. "Yes … it throws me out of my routine, but I suppose … if you wish it—"

Fiona took a deep breath and decided on a new tactic, not wanting a repeat of the garden party. "Henry, think of this picnic as a way to gather more material to work with."

His answer had been unsatisfactorily noncommittal: "I suppose. Of course, I already have more than I can prove in a year's time waiting for me in my laboratory."

Exasperated, Fiona had carelessly thrown out, "I'll help you prove the plants. We'll start a new journal of symptoms just for me. Will you agree to come tomorrow?" She desperately wanted Henry there, as a buffer between herself and Beau.

She was rewarded for her offer. Henry took her hand and brushed a light kiss across the back of it with cool lips. "I'd be delighted to gather plants with you tomorrow, Fiona. For now, I must bid you goodnight. Fresh air tires me, so I want a good night's rest."

Speechless, Fiona nodded. That was easy, she thought. So, the way to make Henry oblige me is through his homeopathy. She'd have to remember that in future.

"Relinquishing this seat, Featherstone?" Fiona's father asked. His once red hair was now faded into blondish-gray, but he was still very handsome, with unlined skin and intelligent blue eyes.

"Yes, and you're lucky. Fiona's game is off tonight." Henry gave Fiona a smile that she briefly returned.

"First deal, Father?"

"We don't have to play cards. I just wanted a chat with my favorite debutante. Have you enjoyed yourself this evening, my dear?"

"Yes, but I missed you at dinner tonight."

"Did you really, or are you simply flattering your old father?"

Fiona smiled and squeezed his hand. "And how *did* Beau manage to get seated next to me? I would have thought—given the reason for this house party—that Lady Amelia would have avoided that."

"Were you displeased? You seemed to be enjoying his company well enough."

"Of course! He is the light to us female moths, each of us drawn against our will, beating our wings tirelessly until, alas, we get burned."

Lord Fairmont chuckled. "That's an odd way to put it, but there's truth in it, too, by God. So, are you immune to his charms by use of these funny analogies of yours?"

"By those and by good, logical sense. I refuse to become another captive in his long line of conquests, Father. I will not be so taken in."

"In truth, I asked Lady Amelia to give him my seat because I want you to be sure that Lord Featherstone is the right man for you. I've noticed that you like him much more than any of the other gentlemen you've met this season, but I want you to be sure of your feelings. If Beau can't weaken them, nothing can. This Lord Featherstone may be the genuine article."

"He might be, but—unlike Mother—if we do not become engaged this season I won't assume the effort is a failure. What's wrong with giving a relationship time? Why the rush in such situations?"

Agreeable Lord Fairmont simply nodded, loath to disagree with his wife's strong opinion on the matter, and Fiona had to be content with his mild assent.

But now, at three thirty in the morning, Fiona's heart was having its say, overriding the good sense that had relegated Beau to nonentity status.

You're more interested in him than you want to admit, her heart was telling her. And no matter how hard she tried to silence it, she couldn't quite do it.

***

Felicity bounced her sister's bed gently, softly calling her name. "Fiona. Time to wake up. Time to get ready for the picnic."

Fiona's response was to put a pillow over her head. She wished the picnic had never been planned because didn't it mean she'd have to come up with another dose of antidote to Beau's mesmerizing charm? Perhaps not, if she stuck close to Henry's side. But what about her offer to see Beau's father?

She groaned into the pillow.

"Come on, Fiona! Aren't you excited? Emily and I think Beau likes you, by the way. He looked at you with complete adoration last night."

The pillow lifted, but only for a moment so that Fiona could say, "When he turned to his left, Lady Clarissa got the very same treatment. That's what he's famous for, after all."

"No, you're wrong. In fact, we had to practically stuff our skirts in our mouths once, when Lady Clarissa had plucked at his sleeve for the tenth time, and this look flitted over his face. If he'd followed his instincts, he would have put his cream pie in her face." Felicity giggled as she remembered.

"You were too far away to see clearly. Leave me alone! I want to sleep another few minutes," Fiona grumped from underneath her pillow.

"I know what I saw! He likes you, Fiona. The two of you, sitting side by side like that, were perfect together."

She got a pillow thrown at her head for the compliment. "You are the silliest girl imaginable. Beau may have liked me better than Lady Clarissa but that doesn't change who he is: a fickle hedonist, who thinks he can win any woman with a single brilliant smile. Well, he's wrong!"

"What's a hedonist?" Felicity asked, grinning. "And my goodness! I've never seen you get so emotional about something that wasn't made of paper and leather!"

"Just go!" Fiona shouted, pointing at the door.

Felicity scooted to the door, but got in a parting shot: "Depend on you to allow love to turn you into a complete witch!" She closed the door before Fiona could respond.

Fiona pulled the covers over her head. "Love!" she muttered. "Why does base attraction always get confused with love?"

***

André had outdone himself with the picnic feast and the early June weather wasn't too warm, even in the sun. Beau was less pleased with the fact that Fiona had chosen plant gathering over sun bathing, and she had barely taken ten minutes to eat André's delicious fare before she and

Featherstone were off again, walking along the periphery of the forest, their heads bent as they searched the ground for plant specimens. What hurt Beau most was that she had said to him only: "How is your father? Does he want me to visit him?"

"My mother will send someone to fetch you when Father has finished eating. Thanks again for your kind offer," he had responded, and had gotten a polite nod in return.

Before he'd had a chance to say more, Featherstone had called out, "Fiona, what plant is this? I've never seen anything like it."

They're on a first-name basis? Beau thought, feeling a pang in his gut that he knew was caused by Fiona's disinterest rather than André's food. Perhaps by the intense hatred he was feeling for Featherstone, as well.

***

Fiona furiously tugged a specimen of chamomilla from the ground. The defenseless white petals showered downward under the violent treatment, and if Beau could have heard her noises of disgust, as she picked up the scattered petals, his gut might have felt better. Idyllic bliss was definitely not something she was feeling, despite previous appearances to the contrary.

Fiona popped the petals in her mouth, chewing them vigorously and hoping that they would calm her nerves as well as a tea of the whole plant would have done.

"What are you eating?" Henry asked, coming to stand beside her. He had a basket half-full of their pickings in one hand, a dead ant in the other.

She swallowed the bitter mouthful with difficulty. "Chamomile. It works wonders in tea, and I'm hoping it'll take away my stomach pain in raw form as well. It would be an excellent plant for you to prove." She stood and brushed dirt from the unearthed root off her skirt.

"It's been proven already, but here—" Henry held out the basket and Fiona placed the daisy-like flower carefully on top. "I'll make a fresh supply. It's quite useful to have on hand."

Fiona looked over her shoulder, distracted by movement, and saw that one of the Beaumonts' servants was approaching.

"I told Beau I'd look in on his father, to see if there might be an herbal remedy that would help him. Do you know of any homeopathic remedies that might help a chronically ill person?"

"Since I'm a researcher, not a physician, I'll decline giving an opinion," Henry said matter-of-factly.

"Oh. I thought—" Fiona's brow puckered as she hesitated. "Maybe Lord Beaumont has a symptom that reminds you of one of your provings. That would be similar enough to make a case for using a particular remedy."

"It's not that simple. A strong case needs at least three similarities, and many remedy symptoms overlap each other."

The servant had reached them by then. "Miss Fairmont, I was sent to fetch you. Lord Beaumont will see you now."

Fiona nodded, but before leaving she said, "Henry, do you ever see yourself helping people concretely with homeopathy?" It wasn't asked critically, but with simple curiosity.

"By proving these substances and sharing the information with *physicians,* I am already helping people," Henry replied, frowning. "But I do not presume to know anything about diagnostics. That is an art in and of itself."

"Don't take offense!" Fiona gave him a rueful smile. "Perhaps I meant: Will you ever become a physician of homeopathy?"

He gave her a quizzical look. "I'm a peer of the realm. Of course I won't."

"I see."

She turned and followed the servant toward Castlewood, her mind turning over this new piece of information. She wanted to understand why she felt disappointed in Henry, particularly when his explanation made perfect sense, and realized it was because he lacked a certain warmth that, until now, she had assumed he possessed. His passion was with the homeopathic process itself, not the end result of healing, and she realized he had a rather coldly scientific approach to it all.

Fiona's regard for Henry didn't slip with the realization, but she had to make a shift in her thinking of him: less philanthropic, more scientific. It was all still good.

***

Beau was waiting for Fiona just outside his father's door. "Have you ever been in a sickroom before?" he asked, wanting to properly warn her if the answer was no.

"Yes, my grandfather died three years ago. I've loved plants forever, but his illness was what started my interest in their medicinal qualities. One day I visited him after I'd been picking lavender, and my fingers and clothes still smelled of it. He said the smell made his headache better. I've been learning about other herbal remedies ever since."

Beau turned toward her, his hand on the doorknob. "What's on your hands and clothes today? I ask because it smells very good."

"I believe you're smelling a combination of bergamot and mint. I make my own oils." Fiona's serious green eyes gave nothing away, but if Beau could have felt her pulse at that moment, he would have known how profoundly his compliment affected her.

He held her gaze for a moment. "I thought maybe you figured out a way to bottle sunshine, for it reminds me of a warm, summery breeze," he said, finally turning the knob and ushering her into his father's room.

The room was stuffy, largely because of the blazing fire, but there was also the inevitable smell of sickness despite its spotless cleanliness and the fresh flowers on the bedside table.

After Beau introduced Fiona to his parents, Lady Margaret said, "My dear, you are every bit as beautiful as the papers say. What they don't mention is that you are just as beautiful inside as out. This is quite kind of you."

"To go out of your way for an old man who has one foot in the grave is beyond kind. You're saintly. And my wife is correct in saying that you are beautiful," Lord Beaumont agreed, giving her a rheumy wink.

"Please don't credit me with saintliness. This interest I have in herbs is inherent—a part of me. My mother might call it a compulsion. Now—" Fiona sat in the chair next to Lord Beaumont's bed and took one of his frail hands, "—I already know that I want to make a potpourri for your room, one that has lavender, rosemary and eucalyptus in it. But tell me what's ailing you the most, so that I can know what else to bring."

Beau watched their exchange from a few feet away, arms crossed over his chest. His mother had left to greet their guests, so his thoughts ran unimpeded: Fiona was one of the most unaffected, elegant, and *kind* women he had ever met. Her beauty was unparalleled in his experience. Even here, in this dismal sickroom, the firelight had found the highlights in her gorgeous hair and danced freely through the shiny locks.

Beau started when Fiona turned to him, smiling in amusement and saying, "You're a million miles away!"

"What?"

"I told her I couldn't remember my boring old ailments enough to talk about them, and she said you'd jog my memory," Lord Beaumont said, his thin face pulled into a skeletal smile. "See? I told you they were inconsequential. He can't talk about them either."

Beau cleared his throat, amused that his father was flirting. It was totally out of character, too. Unlike his son, Lord Beaumont's reputation had not been that of a rake prior to his marriage. He had had mistresses, certainly, but only a few select relationships. Once Lady Margaret Edwards had entered his life, he had thereafter had eyes only for her. But Fiona had that effect. Even as serious as she was, she was like a warm sun after a week of gray drizzle. One felt drawn to her, even though she was doing nothing to court attention.

Beau drew near and sat carefully on the end of the bed. "Mother and I can fill her in on the details, Father. Don't tire yourself."

"I'm not tired. She really made me forget! You are one of the loveliest creatures I've ever had the pleasure to meet, young lady. Just to lay eyes on you is a balm itself. Thank you kindly for coming to see me." After so many words, he took a deep, raspy breath, seemingly worn out.

"You're too kind, sir," Fiona said, gently rubbing the bony hand. "I'll make your potpourri the minute I get home and send it around this evening. More will follow after I've consulted with your family. Rest now, and I'll be back to see you soon."

"I'd like that very much," Lord Beaumont said softly. He closed his eyes, and Beau and Fiona left quietly.

"We'll find my mother. She'll tell you everything you need to know. Afterward—" Beau stopped just short of exiting into a garden where Lady Margaret and Lady Amelia could be seen sitting together on a wooden bench, their backs to them. "Could I tempt you with a walk? We have a lilac garden on the other side of the house that I think you'd enjoy seeing."

"I love lilac," Fiona said hesitantly.

"You can pick as much as you like. Enough for Featherstone's proving and enough for your potpourris. We have plenty."

"So you approve of Lord Featherstone's work?" she asked curiously, as they stepped out into the rose garden.

"It's not for me to approve or disapprove it. I admire his dedication." Even if he thought Featherstone's work was complete hogwash, Fiona could pick the lilac bushes bare if she wished to.

"He's told me some miraculous stories of cures. Mostly second hand, of course, since he doesn't actually treat people."

"He doesn't?" Beau asked, inadvertently mirroring Fiona's earlier feelings of surprise. They reached the bench where the two ladies sat. "Mother, Father is as vain as he ever was and will not tell Miss Fairmont what ails him. You need to tell her when you have a moment." Smiling at Lady Amelia, he added, "Have you had a nice visit?"

"Indeed!" Lady Amelia exclaimed. "I never knew your mother liked Rembrandt so much. I'm loaning her my Frans Hals portrait. He's not as good as Rembrandt, certainly, but I adore the one painting I have of his."

Lady Margaret demurred. "It's so kind of you, Amelia, but—"

Lady Amelia held up a hand to shush her. "I want to, dearest, if it will make you more comfortable during this difficult time. I know you wish to talk privately with Miss Fairmont now, so I'll go see what Hassie is doing. I'll probably find him asleep with a colony of ants taking up residence on his shirtfront."

"I'll walk with you, if I may, Lady Amelia," Beau said, wanting to give Fiona and his mother privacy. To Fiona he said, "I'll retrieve you in half an hour."

Lady Amelia tucked a hand under Beau's elbow and walked with him toward the other guests. "What's happening in half an hour?"

"Nothing in particular. I don't want Miss Fairmont to have to search for us," Beau lied, not wanting to make the lilac garden a public expedition.

He found the picnickers seated on blankets under the vast horse chestnut tree nearest the pond. They appeared happily relaxed, except for Lady Clarissa. Beau noted with amusement that she had attached herself to the only other single man, Featherstone, but her glazed eyes told a story of boredom. Henry appeared so enthralled with telling her about his plant finds—they were spread out on the blanket between the pair, and he was pointing out details as he talked—that he didn't seem to care that he was boring her.

Lady Clarissa saw Beau and caught her lower lip between her teeth. "Finally! You've been gone forever!"

"Giving Lady Clarissa a horticultural lesson, Featherstone?" Beau asked, grinning.

Henry regarded him coldly, obviously displeased at the interruption—by his family's sworn enemy, no less. "Yes."

Lady Clarissa held out her hand to Beau, and he helped her to her feet. Ignoring Henry completely, she said, "Let's take a stroll around the pond."

Beau nodded agreeably, but caused Lady Clarissa's face to fall immediately after by inviting Henry to come along as well.

"But where's Miss Fairmont? Is she coming back soon?" Henry asked.

"She's with my mother, getting an update on my father's condition."

Lady Clarissa eyed Henry sternly. "All this talk of medicines and sickness is giving me a headache. If you come with us, you may *not* talk about your plants anymore."

Henry grinned sheepishly, and Beau could have sworn that he saw admiration in the man's eyes. "I have just the remedy for your headache, Lady Clarissa," Henry teased.

She shook her head in exasperation, but her lips tipped up in the barest smile. "One more word and I'll shove you in the pond. Don't think I won't!"

Henry stood too, his spindly legs making him look slightly spidery. His foot trampled one of his plant specimens, as he said, "I apologize for boring you, Lady Clarissa. I'm afraid my interest in the topic—and your charming company—carried me away. Please forgive me."

"You're forgiven ... and you might want to take your foot off that plant before it's crushed and useless," Lady Clarissa scolded. She turned away, taking Beau with her, but not before he'd seen a look of unmistakable yearning on Henry's face. Interesting ... he had never seen Henry look at Fiona that way.

Lady Clarissa plucked at his sleeve, pulling him away from his musings. "I can't tell you how relieved I am that you rescued me. He kept going on and on. I couldn't even excuse myself because he never let me get a word in."

Beau bit back a smile. "He's a man dedicated to his cause."

Lady Clarissa gazed up at Beau flirtatiously. "Your cause, on the other hand, is something I can sink my teeth into."

"My cause?"

But Beau knew where Lady Clarissa was leading the conversation, and for many years, he had encouraged women to make suggestive comments. In fact, before he had met Fiona he would have replied, "My cause awaits your membership, my lady," or some such drivel. But now he felt a bit of shame that this woman—who barely knew him—slipped so easily into provocative language with him.

Lady Clarissa's girlish laugh interrupted his self-contemplation. "Coyness is not a known characteristic of yours, Beau. 'My cause?' You are too funny! Must I spell it out for you? Does your charm really exceed your intellect?"

Her words stung, but Beau knew he deserved them. He decided that bluntness was the best course of action. "My cause has shifted, and that is why I asked. I was curious to see if you had perceived the change, or if you were going on old information. You see—" He turned toward Lady Clarissa and brought her hand to his lips for a kiss. "While I think you perfectly charming, I will not act on that impression because my heart has finally been irrevocably captured."

"Your heart—do you mean you have already secured a new mistress?"

"No, I—"

His words were lost because at that moment Henry called out. He had run to catch up to them, and apprehension was etched on his face. "Excuse me, but I need to get home. My hands," he said, holding out hands that were streaked with the beginnings of red, blistery lines. His face, too, had a red streak forming under his nose, where he had smelled a plant cutting. "Will you tell Miss Fairmont that I've left?"

Lady Clarissa ducked behind Beau. "Is he contagious?"

Beau ignored her. "I daresay you touched poison oak. But why don't I lead you to Miss Fairmont? I'm sure she can help with one of her herbal remedies."

Henry waved a contemptuous hand. "What I need is a good homeopathic remedy. Poison oak, you say? I can't remember if I've proven that or not without my notebook. Miss Fairmont might remember. Perhaps you *should* lead me to her, so that I can ask her."

"She's this way," Beau said, motioning. He briskly led Henry toward the rose garden where he had left Fiona with his mother. He was sorely disappointed that the lilac garden would have to wait.

***

Lady Clarissa didn't follow since she wanted to stay as far away from the contagion as possible. Besides, Beau's admission had given her a lot to think about as she made her way back to the group of picnickers. She now possessed one of the best pieces of gossip to surface in years: Lord Albert Beaumont, the most famous rake of the day, was finally out of commission. And she would bet her entire estate on the fact that his heart was taken by Miss Fairmont, debutante extraordinaire who tolerated the season's parties as well as the Prince Regent tolerated boredom—barely, if at all.

***

Fiona saw the two men approaching first and gestured to Lady Margaret. "Something's wrong," she said, standing.

"What has happened?" Lady Margaret asked in alarm, and Fiona's heart went out to her, knowing that the poor woman's first thought was probably that her husband had taken a turn for the worse.

Fiona saw Henry's facial redness and knew immediately what the problem was. "Oh, dear! It's a case of poison oak rash," she said to Beau's mother. To Henry she said, "Oh, Henry, I should have warned you."

She felt ashamed for her carelessness. She had been so caught up in her nerves over seeing Beau again that she had forgotten to give Henry proper warnings about the plants that he knew nothing about. She took his sleeve and examined his hands, saying, "Don't scratch—no matter how itchy you feel—or you could develop infection. Lady Margaret, does André keep chamomile in his garden or should I go pick more from the forest? I need a strong tincture made, and some towels to wrap his hands in. Henry, you'll need an oatmeal bath when you get home."

"No, what I need is a homeopathic remedy. Do you remember if I've made a remedy of poison oak, Fiona? I can't."

"If not, I'll certainly help you make one. In the meantime, let's get some chamomile on your hands fast—it will help to lessen the itchiness immediately, and will lessen the severity of the rash."

"Featherstone, my mother will show you to one of the guest rooms while Miss Fairmont instructs André about the tincture," Beau said. "Miss Fairmont, follow me to the kitchens."

Henry didn't move. "There's no need for the delay," he said curtly. "I need only to get home."

"Soon, Henry. Please, trust me. I've treated these rashes before. The chamomile is an excellent first step. You'll get the remedy very soon." Without waiting for his response, Fiona turned and followed Beau, leaving Henry in Lady Margaret's care.

***

André turned from his task of clipping dill when he heard them approaching. "Ah! I knew it! You've come back for the extra pear-anise crème brûlée. It was truly a masterpiece, was it not?"

"Yes, everyone exclaimed over it, but that's not the purpose of this visit. Miss Fairmont wants to know if you grow chamomile," Beau said.

André's dark eyes clouded with disappointment, and Beau knew that he had not praised enough to satisfy. André wasn't happy unless his creations were the sole topic of a conversation. The Beaumonts put up with his vanity, though, because his cooking really was that good.

"There's more crème brûlée? I feel like I've just discovered a hidden present under the Christmas tree," Fiona exclaimed, and Beau knew that she had just won André's heart and loyalty forever.

André beamed at her and motioned for them to follow him to another corner of the garden. He moved more quickly than his perfectly rotund frame usually allowed, and showed off the healthy patch of chamomile with a flourish of his hand. "You may have as much as you wish, mademoiselle."

Fiona bent to pick the chamomile, and André's eyes widened. Curious, Beau stepped into his line of vision and the sight made him swallow hard. André was watching Fiona as she knelt on the flagstones, her perfect breasts plumping tauntingly against the confines of her dress's stylishly-cut neckline.

"Like two perfect twin soufflés, delicate as spun sugar," André whispered.

Beau cleared his throat and André looked up guiltily. "Apologies," he muttered, averting his eyes.

Fiona, unaware of the stir she was causing, handed André the picked herb. "Will you boil them, please, André?"

He gave an ostentatious bow. "It is my greatest pleasure, mademoiselle."

Beau helped Fiona to her feet while she nodded her thanks. "Miss Fairmont, while André is busy boiling would you like to see the lilac garden? We won't be long, and you may pick as much as we both can hold."

She was busy brushing off her skirt and didn't answer at first. After a few moments she looked up. "I suppose we have a few minutes, while it's boiling," she said slowly.

"We'll be back in fifteen minutes," Beau told André, tucking Fiona's hand in the crook of his arm and leading her to the gate before she had a chance to change her mind.

As they left his garden, André called out, "Miss Fairmont, that crème brûlée awaits you when you return."

Her "thank you" was probably not heard, Beau was walking her so quickly. Nothing—not crème brûlée, not a rash, not a hot sun—was going to stop him from getting Fiona to the lilac garden this time. He had recently discovered the Robert Burns poem "O were my Love yon Lilac fair," and the outing felt important.

7.

Beau led Fiona out of the gated herb garden, along the tall stone wall that protected it from rabbits, deer, and other herb scavengers. At the end of the wall a gravel path led away from Castlewood down a grassy hill. Fiona could see the picnickers far off to her right, the pond just beyond them glittering in the sunlight. Closer and to her left, she saw the lilac garden, an intimate but large grouping of tall lilac shrubs that she could already smell.

She breathed deeply. "That smell. It's magnificent."

"Wait until you're surrounded by it. One almost feels intoxicated."

The gravel path split off and they turned with it to the left and passed under a beautifully crafted archway made from thick, twisted vines interlaced with ivy.

They walked to the middle where an intricately designed wrought-iron table and two chairs were tucked cozily under a tall, freestanding lilac bush in full bloom. Fiona closed her eyes, inhaling so much of the sweet air that she got dizzy. "I see what you mean. I'm lightheaded." Opening her eyes, she added, "I'm lucky to see it in bloom. Lilac only lasts about three weeks, doesn't it?"

"Ours lasts six because our gardener planted three varieties, one an early bloomer, one a standard bloomer, and one a late bloomer." Beau released her arm and turned to face her.

Fiona noticed that with his head directly in the line of the sun he looked more godlike than ever. The sun played off his black hair, giving it celestial, purplish highlights. His eyes and nose were in shadow, making his blood red lips and white teeth stand out in stark comparison. In that moment, perhaps because of the strong smell of the lilac, perhaps because of the privacy of the magical garden, Fiona wanted—yearned—to kiss those lips. The feeling was so strong that her heart ached with it and her lips parted with the quickening of her breath. Beau must have recognized her desire, because he responded before she could think to stop him. He bent his head and kissed her.

The kiss was gentle, a soft melding of their lips, and Fiona's knees felt weak with the deliciousness of it. She sighed softly, knowing she should pull away, but unable to. How could she act sensibly when he smelled even better than the lilac?

And then she felt Beau's tongue lick along the curve of her upper lip and a curious sensation jolted deep within her that shocked her at the same time it tantalized.

She gasped and pulled away, and Beau's eyes slowly opened.

He looks like he just tasted that crème brûlée, Fiona thought, and in the next second she realized that she must look the same, since his mouth was more delicious than any dessert. He didn't say anything, apparently waiting for her to speak first.

Should she slap him? No, she shouldn't. That kiss was too spectacular to warrant such a punishment. She would be grateful for the experience of it forever.

"The chamomile," she murmured, forcing herself to turn away from him. "I know the way back. You must need to attend your guests by now."

"I—" He took a step forward as if to go with her.

"No, please. I know the way," Fiona insisted, staying him with a raised hand.

And he let her go.

***

Halfway up the grassy hillside, Fiona realized that she was holding her breath. She stopped and took a deep inhalation, barely smelling the lilac now. She glanced behind her, confirming that Beau was still out of sight, then reached up and explored her lips with tentative fingers. Their ordinariness surprised her, for she had expected to feel the same heatedness on the outside that she was feeling from within.

That kiss.

It had thrilled—no, even that description was too bland. That indescribable kiss had taken her tidy opinion about what love should and should not be and had turned it on its head. Beau's delicious breath—like fresh cut apples and pinched rosemary—and his warm, firm lips had seared her soul, marking it forever.

She remembered his tongue licking along her upper lip and, as if it was happening all over again, she felt the same sizzling sensation. She had been so startled that she had pulled away, but now she fervently wished that she hadn't ended the kiss so quickly. What would she have felt next?

His face afterward had fascinated her, too. Lids half shut, lips slightly parted, gaze intense, he had taken a slow, deep breath as he looked at her. She had expected him to speak, to say something—anything—to explain what had just happened, but he hadn't. So she had left, but she wasn't the same woman who had entered that garden. For now she understood something that she had never realized before: that attraction has the power to make all else seem inconsequential. That kiss, if she allowed it to, could change the course of her life. It had the power to make her discount every prejudice she had ever held against Lord Albert Beaumont.

But she wouldn't allow it to.

Fiona hurried the last few steps up the grassy incline toward the kitchen, on her way to helping Henry. Dear, easy-to-understand Henry, whose single-minded devotion to homeopathy so endeared him to her. Their relationship was one in which she would never experience a wildly beating heart or deep cravings, but it felt safer to her. More stable. And now she would focus on getting him comfortable and home, almost as if they were already married. It felt right.

"It is almost ready, my dear lady," André said when he saw her. "Crème brûlée while you wait?"

"Yes, thank you, André," Fiona said. But it didn't taste nearly as good as that kiss had.

Ten minutes later, she followed a servant up a flight of stairs to one of the guest rooms. The servant carried a large pot filled with chamomile-soaked towels, and nodded to indicate the room where Henry waited.

Fiona opened the door, and Henry walked toward them, impatience furrowing his brow.

"Do you know whether or not the stables have been alerted that I'm leaving? I want my carriage brought around without delay."

"Where should I put this?" the servant asked.

"Never mind that! Is my carriage being readied?" Henry barked.

The servant put the pot down with such haste that some of the chamomile solution slopped out onto the carpet. "Oh! Ah ... I'll go see, my lord."

Fiona, watching the scene in consternation, murmured a hasty "thank you," as the servant left. When she and Henry were alone, she didn't quite know what to say to this man whom she suddenly didn't recognize. She let him speak first.

"This whole day is a debacle. I should never have agreed to this ridiculous picnic in the first place," he fumed.

Fiona took a chamomile-soaked towel out of the pot and wrung it out. "Henry, why don't you sit down," she said warily. "While you're waiting for your carriage, let me drape these over you face and hands."

He made a noise of irritation. "If you must." He sat down and held his hands stiffly out in front of him, and Fiona began to wrap them in towels. "Will you come with me? And make the remedy for me? My fingers feel as if they're stiffening. I only hope that this delay will not cause a setback in the cure."

"Did you or did you not hear me say that I've treated these types of rashes before? I seriously doubt that the chamomile will cause a 'setback.'" Fiona motioned for

Henry to lean his head on the back of the chair so that she could put a towel over his reddening upper lip.

He obliged her, saying testily, "The point is, as I've told you before, Fiona, that herbs are not as powerful as homeopathy. This little exercise is a supreme waste of time since a *cure* awaits me fifteen minutes away. I honestly don't know why you insisted on this."

Fiona dropped the towel over Henry's face with less gentleness than she normally used in such situations. "For heaven's sake, Henry. I was trying to help you."

"Next time, don't, as you know I have no faith in herbs," came the muffled reply.

Fiona's look of disbelief was completely wasted since Henry couldn't see it. "No, I certainly won't." She turned away from him and tried to sort out the mix of emotions that she was feeling. This blunt rudeness wasn't something that she had expected in him. It had a petulant, tyrannical quality that she detested.

Did this aspect of his personality present itself every time he became upset by something? She hoped not.

***

Henry excused himself from the house party for the duration of his cure, so Lady Amelia invited Beau to join them for dinner again, to even their numbers.

Fiona had spent a fascinating afternoon in the laboratory making a remedy out of poison oak for Henry. His meticulous notes had made it easy. The hardest part had been avoiding direct contact with the irritating plant.

Now back at the Hasseltons', Fiona was reading in her room when she heard a knock on the door. She looked up as her mother entered, already bejeweled, perfumed, and dressed in high fashion for dinner.

Lady Winifred eyed Fiona's book with disapproval. "My dear, why are you not getting dressed? We meet for dinner in thirty minutes."

Fiona tried her best to keep defensiveness out her voice. "Twenty minutes is all the time I need to dress. "I'll ring for—"

"In a moment, dear," her mother interrupted. "Give me five minutes first. I wish to clarify something I said earlier because I may have given you a wrong impression when we last spoke about him." She stopped, and Fiona raised one eyebrow expectantly. What she heard next was a total surprise. "Beau would be the catch of the season. He appears to like you very much, and I believe that he may soon ask you to marry him. I think you'd be a fool to refuse him."

Fiona did not attempt to hide her irritation at this change in her mother's advice. She knew it came from her mother's loathing of Henry. "What about his reputation? His inclination to take on new mistresses the way other men buy new clothes?"

"All men take mistresses, Fiona."

"Henry wouldn't," Fiona retorted, saddened by the confirmation that her father must be included in that group of men who would. "You're only saying this because you hate him so."

"I do not dislike Lord Featherstone. What I find abhorrent is that he doesn't appreciate you."

"Does this appreciation, that you insist is so important, include faithfulness and respect? Or is it the shallow variety, which allows a man to take a mistress? No, thank you! I want steadfastness and loyalty and trust, not the *false* appreciation that most men have mastered as part of the courtship dance. Henry is quite extraordinary in that he doesn't care to learn those steps."

Lady Winifred winced. "Is that how you truly feel?" At Fiona's nod, she added wearily, "Then I'll go, and say no more about it."

***

Beau lay on his bed, hands laced behind his head, staring

out at the morning sky. The dark box created by closed bed curtains had quickly grown tedious after hours of insomnia, so he had thrown them open to give himself a distraction. The bluish-gray early light was something he rarely saw, but this bout of sleeplessness, based in fear, had been relentless. Its cause? He had finally acknowledged, at last night's miserable dinner, that Fiona might very well slip away from him. No, not slip. She would turn from him deliberately, choosing to do so. He might never again taste that ambrosial mouth.

He was going to see her again today, but only thanks to Michael's archery talent. The one conversation Fiona had shared with him, at last night's wretched dinner, had been about—of all things—archery. Lord Hasselton had mentioned having an archery contest if the weather continued to hold.

Beau had replied, "Are you a betting man? If so, I lay good odds that my brother could beat every person at this table."

"That's hogwash! He's still a babe—off to Eton just last year," Lord Hasselton expostulated.

"Your brother? I didn't know you had a brother." It was the first time Fiona had addressed a comment directly to him all evening. "Where was he this morning?"

Beau rewarded her attention with his best smile. "Picnicking with adults isn't his idea of fun. He stayed out of sight purposefully, I'm sure of it."

"A child, and an expert archer?" Fiona asked.

"He's twelve, but will surpass me in height by fourteen, if not sooner. He's strong for his age."

Fiona looked across the table at her host. "Lord Hasselton, you're a neighbor of the Beaumonts. How is it that you do not know of this great archer in your vicinity? Could it be that he doesn't wish to be on exhibition?"

"He'll love every minute of showing us his talent. He'd have done so before now if he'd had the opportunity," Beau said, feeling the sting of her words. He supposed he should have asked Michael's permission to plan such an event, but surely he wouldn't mind. Would he?

Lord Hasselton settled the matter. "Tomorrow at one we'll start on the front lawn. I'll have targets set up at various distances. We'll see if Michael can beat us. My money is against him. No twelve-year-old can beat me!"

"I think I saw your brother yesterday," Fiona said. "Is he fairer than you? Nice looking?"

The thought of Michael's preadolescent lanky limbs, and the two missing teeth that made his grin comical, made Beau smile. "I suppose one might say he's nice looking. He's definitely fairer than me. Where did you see him?"

"Running through the woods. Lord Featherstone and I found some of our best plants at wood's edge."

"How is Featherstone? Any better?" Beau asked.

"I left him with his remedy this afternoon. I won't find out if it worked miraculously until tomorrow."

And then she had stopped talking, had clammed up so thoroughly that she had not even said a rote "excuse me" after she'd accidentally flipped the salt cellar spoon out of its silver container and next to Beau's plate while putting down her wine glass. She'd picked it up and put it back without a word or a smile.

As the ladies were preparing to leave, Beau had leaned over to say, "Give Featherstone my wish for a speedy recovery when you see him tomorrow."

She had given him a brief nod, her eyes refusing to meet his, and had immediately turned to ask her father a question.

It had been a bloody awful dinner, that was a fact.

***

"Not again! I can't believe it. What's your trick?" Lord Hasselton shouted. He clapped Michael on the back, almost toppling him even though they were almost the same height.

"A lot is how you hold your wrist, sir. It has to be straight but not rigid," Michael said.

"Well, here. Show me." Lord Hasselton aimed an arrow and froze, giving Michael a nod. "What now?"

Michael frowned. "Your wrist looks right, sir. Maybe it's your elbow." He gave Lord Hasselton's elbow a gentle tug, moving it out an inch. "Now try."

The arrow hit four inches below bullseye and Lord Hasselton groaned. "You were right, Beau. Michael here has either sold his soul to the devil or been possessed by Cupid. Either way, we don't stand a chance against him. Here, Fairmont, you have another go."

The contestants included Beau, Michael, Lord and Lady Hasselton, and Fiona's parents. The Skeffingtons were watching the contest in comfy chairs set up just for that purpose. Michael pointed out two girls watching from the second floor sitting room, and Beau guessed that one of them was Fiona's sister—the one who took a long time to recover from measles and fainted at the sight of leeches.

The Richlands were notably absent, and Fiona had chosen to play nursemaid to Henry rather than join the archery contest, putting Beau in one of the blackest moods he'd ever experienced. Yes, Featherstone's illness meant he'd be the substitute guest for dinner again that evening, but he didn't relish the prospect of being the sole recipient of Fiona's cold shoulder again, only to return home with his tail between his legs at evening's end.

Something had to be done. But what?

"You seem out of sorts today," Lady Amelia said, coming to stand beside Beau as some of the others took pointers from Michael.

"Do I? Lady Amelia, how much longer is your party to go on?"

"Oh! Let me think—another two weeks. Everyone is due to leave at the end of the month and we're halfway there now."

"Would you consider me inexcusably rude if I invited myself to the remainder of your house party?" Beau had a plan forming and its success hinged on his not having to manufacture any more outings or contests, for those could be avoided—as today's contest proved.

"Of course! I mean, of course you can come! I—we'd

be honored to have you join our party, Beau!" Lady Amelia seemed to mean it.

"Despite the fact that the Richlands dislike me?"

Lady Amelia shook her head. "I've told Lady Richland that bygones should be bygones. They need to let go of this ancient grudge. It's all nonsense if you ask me. We'd be honored to have you stay with us, Beau."

"Lady Amelia, thank you, and the honor is mine." Beau took her hand and brought it to his lips. "I'll return by five o'clock." Which meant he needed to bring the archery contest to a close, get Michael home, and get Smithers to commence packing his trunk. "Michael, we'll leave in ten minutes!" he called to his brother.

"Michael, come again tomorrow if you like—if the weather holds," Lady Amelia said. "I'm sure we could learn much more from you."

Michael looked slightly dazed, probably due to the many wrists, fingers and elbows that he had adjusted—to no avail. Beau could tell that the archery contest's end was long overdue in his brother's mind. His haste in packing up his arrows was almost comical.

Lord Hasselton noticed it too. "You going to come back and continue our lesson tomorrow, Michael?" he asked, managing to keep a straight face.

"I ... no, sir, I don't think so. I think it's going to rain," Michael said, looking to Beau for confirmation.

"But I think I'll get the hang of it with one more day! We could set up a target in the ballroom if it's raining," Lord Fairmont said, adding to Michael's panic.

Bad mood withstanding, Beau took pity on his brother. "As enjoyable as this was, I think Michael has had his fill of tutoring for a bit." He started to explain that Michael's time was largely taken up by artistic pursuits—he was in the process of completing a charcoal drawing of Merlin—but the words never left his mouth because a carriage came into sight, rolling to a stop in front of the Hasseltons' mansion.

They all watched as Fiona emerged from it and quickly disappeared through the front door without sparing a glance in their direction.

"I wonder if that poor fellow's feeling better," Beau heard Fiona's father say.

"Those types of rashes can linger for days and days," Lady Winifred answered, and Beau would have sworn by her tone that she wouldn't have minded if Featherstone's did just that.

Beau leaned down to pick up the extra bows they had brought. "Ready, Michael?"

Michael said the awkward goodbyes typical for his age and they left for Castlewood.

***

Fiona couldn't remember when she'd been in a worse mood, and the reason for it smarted—considering how she had sung Henry's praises just the night before.

His behavior on this particular morning had been nothing short of despicable. In an angry voice, he had rained blame down on her the moment he had laid eyes on her.

"You made it incorrectly," had been the first words out of his mouth.

Fiona had been so taken aback that she had momentarily lost her power of speech, and Henry had taken her silence as an admission of guilt. "If you couldn't follow my written instructions, why did you pretend to? I would have rather made it myself than been made to suffer longer."

"Your instructions were perfectly clear," Fiona said, still standing by the door. Genius or not, there was no excuse for his nastiness. She was tempted to turn around and leave without another word, but his next words stayed her.

"Perhaps you *thought* so. Nevertheless, I'll try again today." He stood with a groan and limped slowly toward the bell pull, wincing with the action of pulling it.

"You'll do as you wish, of course. Is there anything I can do to aid in your comfort before I go?" Fiona asked coldly, wondering if the rash had spread to his legs. Judging by the way he moved, it was all over him.

"Go? Go where?" he asked in alarm, falling heavily back into his chair.

"Back. To the house party."

"But I need your help in the laboratory—since my fingers are so clumsy and useless. I'll tell you exactly what to do." He sounded more weary than angry now. "Please, Fiona," he added as an afterthought.

As least he had said please.

"Has your rash spread, Henry?" When he shook his head, Fiona bit back a groan. Were all men such babies under duress?

A servant appeared in the doorway of the morning room in response to Henry's summons. "Have Dawson meet me in my rooms, Mildred. It seems I must dress, after all."

The inherent accusation in his words made Fiona finally lose her temper. Her eyes blazing, she said, "I will make the remedy while you watch, and you are not to say one word unless I'm straying from your written instructions. If I do not stray, and if you have not seen anything to fault in my method, I expect a groveling, lengthy apology because you, Henry, have been inexcusably rude to me this morning. Do you even realize it?"

Henry stared at her, dumbfounded, while the servant made a hasty retreat.

"You don't, do you?" Fiona continued, amazed and saddened. When Henry still didn't answer her, she added, "I expect you to keep a civil tongue in your head for the rest of the morning."

They rode to the laboratory in the Fairmont carriage. Fiona had chosen to ride instead of walk that morning, thinking that taking the carriage would allow her time to join the archery contest later in the day. Now it looked as if she'd miss it altogether.

An uncomfortable silence fell between them on the way to the laboratory. Neither of them wanted to continue their argument in front of the Hasseltons' footman, who had taken Anna's place as chaperone that morning and was driving the carriage.

But Henry finally spoke. "I apologize if I offended you, Fiona. My tone inadvertently mirrored my discomfort, which is extreme. But next time, if my instructions are not clear, please tell me."

"They were clear!" Fiona said heatedly. "If the remedy is incorrect, it is because the plant I used was incorrect, not because I made it incorrectly."

"You identified poison oak as the culprit. I trusted that you knew that much."

"You trusted that—oh!" Fiona fumed, so angry she wanted to scream. She was embarrassed too, since the footman could hear every word.

Henry remained calm. "I don't know why you're so angry. Was it poison oak or not? It's important to determine that before we make the remedy again."

The crazy thing was that, rude or not, he had a point. Was it poison oak? Or might it have been poison ivy? She had jumped to the conclusion of poison oak because she had seen it while they gathered plants together, but Henry had gathered by himself while she tended sickly Lord Beaumont. Nevertheless, it was the *way* in which he spoke, without warmth or appreciation for her kind impulse to help him in the first place. Empathy was completely absent. And, sadly, he saw no fault in his behavior.

"It might be poison ivy. The symptoms are nearly identical. Can you take two remedies together? I'll make them both."

Henry exhaled loudly in exasperation. "If I see that you make them both correctly, I'll take the poison ivy remedy today. Otherwise, I'll try poison oak again."

They reached the laboratory and Fiona got out first. She grabbed an empty basket from the pile by the greenhouse door and turned to face Henry. "I'll have to go find the poison ivy," she said, turning toward the nearby woods.

"I'll wait inside. Please hurry," Henry said, but he got no assurances in return.

Fiona swiped an angry tear away as she headed for a nearby grove of trees. The idealistic bubble that she had built around her relationship with Henry had officially burst, wetting her face with unexpected tears and tightening her throat, but she recovered quickly, her cynical streak coming to her rescue.

What did she expect? Perfection? No man was perfect, and she had been foolish to think that Henry would fall outside that tenet. She now knew that he could be unreasonable under certain circumstances, but wasn't that still preferable to pretense, unfaithfulness, and the ennui that enveloped so many relationships? She would always be fascinated by Henry's work, always respect his intelligence, and could continue to believe that he was a faithful sort of man. But how well would she tolerate unfair and ill-tempered accusations in a husband? She suspected that such things could damage a wife's soul over time.

Fiona sighed as she clipped the ivy, taking care that the sticky yellow fluid didn't touch her skin. She hated that her mother might be right about Henry, but was she right otherwise? If Beau asked her to marry him should she accept? Of course not! It was irrational to think that Henry's imperfections in some way lessened Beau's many faults.

But a memory of Beau's sunlit head, bending close to kiss her, sprang to mind, and her gut clenched with pleasure. As a hummingbird is drawn to nectar, she wanted another taste of his lips. No, more than a taste. She craved a thorough exploration of his delicious mouth.

Fiona swallowed hard, shocked that her heart was pounding from the memory. Was she so weak that she, too, would become one of Beau's conquests? After all her sensible talk, would she allow her actions to fall short of sound logic?

She shook her head and sighed, wishing for simplicity yet knowing that it would never transpire.

The rest of the morning was a blur. Henry didn't talk while Fiona made the remedies, since his instructions were—once again—followed to the letter. After he had taken the poison ivy remedy, and while they were riding back to his house, he said, "A 'thank you' is in order."

So his bad mood had passed, but the damage was done.

"You're welcome," Fiona replied, giving him a perfunctory smile.

They were silent the rest of the ride, but while the carriage was pulling to a stop in front of the Richland estate, Fiona said, "I'll leave you now, Henry, so you can rest. Tomorrow I'll come by at the usual time to see how you're faring."

He gave her a worried glance as he got out. "Goodbye, Fiona. Again, thank you."

Fiona nodded, her serious eyes daring him to acknowledge that his behavior had been unacceptable, but he stepped back from the carriage and ordered it forward without another word, a sudden breeze blowing his thin brown hair into his eyes.

8.

Lady Clarissa returned the square piece of chocolate to its paper nest and took the round one with a dot of icing on top instead. She bit into it before speaking. "Whom do you think I met at the Hasseltons'?" she asked, closing her eyes and whimpering as creamy caramel cascaded into her mouth.

Daphne watched in disapproval as her guest examined the box again, this time picking out a sugar-coated almond. Lady Clarissa was plowing through her entire box of candy. In fact, she was a veritable pig who conversed even when her mouth was full of chocolate. Her hastily scribbled note, delivered on a card that morning, had been too tempting to reject. It had said: *You will want to hear what I have to tell you.* Was that true, or did this woman worm her way into tea invitations in order to eat other people's expensive confections? "I can't begin to guess. When you're finished swallowing, why don't you tell me?" she replied coldly.

"Lord Featherstone was there. Have you heard of him? 'The Mad Scientist,' they call him, and if any man has determined a way to make love to a plant, it's he. But no, another person was there too. A neighbor of the Hasseltons'. Can't you guess?"

"No."

"The most deliciously handsome man in all of England?" Lady Clarissa teased, giggling. "One with whom you were recently aligned?"

Daphne's stomach clenched in hatred. "Lord Albert Beaumont," she said neutrally.

"Yes!" Lady Clarissa squealed, almost wriggling off the settee in excitement.

"News of his whereabouts doesn't interest me in the least. I haven't thought of him since our estrangement."

It was a lie.

The truth was that she had not *stopped* thinking of him since that horrible ending. Gossips had cruelly pointed out that their affair had been his shortest on record, something that had made more than one infuriating female titter at her from behind a fan. Worse than that, a repetitive nightmare haunted her. In it, a replay of their first night together began as it truly had, in a darkened carriage on the way home from a ball. They exchanged hungry glances while Beau's friend Ferguson was with them, but as soon as he was dropped at his destination they began to make love in the carriage. Nightmarishness intruded on the memory when the Beau in her dream pulled roughly away from her and banged on the roof to signal to the driver. Glancing back at her, he shook his head in disbelief and leapt from the carriage before it had come to a complete stop.

The nightmare's first appearance caused her to wake up gasping, tears of anger wetting her pillow. By the tenth repetition, the seed of hate that his careless dismissal had sown had grown into a massive tree.

Lady Clarissa brought her out of her musings. "It isn't his whereabouts I'm here to tattle about."

"Oh?" Daphne feigned a yawn. Inside she was seething. If this hussy was about to brag that she was Beau's new mistress she'd throw tea on her. She'd have no compunction since the milk had cooled it. She'd aim for the face, too.

"He has a new interest—a debutante—and this one looks to be the real thing. I predict a marriage will come out of it," Lady Clarissa said, unwittingly sparing herself a tea bath.

"It's probably a rumor."

"It's no rumor. He told me so himself. Don't you want to know who's finally captured his heart?"

Daphne forced another yawn. "I suppose you'll tell me whether or not I do. You're positively bursting to tell."

Lady Clarissa didn't answer immediately, instead dropping a fourth spoonful of sugar into what had to be an already sickly sweet cup of tea. "It's—" She took a sip, swallowing noisily, "—Miss Fiona Fairmont." She returned her cup to its saucer, her large brown eyes never leaving Daphne's face.

But Daphne wasn't going to give her the satisfaction of an emotional reaction. She was far too expert at hiding her feelings for that. A faint crinkle of the brow, to show an appropriate mixture of borderline interest and cynicism, was all Lady Clarissa would see.

"That bluestocking? He's feeling a challenge. Once he wins her devotion he'll grow bored."

Lady Clarissa smirked. "I don't think so."

Daphne shrugged in disinterest, so Lady Clarissa leaned forward, displaying her massive chest—much to Daphne's annoyance—and said, "He told me his heart was attached when I ... well, you know." She straightened back up and gave a confidential wink.

Ah! So the pig *had* tried to bed him and had been given this cliché as an excuse.

Daphne smiled at the prospect of inflicting pain on this woman who had grown so irritating. She enjoyed causing pain, and Lady Clarissa's rejection by Beau was too good an opportunity to miss. "It's a well-worn excuse. I'm surprised he doesn't have better," she said, and Lady Clarissa's astonished gasp was as satisfactory as she'd hoped it would be.

"He gave me no excuse. Believe me, if his heart hadn't been engaged by Miss Fairmont, he would have been in my bed by night's end." Anger now flashed in Lady Clarissa's eyes. She stood. "I'll take my leave now. And I hope the gossips leave you alone soon. It must be so unpleasant to be the source of such ridicule. As a *courtesan*, it must have made it difficult for you to find a new lover."

Daphne didn't rise—or in any other way acknowledge Lady Clarissa's departure. Something inside her had snapped.

She had always ruled her lovers by keeping them uncertain of her feelings, by intimidating them and making them feel as if they were never quite good enough. It worked like a charm with the right sort of man and she had been hopeful that Beau was just that type. She had wanted to destroy his easy confidence and be the one to do the dismissing after she'd finished with him. But he had not cooperated. He had fled, and in such a public manner that she was finding it difficult to regain her power. She had not had a lover since, not for lack of trying. Well, now it was time for delicious revenge. She had confidence in the knowledge that his pain and suffering would banish her own.

***

Beau refused a second brandy, wanting to keep his head clear, his senses sharp. Dinner had been nothing short of a miracle because Fiona's cold shoulder had completely thawed. She had chatted unreservedly with him, and had also promised to share a newly discovered, favorite poem with him after the men rejoined the ladies.

"Not partial to brandy made of pears, eh? It is a little different," Lord Hasselton commented.

"The brandy is excellent. Italian?" Beau asked.

"As a matter of fact, yes."

Beau listened as Lord Hasselton launched into a tale of how he had discovered the brandy—in various fruit flavors, cherry being his favorite—at an Italian monastery during his travels as an unattached young man. He'd been buying from them ever since. Twice, Beau had to stop his fingers from tapping impatiently on the table. What if Fiona changed her mind and decided to retire early?

But they were finally back amongst the ladies and there she was, looking almost as she had when he had first laid eyes on her because her back was toward the door and her lovely hair was shimmering in candlelight.

***

Fiona was playing Commerce with Lady Amelia and her mother when Beau entered, but she could see his reflected image in the darkened windows as he approached. He rested his hand on the back of her chair. It didn't touch her, but its nearness made her heart beat faster.

"Is that the book of poems you were telling me about?" Beau asked, pointing with his other hand to a small book on the card table in front of her.

"The very one," she said, smiling up at him. "Here," she continued, picking it up, "See if you can guess my favorite while I finish my game."

He laughed, a sound powerful enough to send thrills cascading down her spine. "I'll do that, but give me a hint. Will your choice surprise me or will I say, 'Ah, of course?'"

"I don't know your perception of me well enough to answer that," Fiona said, handing him the small book.

His fingers left a trail of heat on the side of her hand that made examining her cards nearly impossible. Instead, she watched as he opened the book and began to read, not stopping even when he reached the window seat and sat down. After a few moments he glanced up, his dark eyes assessing her as he judged her favorite, and she tore her eyes away and stared at her cards without really seeing them.

"Beau likes poems, dearest?" she heard her mother ask, but Lady Winifred might as well have said outright, "He'll think you're a bluestocking, dearest."

She stole another glance at Beau before answering. "He likes poems."

"Which book of poems is it?" Lady Winifred pressed.

They were John Donne poems, some of them considered quite risqué reading, but Fiona could never be faulted for prudishness. She formed her opinion of a poem based on its own particular merit, not on some stuffy edict about it. Nevertheless, she was grateful that her mother wasn't familiar with Donne.

Fiona picked a card from Lady Amelia's hand and discarded before answering. "John Donne."

"He *seems* interested enough," Lady Winifred said, picking one of Fiona's cards and rearranging her hand. "It's not often you find a man willing to discuss poetry with a woman, though. They usually only want to shower us with readings or memorized verses."

"Generally true, but Hassie knows not to dare!" Lady Amelia agreed, taking her turn. "Poems give me a headache. The language is too obscure, and requires too much effort." She put down a match and chose another card, this time from the pile of cards in front of them. "Amazing, I drew my card. I'm out!" she said, putting down her last pair. "Shall we play again?"

"The archery lesson tired me, I'm afraid," Lady Winifred demurred, politely stifling a yawn.

Fiona was grateful not to be asked to play another round. She wasn't sleepy; just curious to find out what poem Beau was reading, since one eyebrow was raised and a ghost of a smile tipped up the corners of his perfect mouth.

"That must be why I'm sleepy too," Lady Amelia exclaimed. "Beau, you'll have to tell Michael that he wore us to bits with his lessons," she called over to him.

Beau nodded distractedly, too immersed to do more than glance up briefly. "I certainly will."

Fiona excused herself from the card table and walked to the window seat, to sit next to him. "Which one are you reading?"

"'Twickenham's Garden.' If I were to stereotype you I'd say you liked it or 'The Primrose' best, but somehow I think you are going to surprise me."

Fiona smiled. "Two worthy poems, but neither is my favorite."

"Which then, or will you make me guess again?" Beau said, closing the book on his finger and giving her his full attention.

Her heart skipped a beat. It wasn't an unpleasant sensation, but certainly distracting. And she wasn't able to give Donne proper attention because her mind was crowded with memories of Beau's soft lips, his tongue ... and how wonderful he smelled. She took a deep breath. "Do guess. For fun."

Beau reopened the book and scanned the titles, that tiny smile still in place. "'The Fever,'" he finally guessed, looking up.

"Another worthy poem, but no—" Fiona took the book from Beau's hands and flipped through it, easily finding her favorite. "This one."

He leaned closer to see. "'The Flea?'"

"Yes."

Beau took the book back and read, taking his time, his face not giving anything away. When he was finished he looked directly into her eyes again, and Fiona wondered when exactly she had become so shameless. She was flirting—with the poem, with her eyes, with her interest—but for the moment she didn't care. Tonight she wanted Beau's attention too much to stop.

We are all creatures driven by impulses, she thought, remembering her dear tabby's response to a tomcat that had come prowling last spring. But what separates me from Cleo is that I can choose. Cats are driven by unstoppable impulses to see a flirtation through to the end, whereas I can choose to stop. And stop I will—tomorrow—because I know this isn't real.

"Do you like the poem?" Fiona asked.

"I do. Unrequited love made better by the knowledge that his blood mixes with hers in the flea. Their blood mixing together, no less intimate than—" he trailed off, the words "making love" obviously not in the vocabulary that he used with debutantes. "It bypasses sugary, fawning blather, and is one of the best love poems I've ever read."

"I'm glad you like it. I agree that the lack of ... sugar ... makes it powerful. Did you feel its angry tone?"

"Anger, or frustration perhaps. If their blood has mixed, why can she not see that intimacy has already happened, and allow it to happen in its more natural course throughout their lives?"

"Yes. Exactly."

"Last night, Miss Fairmont. I was sure you were angry with me. Were you?"

Fiona's heart lurched. Poetry was a safe topic, but now he was headed onto dangerous ground. "Angry with you? Why should I be?"

"The kiss, perhaps?" he whispered, leaning closer so that only she could hear the words. Fiona was freshly struck that he was the most divine-smelling man on earth.

"The kiss didn't anger me," she whispered back. She knew she should pull back, out of the aura of his captivating scent, but for the life of her she couldn't.

"Then why did you barely speak to me?" Beau asked, his tone of voice not accusing in the least. He might have been asking her how she liked the trout they'd eaten.

Fiona gave him a rueful smile. "Blame my mother for that. She had just informed me that I should accept a marriage proposal from you—if you gave one—and I felt the need to punish her."

"Your *mother*—" Beau murmured, taking in the full implications of her explanation. And then he laughed, attracting everyone's attention. Lady Winifred, who had been watching their exchange out of the corner of her eye while pretending to listen to her husband's account of the ideal saddle, used his laugh as an excuse to stare directly.

Fiona continued. "I apologize if I seemed rude last night."

"Rude was the least of it. Cruel."

"Cruel? You expect me to believe that a man such as yourself can be hurt by one woman's aloofness? That's a bit farfetched." She was still looking into his eyes and she saw them change slightly. Some of the amused enjoyment went out of them. Not all, but enough to see the difference.

"What type of man am I, Miss Fairmont?"

"A man who's had more than his fair share of adoration," Fiona answered honestly.

"My share, no matter the size, means nothing if I can't attract those who matter."

Fiona considered his now-serious face. Minus the cynical amusement, its beauty almost winded her.

"I *matter*? You barely know me."

"I know you."

The simple phrase was like music to her ears, but still she argued. "You're intrigued by my disinterest. If I—like so many others—showed a preference for you, you wouldn't be saying this. It's my nonchalance that interests for its uniqueness, not me for myself."

Beau's puzzled frown was almost more endearing than his smile. "You say that with such certainty. Why?"

She looked away, not wanting to say anything that would ruin the evening and the memory of it; something like, *You're an infamous rake, and I'm not foolish enough to believe a word you say.*

He leaned in close again, softly saying, "What if I told you that our kiss in the lilac garden, as brief as it was, was nothing short of transcendental? I knew you were splendidly unique after your offer to help my father; the kiss sealed my fascination."

His breath, softly playing on her cheek, was delicious, reminding her of that wondrous kiss.

"Please don't. Beyond physical appeal, your power lies in your ability to make a woman feel utterly cherished and desired. But the fact of the matter is that once your brilliant light shines on a different woman, the one beforehand feels diminished ... used. At least I would, so I will never allow myself to fall in love with you. I'm willing to forgo exhilaration for a steadier, less exciting relationship."

"As you would find with Featherstone?"

"Perhaps," Fiona said vaguely. She didn't want to talk about Henry tonight. Not with Beau.

"Can I say nothing to convince you that I'm not as you see me?"

"History is a tattle extraordinaire. Your words, given your history, cannot convince."

"Then I'll have to show you through my actions," Beau responded swiftly.

"Please—"

"Don't tell me not to try, for it won't do any good. I'm determined to make you see." His warm, strong fingers enclosed her hand and turned it up, cradling it in his palm. He smiled appreciatively down at her hand, which was puzzling because he seemed to be looking straight at her stubby nails. But her surprise at his admiration was nothing compared to the way she felt in the next moment, when he looked into her eyes and said:

"Miss Fairmont, I wish to marry you. Will you throw aside stifling doubts and accept my offer of marriage?"

Fiona frowned and shook her head. "I ... you cannot be serious!"

"I am."

She gently pulled her hand back from his grasp, her mind whirling. She was stunned, thrilled, and appalled all at once, if that was possible. Here it was: a chance to shrug off good sense and follow a path that promised exhilaration and passion ... and certain misery. It was tempting, but logic prevailed. "I cannot accept your offer."

"Maybe not tonight, but know this, Miss Fairmont: I'll not stop trying to win you until a minister has pronounced you married to someone else." He took her hand again, holding it so that her nails were on full display. "Fergie told me that your hands are your worst feature, but I must go on record as saying I love them. They are the hands of Mother Earth, Diana, and Joan of Arc all rolled into one."

Fiona laughed. "Joan of Arc? I'm not a warrior!"

"Is that why she was martyred? I thought perhaps she'd healed people too well."

"Many women—and men—have been killed for that exact reason, but not Joan of Arc. She fought the English and they took their revenge accordingly."

"You see? You must marry me so that you can keep me straight on history. And plants. And so that you can introduce me to hundreds of poems that stretch my imagination."

Fiona smiled. "As relationships should never be one-sided, what would you teach me?" Even as the words left her mouth she realized how they sounded. A blush suffused her cheeks, and Beau's slow smile made her breath catch.

He leaned close and whispered, "There would be no one-sidedness."

His words brought the kiss in the lilac garden sharply into focus. No, to be honest, it was the close proximity of his ambrosial lips—mere inches from her cheek—that brought it back. Fiona wanted—desperately wanted—another kiss. Just one. What would one more kiss matter? Tomorrow she could go back to being sensible. But tonight, just for tonight, she could experience one more kiss like the one in the lilac garden. Only this time she'd see it through to the end.

"Indeed, if our shared kiss is any indication," she whispered back. "And yet—" her words trailed off, but she knew he'd take the bait.

Beau's eyebrows rose expectantly, waiting for her to continue. When she shook her head he said, "And yet what?" just as she hoped he would.

"It's nothing." She kept up a pretense of modesty, knowing full well that Beau would not let the matter drop. And as long as Beau played along, she would get another delicious kiss from him.

"It's very much something. *Tell me.*"

Fiona looked into his gorgeous, dark eyes and gave a small shrug. "I was thinking out loud, something that tends to get me into trouble more often than not."

"I appreciate your forthrightness, but don't withhold speech on my account. I'm not judgmental in the least. And yet what? Tell me," Beau asked again.

His persuasion was so ... persuasive. Not that she needed persuading tonight. It was time to get to the point.

"If you absolutely must know, I was wondering how the kiss would have ended—if I hadn't pulled away. Out of a purely scientific curiosity, of course," she said, looking full into his eyes—eyes that had a newly awakened depth that electrified. There was no turning back now.

"All good experiments need multiple trials, do they not?" Beau asked, without missing a beat.

"They generally do," Fiona acknowledged, feeling anticipatory prickles course through her spine.

"Bid your parents goodnight and tell them you're ready to turn in."

"Why?" Fiona asked. But she knew why.

Beau smiled. It was a sensual smile that turned her prickles into flames. "We can be scientists and conduct an experiment. Do it."

"How?" Fiona breathed.

"You'll see," he urged, his voice hypnotic. "Go on."

Fiona stood and walked to where her parents and Lord Hasselton were in conversation, a discreet distance from the window seat. The others had already gone to bed.

"I'm turning in now and wanted to say goodnight," Fiona said. To her ears the words sounded wooden, but thankfully no one looked askance at her.

"I'll walk Miss Fairmont to the stairs, on my way to the library," Beau said. He stood right behind her. "I'll be back momentarily, after I find the book she recommended. Are you three up for a game of Whist when I return?"

"Yes, yes, certainly," Lord Fairmont said.

"When will you be back? Five minutes?" Lady Winifred asked. It was her way of saying *I'm willing to give you five minutes alone, but no more.*

"It shouldn't take me long to find the book," Beau answered.

They left together, Beau taking Fiona's hand as soon as they were out of sight, leading her forward to the library where he pulled her in and closed the door.

"Time is short," he said, stepping close. Their faces were mere inches apart.

Fiona nodded, her heart tripping furiously at his nearness, and then his warm lips met hers.

The deliciousness of him made her weak-kneed, so she reached up and circled her arms around his neck, marveling at the silkiness of his hair. She felt Beau murmur softly against her lips, just before his arm circled her waist, pressing her against his muscular body. His other hand came up and entwined into her hair, gently tilting her head up a fraction more, better to reach her lips.

"What did you say?" she whispered against his mouth, dipping her fingers under his cravat and feeling the heat trapped there, forcing a groan from him.

She wanted to remember every detail of this encounter: the physical sensations, the whispered words—all of it.

"You're a treasure," Beau repeated, but she couldn't answer because his tongue slipped between her parted lips. Fiona responded fervently, her body and mind consumed with pleasurable aches and yearnings the likes of which she'd be trying to sort out for days—weeks. But she didn't attempt to analyze them. The perfection of right now wouldn't permit that.

But a minute later Beau pulled away, his breath ragged. He gazed at her for the space of one heartbeat, but then closed his eyes and rested his forehead against hers. The sweet intimacy of the gesture wrenched Fiona's heart, but his next words reminded her that now she had to re-establish her sensible self.

"I mustn't generate your mother's ire. Or your father's," he said, taking a deep breath as he pulled away once more. "You've undone me," he confessed, the tremor in his voice temptingly believable.

Fiona wished she could believe him. Reaching a hand behind her, she turned the knob to open the door. "I'll go now." She remained where she was, though, watching him. She didn't want to go.

A pained expression flitted across his face, but was gone by the time he said, "Dare I hope that you'll give me a different answer tomorrow? Is it possible?"

Fiona looked away. She started to speak, but shook her head instead.

"I won't give up," he said, as she closed the door.

9.

Jack Whitehead loved his line of work. While his brothers were both slaving away as coal miners in the North country, he had rejected family tradition and moved to London. He had never looked back. His broad shoulders, thick neck and unsympathetic eyes had immediately bought him a job as a doorkeeper at one of the busiest public houses in London, and the thing he loved most about it? Picking the drunken swells up by their fancy cravats and breeches and dumping them in the muddy street when they'd had a bit too much. He usually gave them a kick, too, while he had them down.

One of the more unscrupulous moneylenders had seen such a kick and had offered Jack a new, more lucrative position. If someone didn't pay a debt on time, Jack was sent to give that unfortunate person a strong message. He liked beating up the rich so much that he started his own business on the side, hiring himself out for the types of jobs that were generated by vengeful minds. And because there was always someone holding a grudge, and because word had gotten out that he took pride in his work, he stayed busy. In fact, Jack sent more blunt home to his mother in one month than his brothers made together in three.

"You wanted to see me?" he said now, his hat still on his head, his stance aggressive. There was no need for manners and pleasantries in his profession.

"Yes. I've heard of your services and wish to employ you," Daphne said.

Jack folded his thick arms over his chest. "I gets half now, half when the job is done. Who is it and what's his address?"

"He's currently at his country residence—"

"That'll be a hundred pounds more. Travel expenses," Jack interrupted.

"I'll give you whatever it takes. The man is Lord Albert Beaumont. I want you to make him suffer dreadfully. Make his beautiful face a bloody fright—along with the rest of him. Can you do it?"

Jack gave Daphne a look as if to say, *You needn't ask such stupid questions,* and nodded curtly. He had never failed yet, with hundreds of successful cases behind him.

"I'd wait until he's back in town and pay extra to watch, if you allow such a thing."

"Nope."

"Fine. I'll just write my promissory note—"

Jack hissed scornfully. "Cash only, lady."

"You'll have it by this afternoon."

***

Henry woke up feeling bothered. Bothered by the fact that, while the remedy seemed to have helped tremendously, it hadn't given him the miracle cure he had hoped for since his hands were still scabby and a bit itchy. He was also bothered by Fiona's coldness from the day before. He had watched as she made the remedies, perfectly following his written specifications, and he had thanked her accordingly. But his appreciation had obviously not appeased her because she hadn't come back this morning to inquire after his health. Maybe she planned to see him later that afternoon, but what rankled was that he didn't know that for sure.

He had come to count on her faithful morning visits. She was an excellent assistant—despite what he might have made her think with his recent scolding. Her natural inquisitiveness and easy understanding of scientific rules and terminology was certainly a boon to his research. He just wished that she would stop trying to treat complete strangers. It was one thing to treat oneself or a family member, but old Lord Beaumont, with whom she had no connection? Such behavior was inappropriate for a young woman of gentle breeding. Not only did it put her on the same level as a skilled laborer, it set her up to have conflicts with the man's regular physician.

Henry was in the process of getting the first shave his irritated upper lip had been able to tolerate in days, when his aunt burst into his room, providing a sharp distraction from his thoughts.

"Are you going to let that horrible rake steal Miss Fairmont right out from under your nose?" she asked, and it was a testament to Dawson's skill that her startling fury didn't cause him to nick his master's face with the razor.

Lady Richland continued, closer now, her hands aggressively positioned on her hips. "Last night he flirted with her unabashedly, taking complete advantage of your absence. He's part of the house party now—a fact I abhor. I would quit the party altogether if I didn't feel the need to keep an eye on him! The Hasseltons are stupidly blind to the fact that he's an immoral scoundrel, just because he played with their sons. And to be quite honest, I thought better of Miss Fairmont. Her encouragement of his attentions was a nasty surprise."

Henry shut out the sight of his aunt's agitation by closing his eyes. "It's nothing. He doesn't seriously pursue maidens. He's bored and Fiona's too beautiful to ignore."

Now he could hear his aunt pacing, as she said, "Your opinion is correct in only one respect: he's certainly not ignoring her. He read poems with her and they sat far too close together on the window seat. If you had seen them you wouldn't say it was nothing!"

"Please calm down," Henry said, as Dawson wiped soap remnants from his face with a towel.

"Don't tell me to calm down, as if I was a child! I think he's planning to propose, and this time it's real. He's older now, and I've heard rumors that his father wishes to see him married before he dies." Lady Richland came to a stop right in front of him. "Are *you* planning to propose to her?"

Dawson helped Henry into the old, loose-fitting jacket that he habitually wore to the laboratory. "Eventually, I suppose."

"Suppose nothing!" his aunt raged. "Just do it, before it's too late!"

Henry didn't answer since he was unable to think of a polite response. Instead, he stuffed Hahnemann's *Organon of Medicine* into his satchel and buckled it.

"I arranged your introduction to Miss Fairmont and—until last night—everything was going according to plan. I expect you to propose to her today," Lady Richland demanded, her finger jabbing the air for emphasis. Then she added, a little more gently, "You're too immersed in your hobby to bother finding a wife. Don't ruin this perfect chance to make a splendid match."

"We'll see," Henry said, throwing the satchel strap over one shoulder. He brushed past her and exited his room, but he didn't move quickly enough to miss her parting shot.

"I expect to hear news of your engagement at dinner *tonight.*"

He continued to walk briskly, grateful that he finally felt well enough to return to his laboratory. But as he neared it, his steps slowed, his mind deep in thought. Why not propose today? Fiona was a beautiful, intelligent woman who seemed to genuinely like him—despite yesterday's uncomfortable interlude. She could make an excellent life partner once their one small difference in philosophy was dealt with, which—as her husband—would be easy enough to amend; he'd simply not permit her to treat strangers.

Henry smiled as he unlocked his laboratory door. He rarely did anything his aunt told him to do, but this time he might just be able to comply.

***

Fiona awoke and stretched luxuriously. That kiss's power had kept her in a strange, half-awake state all night. She fell asleep, only to dream of the kiss until her body's very real tingles woke her up. Then she drifted off to sleep again and it happened all over. Despite her lack of connected sleep she felt energetic—almost too much so—and as she got out of bed she chided herself for allowing Beau's kiss to work such magic on her.

Today she would slip off the flirtatious mask from last night and return to what she knew to be comfortable, sensible, and safe.

She would breakfast in her room, read, and eventually go see Henry. Although she would deny that she was avoiding Beau, her morning and afternoon plans nevertheless left no room for any chance encounters with him.

Her mother, true to form, disagreed with her perfectly planned day. She knocked on Fiona's door just after noon, opening the door before Fiona could respond.

"You *are* here! Did you rest well, my dear?" she asked, breezing into the room.

"Like a log," Fiona lied, looking up from her book. "I'm later than usual going to see Henry—"

"Henry! You wish to go to that musty old greenhouse on this fine day? Celebrate that the rain was short-lived. Just this once, don't go. Beau has invited you, me, and your father to go for a ride. He said he'd take us to see the waterfall. There's only one in this county, you know."

"You and Father go. I want to see how Henry is faring."

"But, Fiona, you can visit him this evening. Please come with your father and me! I thought—" Lady Winifred stopped, clasping her hands in front of her.

"You thought what, Mother?" But Fiona knew what. Her behavior last night had naturally given her mother hope that she was allowing Beau to court her. In the light of day, last night's motives—to flirt with and kiss the irresistibly handsome Beau—shamed her, and she avoided discussion of them by quickly changing the subject.

"I would like to see the waterfall, too, I suppose, but first I want to visit Henry. Lady Richland sent me word that he's back in his laboratory today. Perhaps he could come as well."

"But, dearest, I don't think that's what Beau had in mind, and your behavior last night causes me to be surprised by this turn of events."

There it was. An explanation was required, much to Fiona's embarrassment.

"I'm not going to marry Beau, Mother, so you can stop hoping for that," she said gently. "I flirted with him a bit, yes, but it wasn't serious. It's best if you and Father go without me to the waterfall." She stooped to retrieve her sturdiest shoes from under her bed. She and Anna were planning to walk to the greenhouse since the rain had stopped.

"Just flirting? But that's … isn't that unfair to Beau? You're playing with his affections," Lady Winifred chided.

"Trust me. He knows it was a game," Fiona insisted, and bid her mother goodbye.

***

Half an hour later a sorely disappointed Beau drove Lord and Lady Fairmont through the gates of the Hasseltons' estate, on their way to see the waterfall.

Doesn't she crave me as much as I crave her? he thought glumly. *Hell and damnation, what will it take to win her?*

"It's a fine day, is it not?" Lady Winifred said, shaking him out of his black reverie.

Her stilted question, asked despite the fact that the topic of weather had been thoroughly explored before they got into the curricle, made Beau call a fast halt to his self-pity. He refused to let his disappointment make him churlish. "Indeed. Have either of you seen a tiered waterfall before? This one has large boulders in the stream below it. If you don't mind damp clothes, we can stand midstream and feel the spray."

***

Fiona gave a hasty knock on the greenhouse door and let herself and Anna in without waiting for Henry to answer. He turned and gave her an uncharacteristically big smile. Fiona laughed. "Henry! You must be feeling better to give me such a smile."

"Yes, better. My hands aren't quite themselves yet," he said, holding them out to show her. "But the remedy helped speed the recovery overall."

"That's good news. What are you working on, then?" she said, coming to stand in her usual spot in front of his work table. Her arm brushed his and he started, which startled her in turn. *Why is he so jumpy today?* she wondered.

Henry took a step away from her. "I'm dissecting that ant I collected, trying to determine which part is the best one to make the proving."

"And how is the onion treating you?"

"I stopped that when I fell ill, since I didn't want to confuse onion symptoms with the symptoms of the rash. I'll start it again soon."

Fiona was grateful that he discussed this setback as he might anything else, without rancor or blame. Maybe his nastiness had all stemmed from his discomfort and pain.

She took a large watering can off the table's lower shelf and began to water Henry's thirstiest potted plants.

Henry cleared his throat. "Fiona?"

She glanced up while continuing to water a particularly dry fern, but pulled the watering can upright when she saw Henry's face. "What is it, Henry? Is something wrong?" she asked, her brows pulling together.

"No, nothing's wrong!" His words squeaked strangely, and he cast a nervous glance at Anna. She sat in her usual place beside the door and was thoroughly occupied with a sewing task, so he continued quietly, "I'm very grateful that you came back today. I feared that I had somehow angered you—"

"*Somehow* angered me?" Fiona interrupted, the frown still firmly in place. Were these strange nerves caused by the act of apologizing? To watch him, one would think he'd never apologized to anyone before.

"I shouldn't have spoken to you the way I did," Henry finally acknowledged, and as soon as the words were out of his mouth, Fiona rewarded him with a smile.

"Apology accepted, Henry. Think no more about it," she said, returning to her watering.

But he wasn't finished.

"Fiona, this uncomfortable episode has made me realize something."

"What's that?" Fiona murmured, dipping her hand into the can and gently flicking drops of water onto the fern's fronds.

"I'd miss you dreadfully if—" Henry paused to clear his throat again, then said in a rush, "Would you do me the honor of becoming my wife?" He was half-turned toward the table and still had the ant in his hand.

Fiona's mouth wanted to gape open, but she didn't let it. She stared at Henry's profile, noting that he looked more worried than anything else. She couldn't help comparing this scenario to last night's, during which Beau had held her hand and whispered fervently that he wouldn't stop trying to win her. *His* eyes hadn't been worried, but had burned with a passion that had permanently seared her soul, marking it despite her best attempts to shield it.

Fiona put the watering can down and walked back to the work table, watching Henry's averted face, hoping that he'd turn to face her. When she was within a few feet of him, she said, "This seems very sudden, Henry."

"Yes, it is!" he agreed, still staring down at his ant. He placed the ant on a piece of wax paper and glanced up, finally meeting her gaze. "But it's what I want. Am I too late? Have you already accepted an offer from Lord Albert?"

"You're not too late," Fiona said, winning a grateful smile from him.

"Do you accept my offer, Fiona?" he asked, and the strongest emotion evident was wistfulness.

She gave Henry a considering smile, her thoughts roiling. Here it was: the proposal. The reason she had come to this house party. Ironically, her mother would no longer welcome this turn of events. She wanted Fiona to marry Beau, which made Fiona doubly wary of him since she and her mother had never agreed on anything.

Beau was not the sort of man who would make a good husband, and the faster he was out of her life the better. An engagement to Henry—and it could be a nice, lengthy one—would be the best way to accomplish that goal. She didn't trust Beau's determination to keep up the fight, once an engagement was in place. That claim was one of his ploys—calculated or not—to rile a woman's heart. And she was not a woman to be riled in such a way.

"I accept, Henry," she finally answered. Her heart gave an unpleasant lurch at the same time that Henry gave a relieved sigh.

He clumsily took her hand and kissed it. "Thank you, Fiona," he said quietly. "You've made me a very happy man today." He leaned forward and gave her another kiss on her cheek, then released her and turned back to his ant.

Fiona stood, stunned. Had she really just gotten engaged? She felt so strange, like she sometimes did when she couldn't find the right word for something, or when she'd had too many glasses of champagne. Foggy-brained. Numb.

Henry's the sort of husband you want, she told herself firmly, picking up the watering can again. Be grateful that he's *not* the sort to give premature words of love. Our love will grow slowly, establishing firm roots; it won't be the unreliable kind that burns out after six months.

Fiona forced cheerfulness into her voice, saying, "Henry, I like the idea of a longish engagement,"

But Henry's mind had long since moved back to his ant, and he looked up, frowning in puzzlement at her pronouncement. "I'll leave all the arranging to you, if you don't mind," he said, waving a hand dismissively.

"Oh. But won't you arrange the banns?"

He threw her a quick smile. "Of course. Let me know when to send word to our churches. The rest is up to you."

"I know you want to get back to your ant, but will you agree to a picnic—to celebrate our engagement—sometime in the near future? We could go to that waterfall my parents are visiting today. Perhaps gather some new plants for proving—avoiding the poisonous ones, of course!"

"Of course," Henry agreed, reliable as ever.

***

This time Fiona knocked on her mother's door. She knew the waterfall expeditioners had returned because she had heard their voices, boisterous from fresh air and good spirits, in the front hallway. Her mother had actually laughed—a rare sound indeed—at something that Beau had said. Fiona hadn't been able to hear his funny comment through her closed door, and had rushed to crack it open. But the party had already scattered. Her pang of frustration surprised her and made her feel grumpy. *What had he been saying?*

"Come in!" she heard her mother sing.

"Should I come back? Do you need to rest after such a long outing?" Fiona asked, standing in the doorway.

"Not at all, dearest. Come in! How is Henry?" her mother asked, relaxing on her chaise longue with her ankles crossed daintily before her.

Fiona sat next to her mother's outstretched feet. "He's much better. Hard at work again." She examined her nails, absentmindedly running a finger over the edge of one nail. "Mother—"

A lengthy pause prompted Lady Winifred to say, "Yes, dear?"

"Henry proposed today." Fiona looked up and noticed that much of the joyful light had gone out of her mother's face, a fact that saddened her.

"Did you accept?"

Fiona nodded.

Lady Winifred grasped Fiona's fingers—too tightly. "Are you happy? Are you sure about this?"

"Yes, Mother. Henry isn't perfect—no man is! But I respect him and genuinely like him. I'm sorry you don't understand."

"Don't worry about me. Now that you've made your decision, I'll be happy for you," Lady Winifred said, unclenching Fiona's hand and giving it a pat.

"Henry's left all the wedding planning to me, and I—"

"Smart man," her mother interjected. "Your wedding will be spectacular. You can count on me to make it so. What do you think of a December wedding?"

"December in a few years would work very nicely."

"A few years?" her mother cried. "Dearest—"

"Mother, I'm engaged. Be happy with that and don't push for a quick wedding. I won't stand for it."

Her mother sighed and closed her eyes, shaking her head. But a second later she reopened them and said, "I missed you today. You would have enjoyed the outing."

"Henry and I are planning a trip to see the waterfall," Fiona responded glibly. "We'll celebrate our engagement with a picnic there."

"That's lovely." Lady Winifred didn't sound like she meant it.

"The waterfall is worth seeing, isn't it?" Fiona pressed.

"Yes, but to be frank the best part of our outing was Beau's company. He's astonishingly good fun. Oh, Fiona! He told us about his proposal. I wish you could have given him more of a chance before accepting Henry." Disappointed tears sprang to Lady Winifred's eyes.

"You're crying about this? When you were telling me to be wary of him only days ago?" Fiona said in exasperation.

"I know him better now. He's a good-hearted man, Fiona. And he appreciates you."

Fiona stood. "I'll let you rest now, Mother."

"I'm sorry, Fiona," her mother said, swiping at a tear. "I want you to be happy."

"I *am* happy," Fiona exclaimed irritably. "If anything saddens me it's that—once again—we do not see eye to eye about something that's very important to me. I suppose I should stop expecting that."

And with those cruel words she left, making a point *not* to slam the door behind her.

10.

Beau knew something had changed the minute he joined the before-dinner gathering in the drawing room. There was a charge in the air, a subtly disheartening resonance that he noticed immediately.

And it was the elderly aunt of Lord Aldwinkle, fill-in guest since Lady Clarissa was in London, who confirmed his misgivings.

"Did you say they got engaged?" she shouted, cupping her ear.

"Yes, dear, that's what I said." Lady Amelia nodded vigorously to give visual reinforcement to her words. "Ah, Beau! I was just telling Lady Boswell the news. Miss Fairmont and Lord Featherstone became engaged today. You've met Lady Boswell, certainly?"

"I have," Beau said without missing a beat. He brought Lady Boswell's gnarled old hand to his lips while his mind churned over the news.

"You've turned into a sinfully handsome man. Are you as naughty as the gossip papers say?" Lady Boswell asked gleefully, her too-loud voice heard by all the guests.

Unfortunately, Lord and Lady Richland chose just that moment to enter, their nephew just behind them, and Lady Richland did not waste the opportunity to give Beau a haughty, disdainful glance. Henry followed it up with a curt nod and Lord Richland, a man who generally let his wife speak for him, didn't acknowledge Beau at all.

Beau indulged a wicked urge. "And then some," he said loudly, causing Lady Boswell to cackle happily.

"There was a rake such as you in *my* heyday who—" she began, but Lady Amelia interrupted her.

"My dear, we built the fire just for you. Your daughter-in-law told me that you get chilled, even in warm months. Would you like to come sit over here?" She pointed to a comfortable armchair.

"Eh? I suppose," the old lady said, thankfully letting the subject drop.

Lord and Lady Skeffington entered then and were thrilled to see one of their own generation in the form of Lady Boswell. They gravitated toward her and sat, three white heads bending close together, making Beau smile despite his aching heart. Surely that many years' worth of experience could together produce something prophetic by dinnertime, if they weren't talking about gout and regrets.

But his smile disappeared when the Fairmonts entered. Fiona was ravishing in an off-white gown that perfectly complemented her coloring. Her fiancé stepped forward, taking her hand in his and bringing it to his lips. She smiled at something he said, and Beau's heart sank.

Bloody hell! Had last night been a figment of his imagination? It was as if it had never happened, but—if so—what did *that* mean?

Not wanting to appear boorish or sulky, he stepped forward and took Fiona's hand. "Miss Fairmont, I believe congratulations are in order," he said, dropping a kiss on her gloved hand. "And yet—" he added softly, borrowing Fiona's phrase from the night before.

"Thank you," she responded dispassionately, moving away to meet Lady Boswell, and completely ignoring his reminder.

Beau forced himself not to stare after her. Two images churned together in his mind unchecked: her face after his stolen kiss of last night, desirous and full of wonder; and her face just now, cool and detached.

Had last night been just a game to her? Perhaps the whole evening had been a scientific experiment in her mind, to see if she could—could what? Bring the infamous Lord Albert Beaumont to his knees? Could she be that heartless? That calculating?

Thankfully, dinner was announced.

Lady Amelia placed a hand on Beau's arm, her face worried. "Beau, since Lady Clarissa is in London—as is every other young woman in the vicinity—I asked Lady Boswell to partner you at dinner. Even numbers, you know."

"I look forward to Lady Boswell's company, Lady Amelia." And, in truth, Beau was grateful that no young woman would be vying for his attention tonight at dinner. His heart thoroughly engaged by the elusive Miss Fairmont, he didn't have the stomach for flirting with anyone else.

He sat next to Fiona at dinner as usual. She was perfectly amiable, but it was as if they had never shared anything more intimate than that first dance. He kept up a stream of small talk and smiles, but inside he seethed with pain. Not just for himself, but for her as well. Did she really want to spend the rest of her life with a man who didn't ignite her passion? For as he watched Featherstone's and Fiona's platonic interactions he knew that would be the case. They were undeniably good friends, but nothing more.

***

Fiona awoke early, her rational mind pulling her out of a dream filled with kisses and warm, strong hands. As always these days, her heart was waging war with her mind. In the dream, Beau had ridden Merlin through the wide double doors of St. John's on her wedding day, just in time to stop her from saying her vows. Henry watched, without any apparent regret, as Beau swept her up onto Merlin, his warm hand splayed on her stomach to steady her. They had cantered out, their lips locked in a kiss that sizzled so thoroughly it had woken her up.

Fiona kicked her twisted covers away from her feet so that she could stand and stretch. "Get out of my dreams, Beau!" she shouted. More softly, she said, "My acceptance of Henry's proposal is based upon common ground and mutual respect. The sort of passion I feel for you would die, especially when you took your first mistress. Then what would I be left with? Bitter regret, that's what."

She threw open her window and took a few deep breaths of cool morning air. Faint sounds of kitchen activity—the rhythmic sound of a rolling pin and low remnants of conversation—floated up from below, but Anna wouldn't be expecting her breakfast summons for hours.

Sleep was impossible. Tired as she was, she knew it would either elude her or push her into more illicit dreams, since her subconscious seemed to be in league with her heart.

Yawning hugely, Fiona closed her window. She would take a walk in the hope that the exercise and cool air would help her regain a measure of calm. It took one minute to slip into her blue day dress, another two minutes to brush her hair and tie it back with a ribbon, and then she left, tiptoeing quietly downstairs and out into early morning birdsong and mist.

She neared the stables on her way to the sunflower garden beyond, preoccupied by a robin that sat on the stable yard fence, chirping loudly.

"Fiona."

She visibly started, and put a hand up to calm her racing heart. She recognized the voice immediately, of course. Beau's rich baritone could not easily be mistaken for another's, and besides, she had heard it so recently in her dream, saying words of love that had pulled her away from Henry forever. *Silliness!* she scolded herself, taking a steadying breath.

"You startled me," she said, turning toward the stable door. "Are you an early riser by habit?"

"No," he answered, leaning a shoulder against the stable doorway. Merlin peeked over his shoulder, saddled and snorting impatiently at the delay. "But when I've had trouble sleeping, a ride usually helps to clear the cobwebs."

He looks tired, Fiona thought, squelching an impulse to go to him and stroke his unshaven face. "I find a walk refreshing in such circumstances. I was on my way to the sunflower garden. I told Lord Hasselton I'd see it so that I could tell him how it compares to the Aldwinkles'. He's fully expecting me to rave about it."

Why am I chattering on like an idiot? Fiona wondered, forcing herself to stop.

Beau reached up to stroke Merlin's nose, never taking his eyes off her. "What about you? Do you always rise this early ... or did you have trouble sleeping too?"

"I'm a bit of an early bird. This hour might be a tad early, even for me," Fiona lied, wishing she had a horse's nose to busy her hands with. Since she didn't, she folded them in front of her.

"Your thoughts are busy with wedding preparations, perhaps?"

"I don't know," Fiona hedged, shrugging. She'd best be on her way, before he caused her to say something she regretted. "I'd best—" she began, gesturing toward the garden, but Beau interrupted her.

"Last night's news caused my sleep loss, especially since—just one night before—" he broke off and gave a shrug and a small shake of his head. "That *was* truly an experiment, wasn't it? You wished to see if flirtation would stop my pursuit of you. You really *don't* think very highly of me."

Fiona bit her lip. "No! It wasn't like that."

"Perhaps you think I have a heart that can't be hurt. That I've loved so freely that my heart is immune to pain. Is that what you think?"

Fiona shook her head, her heart breaking at the pain she saw in Beau's eyes. Pain that she had caused.

"What, then?" he asked softly, closing the gap between them, Merlin following close behind.

"I don't know. It—my heart—was stronger than my will. I enjoy your company very much—too much! And for once I allowed myself to indulge my heart. There, that's the truth."

"Follow your heart, Fiona! A marriage without love, without passion, will be like a slow death," Beau insisted, stopping in front of her.

"The type of love you speak of isn't enough to sustain a marriage. If you believe it is, then you live in the world of romance novels. You're not alone; many people do!"

"So you *want* a marriage in which passion is absent?" Beau asked, doubt etched on his face.

There it was: the question that had tortured her all night. "Passion fades. In the end, compatibility and friendship are what lasts."

"Aren't you over-generalizing? Who has put so firmly into your head that passion has to fade?" Beau asked gently.

"It depends on the couple, of course. I don't trust that any passion felt between *us* would last." Fiona was sorry for the blunt words the second they left her mouth.

Beau snorted. "Back to that, are you? My reputation? I need you to understand something, so I'll be as plain-speaking as you. I've had more affairs than I care to count, but you're only the second woman I've wished to marry. My first proposal was made based on a youthful infatuation; thank God, *it* came to naught. But now I'm a man who knows what he wants, and I find it grotesquely ironic that you, too, have refused me." He reached out and tenderly pushed a lock of hair away from her face. "What can I do to make you believe me?"

Fiona's face prickled where he had touched her. "It's too late. I've already accepted Lord Featherstone's proposal."

She turned to go, but Beau caught her arm. "I won't give up," he said. "You're making an enormous mistake, and I'm going to do my damnedest to make you see that." He let her go, mounting Merlin in one graceful movement.

"It won't change anything." Fiona forced the words despite the bruise they left on her heart.

Beau turned in his saddle to face her. "We'll see."

"My mind is made up. You'll be wasting your time," Fiona insisted. If he'd only leave her alone, she could get on with her life as she had planned it. In truth, she worried that her resolve wouldn't survive a full-fledged onslaught by this man whose mere presence felt like a warm blanket after a chill. She craved his touch, his kiss, his all-encompassing warmth.

"I can be very persuasive," Beau said, finally giving Merlin the signal he'd been waiting for.

Fiona opened her mouth to protest again, but Beau wouldn't have heard. He and Merlin were already out of earshot, Merlin's hooves raising a cloud of dust in their wake.

***

Later that day, in the greenhouse laboratory, Henry noticed that Fiona had stopped her task of re-labeling his bottles. He looked up from crushing leaves with a mortar and pestle to find her looking at him.

"Is anything the matter?" he asked.

"Henry, why haven't you ever tried to kiss me?" Fiona asked, taking him completely by surprise.

He stopped mashing and turned to face her. Hadn't he asked for her hand in marriage just yesterday? Kissing—all of that—would happen in good time. "Opportunities are scarce," he said, tilting his head toward the ever-present Anna.

"I suppose," Fiona mused, her eyes searching his face.

It was the rare woman who clenched Henry's gut and pulled his mind away from his work. Lady Clarissa Cowper's ample curves had threatened to do so, and he had been grateful to be able to use Fiona as a buffer. The only woman who had successfully lured him from his interests was a buxom maid his aunt had employed when he was seventeen. Edna had been dismissed after being caught kissing him. At first he had been furious with his aunt over the dismissal. But once time had cooled his ardor, he had realized that such a lack of control wasn't good for him—for his work, more specifically, for even at seventeen his scientific mind had found diversion with plants and bugs and weather. His feelings for Edna had distracted him, making him lose focus, and he had decided that firm control was preferable to exhilaration. He had long ago decided that the woman he'd marry wouldn't have such a pull on him, and Miss Fairmont, who was now requesting a kiss, fit that bill perfectly. He was more than happy to kiss her, though, since she'd asked.

Glancing at Anna, he saw that she was absorbed in her darning task, so he grabbed Fiona's hand and pulled her clumsily out of sight behind the tall bookshelf. Fiona gasped, which made him smile before he got to the serious business of giving his betrothed a kiss.

***

Henry's lips were firm and warm, his breath clean. Fiona tentatively put her arms around him as he kissed her and was amazed that two male beings could feel so different. Where Beau had been solid muscle, Henry was sharp angles and concavity. But the kiss itself was executed with efficiency and aplomb, and when Henry released her, giving her shoulder a little pat as he did so, her mind whirled in confusion.

She searched her mind for something to say, but she needn't have worried that Henry expected anything more from her. He was back to his mortar and pestle, the kiss apparently as transient and unmemorable to him as a sneeze.

Of course he's not going to say, 'You've undone me,' or other such nonsense, Fiona scolded herself. *His motives—the things that drive him—are far different from Beau's. He has a higher purpose that doesn't include making women swoon with fixed attention and the right combination of words. That was a perfectly respectable kiss, just as I requested, and that's all I should expect from Henry.*

But her heart sank as she realized that the biggest problem with Henry's kiss was that it lacked the taste and smell of Beau's lips and breath. In sampling Beau's deliciousness she had become thoroughly addicted to his essence. Could she stand never to taste him again?

Of course she could! But her resolve caused her heart to ache dreadfully.

***

When Fiona got back to her room, she saw a letter on her dressing table, propped against her vial of bergamot oil. Opening it, she saw that it wasn't a letter at all, but a poem, written in a bold hand.

She read the first line, "Thy lips are as intoxicating as crushed, brandy-soaked cherries," and felt her heart thrill. As she read further, she was awestruck that Beau had so perfectly immortalized their stolen kiss that by the final line, "Our perfectly paired lips are my heaven on earth," she felt lightheaded, and sank down onto the floor to read it through again.

He loves you! Why did you refuse him? her heart remonstrated.

"Stop! Stop! He's never once said he loves me! It's not real," she whispered in desperation, but the argument felt brittle. "Don't let your resolve weaken," she muttered. But instead of throwing the poem away, she tucked it into her favorite plant book.

Seeking any distraction, she went in search of her sister and Emily, who usually took tea together in what had once been the nursery. Now it was a casually refurbished sitting room, perfect for two young ladies who liked nothing better than to read gossip papers and put on mini-plays for the entertainment of Emily's governess.

"Fiona!" Felicity screeched when she saw her, but it wasn't a happy sound. More like a severe scolding.

Fiona stood in the doorway, perplexed at her sister's reaction and waiting for her to explain herself.

"Mother told me," Felicity said, as if that explained everything.

"Told you what?"

"Oh, let's see ... that you refused Beau!" her sister scoffed. Even mild-mannered Emily shook her head in amazement.

"Well, let's see," Fiona retorted, adopting Felicity's rude tone. "I've only known Beau for one week, and—"

"You barely know Lord Featherweight but you accepted him!" Felicity interjected.

"It's 'Featherstone,' and let me explain the difference to you," Fiona said with exaggerated patience. "My engagement to Lord Featherstone will be a respectable, lengthy one, and will give me ample time to properly acquaint myself with him prior to our marriage. We will not rush the marriage, because that's typically what people in the throes of passionate crushes do. I, for one—and I'm just about the only one, except for Lord Featherstone—shun such irresponsible actions."

"But, Fiona, what you're talking about isn't love! Don't you want to be in love?" Felicity said, pleading now.

Fiona opened her mouth but couldn't bring herself to expound her rationales for the hundredth time. She was tired of rattling them off in a world of irrational people. Were she and Henry the only sane ones? Or—

Or what? The alternative—that everyone else knew the truth, and she was the fool—didn't bear contemplation. She shook her head, sighing heavily.

"'Love comforteth like sunshine after rain'" Felicity recited, hands clasped to her breast. "Does Lord Featherstone make you feel like *that*?"

Fiona didn't answer, so Felicity pushed further. "Have you even *kissed* him?"

"That's none of your business, but I'll tell you anyway that yes, I have," Fiona said, shushing the inner voice that yelled, *and it wasn't even one-tenth as good as Beau's kiss.*

"So you *didn't* kiss Beau?" Emily asked wistfully.

"Why would I have?" Fiona retorted, hating that her body tingled at the mere mention.

"I thought—Mother said—"

"Mother said what?" Fiona cried.

"After dinner, when he walked with you on his way to the library—" Felicity broke off, shrugging.

Fiona made an impatient gesture with her hand. "He gave me a little peck on my hand. Nothing of consequence. Casual in the extreme," she lied.

As dispassionate as the kiss was alleged to be, it was still enough to make Emily put her hand over her heart and gasp.

"I have a hard time imagining that it was so ... tepid ... especially since I know how much he likes you," Felicity said, correcting quickly with, "*Loves* you."

"He doesn't love me! He's playing a game. Perhaps he's not even conscious of it, but the fact of the matter is that he cannot rest until he's captured every single, desirable woman's heart. It's his passion as much as homeopathy is Lord Featherstone's passion."

"You're wrong! And I only hope you come to your senses before you actually marry Lord Featherweight," Felicity scolded.

"I'm going to take tea elsewhere," Fiona said, turning on her heel and briskly leaving. Why had she sought out her silly sister's company in the first place? And she'd have to reproach her mother about giving news so freely to Felicity. It seemed that quite a bit too much was being shared.

But as she walked toward the downstairs sitting room, where she could hear teacups clinking and murmurs of conversation, she realized that her appetite was gone. That, and she didn't feel like talking to anyone else. She decided to take a walk, and left by way of the kitchens.

The day was breezy, causing the sun to play hide and seek with the numerous white clouds. One minute the grass would be brilliantly green, only to be darkened in fast-moving strips by the disappearing sun. Fiona's destination was a little pond she had discovered directly in the middle of the sunflower garden earlier that day. It was a solitary but magical place, where one could literally disappear below hundreds of sunflowers by sitting on a wooden bench beside the pond. It was an excellent place to sort out a tumultuous mind.

But as she exited the waist-high sunflowers on her way to the bench, she stopped short, for someone had beaten her to it.

Beau. Fast asleep on his back, with one arm resting on his chest, the other flopped to the ground.

Fiona stood transfixed, watching the slow rise and fall of his chest. He was beautiful even in sleep, breathing deeply through slightly parted lips. She felt her heart quicken at the sight of him, and wasn't surprised in the least by a yearning to kneel beside him and kiss those lips awake. This was the 'love' that Felicity spoke of: a desperate ache to get physically closer; heaviness in the limbs at the thought of moving away. But these feelings would turn into something ugly once Beau lost interest, which he invariably would do. She was the only available woman for miles, so of course he was paying attention to her, but that attention didn't mean what he said it meant.

Taking a steadying breath, Fiona quietly backed away and walked to the herb garden to pick the rosemary she needed to finish Lord Beaumont's medicine.

11.

"Your poem was quite impressive, but you shouldn't have written it," Fiona whispered to Beau, halfway through her cream of carrot soup that night at dinner. Henry was occupied in conversation with Lady Skeffington about the engagement.

"You liked it?" Beau asked, adding before she could respond, "There's more where that came from. I've discovered I like to write poems—or perhaps it's the subject matter I like."

"But you mustn't," Fiona said firmly.

Her impenetrable gaze clutched at his heart. "If anything will loosen your resolve against me, it will be a poem. Of that I'm certain. The one I'm working on now selfishly has to do with my happiness. I describe how you have the power to squelch it forever—depending on which path you take."

"Which path?" Henry asked, turning away from Lady Skeffington in time to catch the last few words.

"Foolish prattle, Henry. It's nothing," Fiona said, taking another spoonful of soup.

Her words bit into Beau's soul and his kneejerk reaction was to take his hurt out on Featherstone. He'd wanted to take him down a peg or two for days, and now he gave in to that instinct. "She's contemplating joining a circus, Featherstone." Leaning closer, he amended, "Ah, but you knew that already."

"Ridiculous!" Fiona rebuked, turning her back on Beau. "Henry, do you like the soup?"

"I ate it all," he answered, looking from his obviously empty bowl then back to Fiona with increased confusion. "What does he mean? Why did he say that?" Henry pressed, increasing Beau's ire by talking as if he wasn't right there, listening.

"I have no clue why he said such a silly thing. You could either ask him or ignore him. I recommend ignoring him." Fiona frowned into her soup. She took several spoonfuls in a row, leaning forward as if trying to be a barricade between them.

But Henry wouldn't be put off. Switching his gaze to Beau, he asked in a contemptuous voice, "Well?"

Beau didn't even try to mute his cold anger. "Well what?"

Henry exhaled loudly and then cleared his throat. "What's this about a circus?" he asked through clenched teeth.

"I was speaking metaphorically, Featherstone," Beau said, his words pure ice. He was tired of Henry's superior, angry attitude, all because of a presumed engagement that had been a complete miscommunication in the first place. He held Henry's gaze, daring him to challenge the inherent insult. He'd dearly love to smash the smug scientist's face to pieces.

But Henry didn't pick up the gauntlet. He gave Beau a disdainful glance before looking away and muttering, "You're mad."

"And you're a coward," Beau said, just loud enough for Henry to hear. Beau knew he had heard because the flared nostrils and narrowed eyes gave away Henry's fury.

A footman chose just that moment to offer duck and roasted potatoes, but after he had moved out of earshot Fiona rounded on Beau.

"Just because Lord Featherstone didn't pick up your childish gauntlet doesn't mean he's a coward. It's the better man who chooses not to fight in such situations," she whispered angrily.

"I insulted him and his family, likening them all to circus performers, and he chooses not to fight? Admit it, Fiona, that's pathetic. If you don't stand up for your family, what kind of man are you?"

"Were you truly hoping he'd challenge you to a duel over such folly?"

"I doubted that sort of passion from methodical Featherstone, but I hoped for some token threat of violence. *Something* to show me he had backbone. Do you truly wish to marry a man who doesn't possess a backbone?" Beau speared a piece of duck on his fork and rubbed it through the orange sauce before popping it in his mouth, his eyes never leaving her face.

"Just because he didn't pick a fight with you over your *asinine* insult, doesn't mean he lacks backbone. On the contrary." Fiona's eyes condemned and shamed. Worse, they held not even a smidgen of pity for what he was suffering.

Their conversation had been a series of indignant whispers on Fiona's part, with softly growled replies from Beau, but the intimacy of it caught the attention of the whole table. Beau looked up and noticed that all eyes were on them—except perhaps Henry's, whose eyes were firmly fixed on his plateful of potatoes and duck.

"Is anything wrong?" Lady Amelia finally asked.

"No, of course not!" Fiona answered—too quickly.

Beau answered with a cursory shake of his head.

"Are you having an argument with Lord Albert?" Lady Richland pressed. "If he's bothering you, perhaps he should leave our company for the rest of the evening."

Beau hadn't realized he could feel such hate, but in that moment he would gladly have strangled the countess if circumstances had permitted it. Luckily, Lady Amelia spoke before he had a chance to pour his hatred into words. "Are you sure everything is all right?" she asked, smiling nervously.

"Of course," Fiona said, but a moment later she angled herself toward Henry, giving Beau a three-quarters view of her lovely back.

Lady Richland gave Beau a knowing smirk that made black dots form behind his eyes.

After dinner he drank a hasty glass of port with the other men and excused himself early, unable to bear Fiona's apparent happiness with her betrothed—and inadvertently granting the countess' wish.

***

Damn, damn, damn. Insomnia again. But Beau was utilizing the early morning hours to pen another poem, in hopes of clearing it from his mind. He wasn't at all sure that he should have Smithers deliver it. His plan wasn't working. Fiona was pulling further away from him, partly due to his immature baiting of Featherstone the night before, but mostly because of something he had no control over: his past.

She appeared determined to go through with this marriage to Featherstone and, he had to admit, it wouldn't be a hideous marriage. They were definitely friends, and friends often made adequate marriage partners. Was it time to admit defeat?

Beau exhaled loudly and stood to stretch. He stepped to his washbasin and splashed his face, noting that he had an ink stain on the side of his hand. Dipping it back into the water, he rubbed it absentmindedly as he yawned. If he could just get one decent night's sleep, then maybe he could better determine how to win her. But sleep mostly eluded him these days.

A knock sounded on his door. "Come in," he called, surprised since the hour was still so early.

A servant appeared in the doorway, a silver platter held before him with a letter on it. "A letter from Castlewood was just delivered, my lord. He said it was urgent."

Beau hastily dried his hands and strode forward, his brow puckered. After tearing open the letter and scanning it, his frown deepened.

Come quickly. Your father is worse.

He was surprised at the handwriting, since he didn't recognize his mother's penmanship, but perhaps the physician was there and had written it. His concern for his mother deepened. Was her grief such that she couldn't write a short note? His father's death was expected and would come as a relief to most of the family, but for the first time Beau realized that his mother might not share those sentiments. His love for Fiona helped him to understand that.

"Tell someone in the stables to ready Merlin," he said, grabbing his boots and sitting to pull them on. He had dressed two hours ago, thinking he would go for a walk, but a sudden inspiration for a poem had stayed him in his room. Now he was doubly grateful for the surge in creativity for he would have hated to have been gone when the note arrived.

"Should I send Smithers to you as well, sir?"

"Don't bother. I'm not going to take the time to shave."

He knew it would take a few minutes to saddle Merlin, so he took the time to reread his new poem. This one exalted Fiona's lustrous hair and discerning gaze. It was his boldest poem yet. Should he give it to her? He reread it again slowly, thinking hard, and then made his decision.

Pulling another piece of paper forward, he dipped his pen in ink and quickly wrote, before he could change his mind:

Smithers, deliver this poem rolled and tied with a green ribbon. Do your best to match Miss Fairmont's eye color. See that she gets it this morning, before she goes on that bloody outing with Featherstone. And then he grabbed his coat and left.

Merlin was jumpy and danced sideways when Beau attempted to mount him. "Whoa," Beau cooed. "Woke you too early, did I?"

Merlin snorted loudly, shaking himself from head to toe, and Beau gave a short laugh. "Maybe one day you'll fall in love. Then time won't have the same meaning."

Beau rode toward Castlewood, pushing Merlin into an easy canter. He'd be there in fifteen minutes if he could persuade Merlin to gallop full out, but so far the canter was all he seemed able to manage. Maybe the muggy weather was to blame. Beau glanced at the skies and wondered if the predicted rain was going to make an early appearance. He grinned cheerlessly at the thought that Fiona's engagement expedition to the waterfall would probably be cancelled.

But he was startled out of his gloomy musings when he caught sight of four horsemen emerging from the woods on his right. They were riding perpendicular to him and they would cut off his way to Castlewood if he kept a straight course. He veered left to buy himself time and space, his mind racing as fast as the many hooves. What were four strange horsemen doing on Beaumont property?—for he had just crossed the stream that signaled the shift in ownership. Castlewood itself would come into view once he topped the clover-rich hill that stood less than a hundred yards away.

And then he realized with sickening certainty that the scribbled note—in a hand he didn't recognize—had been a ploy to get him out in the first light of day. But why? Relief that his mother wasn't suffering unbearable grief was quickly overridden by alarm. Four against one wasn't good odds, despite the fact that he carried a pistol out of habit. Even as he kicked Merlin into a faster pace, he slid his hand into the saddlebag and pulled it out. Its smooth, cold metal felt comforting even as it confirmed his danger.

He could try to outrun them all the way to the stableyard but in Merlin's present mood he doubted he'd be able to do that. In fact, he could hear that the distance was fast closing between them, and he sure as hell didn't want to be pulled from his horse without a chance to defend himself. He had to pray that his hastily laid plan would work.

He wheeled Merlin around to face his pursuers, pulled up short, and took aim at the largest man. "Halt, or I'll shoot," he yelled.

The horsemen quickly reined in with a signal from a heavyset man with closely cropped hair, and Beau switched his aim to this man, the obvious leader of the group. The men were barely ten yards away from him.

"What do you want?" Beau growled.

"For you to put the pistol down, easy-like. We're here to give you a message about your father, that's all," the leader said.

"Right," Beau scoffed. "So give it and go."

"Put the pistol down first."

"No," Beau said grimly, slowly shaking his head. A sudden breeze pushed through the trees and grass, almost spooking Merlin, and he tightened his knees to keep the horse still.

The leader spit into the grass. "You can't win, you know. We're four against your one."

"It'll be three against one, remember?" Beau said, indicating his pistol with a slight nod.

"Blokes like you don't know how to use those. Even if you shoot you'll miss—but put me in a right bad mood, which you don't want to do." It was said with such assurance that Beau wondered for a second if he'd forgotten to cock his pistol. A quick glance told him he hadn't.

Beau relocked his aim on the man's heart. "Keep telling yourself that and you'll be dead soon."

The man's eyes narrowed, but he didn't say anything. All that could be heard was the squeaking of leather as horses arched their backs or shifted from foot to foot. They all stayed dead still for what seemed to Beau like an eternity.

"You'd best give the signal to move away—if you don't want to die today," Beau finally said, after his arms started to ache.

"I'm not afraid of you," the leader sneered. "You don't have it in you to kill."

Beau didn't answer since there seemed no convincing this cold-eyed man.

The leader snorted contemptuously and glanced around at his cohorts. Then he raised his hand to pull his hat on tighter, and it must have been some sort of signal because two of the men turned their horses away.

Beau saw that they were making a wide circle around him; he had to act quickly before he was surrounded. His only real chance at escape was to charge through the two remaining horsemen who were in front of him, and race to Castlewood's stableyard ahead of them. He lowered his aim a bit, intending to shoot the leader's leg. He didn't want to kill the man if he could avoid it, and the noise and pain of a shot leg would hopefully buy him enough time to get away. But when he kicked Merlin forward, the temperamental horse reared, and his shot went higher. He galloped past the leader and saw his surprised face, just before the man fell forward across his horse's neck. Beau feared he had killed him, but he couldn't stop now. Not with his odds at escaping these men still so unfavorable.

The shot spooked Merlin into galloping his fastest, and Beau allowed himself to hope that he could outrace the men. But it was a short-lived hope.

In one fast blur, he saw the rope and felt it at almost the same moment, just before he was roughly jerked backwards off of Merlin. He had no time to react, but even if he had had time, he couldn't have held on to the reins or Merlin's mouth would have been badly hurt from the force and speed of the movement.

Beau hit the ground clumsily, his right leg momentarily catching in the stirrup, which put the entire impact of the fall onto his left leg. He felt rather than heard the snap, and a bolt of pain shot through his leg, stealing his breath. Gasping, he grabbed his leg and rolled to face his attackers.

None of the men were paying any attention to him, even though one of them still held the rope attached to him. They were looking at their leader, who had rolled off his horse and lay in an awkward heap in the grass. His piebald horse had taken up with Merlin, Beau noticed in grim amusement. They both stood twenty yards away, grazing.

"Your leader needs help. You should take him and go," Beau said, looking from one to the other of them, his voice tense with pain.

"Wi' Jack dead, tha bitch'll not pay what's owed. She knows Jack, not us," said a young, blond man, who was missing his two front teeth.

The bitch? Beau thought. And then, "Daphne Tarkington?" he asked in disbelief.

"Dunno," Blondie grunted. The tall man holding the rope shrugged, and the third man shook his head. The leader had obviously kept these hired thugs in the dark. Money was all they had needed to agree to the job.

Beau wanted to know the worst. Was he about to be killed? "Why were you sent?"

"Ta beat y'up," Blondie said, slipping gracefully off his horse and throwing his reins to the tall man. He went to Jack's lifeless form and pulled him over onto his back. Jack's staring eyes and bloody chest told the story of his death. "Cor, 'e's a goner. Won' be able t' hunt no more like this now, will 'e?" the man laughed.

Beau wondered why his head was suddenly spinning. Broken legs didn't make a person dizzy, did they? He glanced down, finally, and saw that his lower left leg was at odd angles to his thigh. That was to be expected. The unexpected was that a bloodstain was spreading quickly up out of his boot, onto his breeches. "Bloody hell," he gasped. "I'd say you accomplished your mission."

"Let's get gone," the tall man said tensely. "Leave Jack. Leave his horse. We don't want no questions asked us going back into London, which him laying dead over his horse would be sure to cause." He held out Blondie's reins, impatiently shaking them.

Blondie gestured toward Beau. "Wha' abou' 'im?"

Beau was busy stripping off his jacket, amazed that his arm movements could increase the pain in his leg so thoroughly. He glanced up. "Please ... can you send word to my family that I'm here? They live just over that hill."

Blondie snickered. "Righ.' An' after tha,' we'll make sure tha' Jack 'ere gets a proper burial." He swung himself easily back into his saddle.

"Let's go," the tall man said, tossing his end of the rope toward Beau. It disappeared into the long grass with a faint thud.

"Wait," Beau called, but they had already turned and were galloping toward the woods.

He knew he didn't have much time. The bloodstain was creeping up and over his knee. His plan had been to tie the arms of his jacket around his leg, but now he used the rope, pulling its loose end toward him and tying it as tightly as he could around his leg, just above his knee. He prayed it would stop the bleeding until someone could find him.

His last conscious thought—as he pulled his jacket over himself to ward off a sudden chill—was that he had never told Fiona he loved her. The poems' many words might have hinted at it, but that wasn't good enough. Fiona saw each poem as another ploy. Another game. One he might play with any woman. He had never said the words she needed to hear. The words that might make her believe him.

***

Fiona yawned and sat up in bed. She pulled the bell cord to signal that she was ready for her morning tea and toast, and plopped back onto her pillows. She was dreading this day ... the outing, to be more precise. She simply didn't have the heart for it, because she knew that Henry would prefer to be in his laboratory. Why had she suggested such a tedious thing?

She yawned again and closed her eyes, deciding to let the arrival of the breakfast tray pull her out of bed, which it did fifteen minutes later.

"Anna, do those clouds look ominous to you?" Fiona asked, with a nod toward the window.

Anna set down the tray and stepped to the window. "They do! The rain is definitely going to make an early appearance. Do you want me to pull these?" she asked, pointing to the curtains.

"No, thanks. I love the rain—especially today," Fiona answered, winning a puzzled look from Anna. "Let's just say I'm not in the mood for a picnic. The rain should effectively cancel my outing, should it not?"

"I think it already has. The cook hasn't given out instructions about preparing for it, at any rate."

"Wonderful," Fiona declared, smiling widely. She could now do what she really wanted to do today, which was to finish Lord Beaumont's herbal tonic and deliver it to him. She'd send a note around to Henry that she'd be by his laboratory later on.

With that happy thought, her sleepiness vanished and she practically jumped out of bed. She picked up her breakfast tray to take it to the table by the window, but frowned at the sight of a rolled piece of parchment, tied with green ribbon, next to her toast rack.

"What's that?" she asked suspiciously, pointing at it. But she knew what it was; she recognized the cream-colored parchment from Beau's other poem.

"Smithers put it there," Anna revealed. "He asked so nicely that I didn't have the heart—"

"That's fine, Anna. I don't expect you to get involved in this." Fiona picked the parchment up. She pinched it flat and tore it into three even pieces, catching the green ribbon before it fell to the floor.

"Return these to Smithers, please, Anna. Don't worry about an explanation. The torn pieces will speak for themselves."

Anna nodded slowly and took the torn parchment.

"Why that look?"

"Oh, no, ma'am. My nose just itched," Anna said, making a hasty retreat.

Fiona picked up a piece of toast and spread it with her favorite orange marmalade, but after one bite she abandoned it on the plate. She half rose from her chair, wanting desperately to run after Anna and retrieve the ripped poem, but after a moment she slumped back into her chair with a loud sigh. It was best that she didn't read it. Beau's poems only served to torture her inflamed heart.

***

An hour and forty minutes later, a dripping carriage pulled up to Castlewood's main entrance and Fiona emerged, a knitted bag filled with two cork-stoppered bottles and a dozen sachets in one hand, her other hand tightly holding her shawl around her shoulders. The wind threatened to blow it off, despite the footman's best effort to shield her with his bulky frame and a flapping piece of oilcloth.

When Patterson, the Beaumonts' butler, opened the door, Fiona couldn't help noticing that he looked positively distressed. Had Lord Beaumont taken a turn for the worse?

"You were summoned as well?" he asked.

His words increased her dread tenfold. "I ... summoned?"

"Please excuse me. I assumed too much. Please come in." He took her damp shawl and led her into the drawing room. "You wished to see—?" he prompted.

"I've come to deliver Lord Beaumont's herbal remedies," Fiona said, fully expecting Patterson to tell her that she was too late with them.

"I'll let Lady Beaumont know you're here," was all he said, leaving quickly after a scanty bow.

Fiona perched on the edge of a high-backed chair, frowning. Poor Lord Beaumont. She hated that he was worse, but for more reasons than the obvious. It would mean that his son would leave the house party. Faced with the prospect of Beau's going, she realized that she'd miss him dreadfully.

She shook her head, ashamed of the thought. Did it mean that she was as addicted to his attentions as every other woman, or that she had deeper feelings that she hadn't allowed herself to admit?

Lady Margaret interrupted her thoughts. "Miss Fairmont, I'm so glad you've come."

Fiona gasped when she saw Lady Margaret's face. It was etched with apprehension, and her eyes were red with recently shed tears. "What has happened?"

"He was found not thirty minutes ago. We've just settled him in his room—"

"Found?" Fiona repeated. Had Lord Beaumont wandered from his bed?

"Merlin returned to our stables, or we might never have—" Lady Margaret pressed her lips together, blinking her eyes to prevent more tears.

Fiona gasped, realization hitting her viscerally, as if she'd been punched. "Beau—?"

"—Is badly hurt. We're awaiting the physician and, even now, Matthews is with him, putting pressure on his wound to prevent more blood loss."

Fiona's throat tightened convulsively. She clutched her bag so tightly that the tonic bottles ground together, threatening to shatter. "May I see him?"

"I'm so glad you asked. His only words so far have been ... well, your name, 'Fiona,'" Lady Margaret said apologetically, motioning her to follow. She started upstairs, continuing, "It's a miracle you've come, really. I don't think he'll be able to rest very well until he's seen you."

This had to be a nightmare. She was about to see Beau—beautiful and vibrant Beau—in a sickbed? It couldn't be true. But the nightmare continued as Lady Margaret opened a door and led her into a tastefully decorated bedroom. A grim-faced man sitting next to the bed glanced over his shoulder at them, but turned back when he'd satisfied his curiosity.

Fiona stood just inside the door, her stomach clenched in fear. She took in Beau's breeches, tossed on the floor, the wetness from the rain causing the blood on them to swirl in varying shades of red and pink. She saw Beau's boots, one of which was cut down its sides, exposing an interior that was stained black. So much blood.

She forced herself forward and finally saw Beau, who lay on the bed, his naked chest rising and falling with each breath, a raw scrape running across it and onto his well-formed biceps. But then she saw his leg, angled in grotesque torsion and partially covered by a thick, bloody wad of cloth that the man next to him was firmly holding.

"Matthews, this is Miss Fairmont, the young lady Beau's been asking for. Miss Fairmont, Matthews is our head groomsman," Lady Margaret said hastily.

"Le' 'im know yor 'ere, miss," Matthews barked gruffly.

Fiona started, unaware that—until Matthews had spoken—she had been staring at Beau's leg, transfixed.

Her gaze traveled to Beau's face and her heart lurched. His pallor was terrifying. Damp hair was matted to a forehead newly beaded with sweat, and his clenched jaw indicated that he was in agony. His closed eyes winced when Matthews shifted the wadded cloth.

"Beau?" she whispered, stepping close enough to cup his face in her hand.

"He might not hear you. He's had laudanum," Lady Margaret said.

Fiona smoothed his clammy forehead. "Beau?" she whispered louder. This time his eyes blinked open and he swallowed convulsively.

"You've come," he croaked.

Fiona nodded, biting the inside of her bottom lip to keep from crying. Her heart felt as if it was about to break open.

"I have to tell you—" he began, but before he could finish, the physician bustled into the room.

"Move aside, if you please." The forbidding gentleman spoke briskly, gesturing impatiently for Fiona to move.

"Tell me later, Beau. Your physician—"

Beau's hand shot out and grabbed Fiona's wrist, staying her, belying his pain and debility. "Wait." He took a steadying breath. "Fiona ... I love you. I had to tell you that."

He released her wrist and closed his eyes, and the physician took Fiona by the shoulders rather rudely and moved her aside. But she didn't complain because Beau's words echoed loudly in her head, crowding out speech and action.

Fiona, I love you. He had been on the brink of death, and the one thing he had insisted on saying was ...

Fiona took a ragged breath and her hand flew to her mouth as comprehension dawned. She'd been wrong. Horribly wrong.

"Let me see, Matthews," the physician was saying, bending over Beau and indicating that the groomsman should lift the bandage.

"He's lost so much blood already. The bone seems to have severed something important. He made a tourniquet, which saved his life," Lady Margaret explained grimly. As the physician took stock of Beau's leg she said quietly to Fiona, "It would mean so much to us if you could stay and help. I wouldn't ask it if you hadn't already shown a healer's instinct with my husband."

A tear trickled down Fiona's face unchecked. "Of course I'll stay." She held out her bag to Lady Margaret. "Here are your husband's herbal medicines. I was coming to deliver them, and—" She stopped, a horrible thought staying further speech. What if she had gone on that wretched picnic? She wouldn't have heard Beau's words. She wouldn't have seen the truth in his eyes.

She had to tell him she'd been wrong about him. Immediately. Before pain or the laudanum or the physician's treatment made him lose consciousness.

Stepping closer again, she leaned down and whispered in his ear, "Beau, I'm so sorry for the things I said. I love you, too." Her heart almost burst with happiness. It felt so right to say the words. So freeing. And it didn't matter that he didn't seem to hear her, having fallen deeper into a laudanum fog. She would tell him she loved him over and over again for the rest of her life. He would hear.

Fiona kissed the unshaven skin just in front of Beau's ear, relishing its rough texture on her lips, then straightened to hear what the physician, Dr. Rufus, was saying. She took a fortifying breath and dried her face. No more tears. She needed to be strong for Beau.

"It *looks* fairly clean, but that doesn't mean that it is," the physician was saying.

"Th' bleedin' 'elped ta clean it, an' it was in 'is boot, away from th' mud. An' I used marigolds," Matthews said.

"Yes, yes! Marigolds are perfect in this situation," Fiona interjected, gazing at the competent head groomsman gratefully. He nodded an acknowledgement but gave no smile.

"That's all very well, but what this man needs is the surgeon. That leg will need to come off. The sooner the better," Dr. Rufus scolded.

Lady Margaret gasped, but he ignored her. "I'll write a quick summary and have Patterson deliver it to the surgeon." He headed purposefully for the door.

"Wait! There are medicines—herbal and homeopathic medicines—that could help to save Beau's leg," Fiona cried.

"Exactly who are you?" Dr. Rufus asked in irritation, glaring at Fiona. "If this man's wound becomes gangrenous, he risks losing his life. His leg needs to come off, before it rots, making him feverish and beyond hope."

"I must ask Henry," Fiona said, almost to herself.

Dr. Rufus paused in the doorway, peering at her impatiently from under his bushy gray eyebrows. "Who?"

"Lord Featherstone. He might know of a homeopathic remedy that could help."

Even before she'd finished speaking, the physician was waving his hand dismissively, his frown deepening.

"That's humbug," he retorted, leaving to summon the surgeon.

Matthews looked at Beau's leg again, seriously considering it before he spoke. "It's th' skin I worry abou'. Th' 'ard part will be keepin' rot away."

Fiona smoothed the fine-grained skin of Beau's injured bicep, her mind racing. "If we use sticking plaster instead of stitches and pour marigold tincture into the wound three times a day—what do you think, Matthews?"

He grunted. "'E'd 'ave ta keep th' leg dead still for weeks. No movin'. 'E might wan' it off ta tha'."

"Lady Margaret, may I call in Lord Featherstone? Before the surgeon—"

She stopped when she saw Lady Margaret give a fearful glance toward Beau's mangled leg, and continued more gently, "I understand your fear, and I feel it too. I love Beau—I do!—and would welcome the amputation of his leg if I believed that he was truly going to get an infection. But I don't, because I also believe in the healing abilities of herbs and homeopathy, something that Dr. Rufus thinks is nonsense. But let me tell you: in all my years of dabbling, I've seen herbs do miraculous things! Do you think … do you think we could just try it? At the first sign of infection we could stop."

Lady Margaret gave her a grateful smile, saying, "I'll put the surgeon off—as long as Beau doesn't get worse. I trust you, Miss Fairmont."

"Thank you," Fiona said fervently, shaking with relief … but also terror. What if the delay cost Beau his life? "I'm going to find your butler and ask him to fetch Lord Featherstone. He has the homeopathic version of comfrey, which knits bones, and I'll also ask him to deliver a letter to my mother. She knows where I keep my herbal tonics."

She left quickly and found Patterson sitting in the front hallway, his head bowed, one bony hand covering his face. She hated to disturb him in such a pose, so she started to back away so that she could find a footman instead. But despite her best attempts at keeping quiet, he looked up. His desolate expression wrenched her heart. "I'm so sorry—" she said.

He quickly stood, his professional demeanor revived. "Miss Fairmont, is there anything you need?"

"Writing paper, ink, and a messenger who can take letters to Lord Featherstone and my mother," she answered.

12.

"I trust Miss Fairmont," Lady Margaret said quietly, stepping into the hallway and closing her husband's bedroom door. An extra dose of laudanum had allowed him to fall into a restless sleep, after hearing the news of his son's accident, but the physician's incensed disbelief threatened to wake him.

Dr. Rufus's eyes narrowed. "You will have to live with the consequences of this decision for the rest of your life. Do you understand that your son will very likely die?"

Lady Margaret motioned the doctor away from her husband's door. "Dr. Rufus, you've been with us for years and I respect your good opinion. But in this instance, if Beau's leg can be saved—" She took a deep breath before continuing. "I'm going to send the surgeon away. I'm asking you to please set Beau's leg. At the first sign of infection we'll reconsider."

"I pray you don't regret this." Dr. Rufus turned toward Beau's room to do her bidding.

"Thank you," Lady Margaret called out, but he didn't answer. She re-entered her husband's room, mixed emotions causing tears to spring to her eyes. That Fiona loved Beau was apparent. She hoped their love was enough to work a miracle.

***

Fiona glanced up when Dr. Rufus entered Beau's room. The doctor eyed her angrily. "If Lord Albert dies because of you, I *will* bring charges against you."

She took a calming breath. "He won't die." She watched as he opened his large leather portmanteau and pulled out two long pieces of wood and one small one.

He rounded on her, the small piece of wood still in his hand. "I've treated men in battle, Miss Fairmont; men who didn't have the advantage of a nearby surgeon. You have no idea what you're doing." He deftly opened Beau's mouth and stuck the block between his teeth. "See that this stays in place. It will keep him from biting his tongue off."

To Matthews he said, "Keep him still. This will hurt no matter how much laudanum he's had."

Not as much as sawing off his leg would, Fiona thought bitterly, but she held her tongue, not wanting to distract the physician from his work.

After examining the break, Dr. Rufus carefully took Beau's ankle in one hand and his calf in the other. He began to move the leg firmly back into alignment.

Fiona held her breath as Beau's body stiffened. He clamped down hard on the bite block, groaning. His hands gripped hers so tightly that she knew she'd have bruises, but she didn't try to pull away.

The setting of the leg was mercifully quick, and Dr. Rufus made fast work of immobilizing the leg with the two long pieces of wood. The worst of it over, Beau's muscles went slack as he lost consciousness. The bite block fell out, leaving a trail of saliva in its wake.

Fiona wiped the spittle off with her fingers, and leaned over to tenderly kiss his lips. "I love you, Beau."

***

Fiona steeled herself before entering the Beaumonts' drawing room, where Patterson had asked Henry to wait. "Thank you for coming, Henry."

He turned away from the rain-drenched window. "I was in my laboratory when I got your message. I knew rain would cancel our outing, so I went there as usual."

"Yes, thank God for the rain. I think I've said that a hundred times today. Listen, Henry, Beau had a dreadful accident this morning. Did you bring the comfrey—I mean, whatever it is homeopathically?"

"Symphytum officinalis." He pulled a bottle from his coat pocket and handed it to her. "What happened?"

"He broke his leg badly. The bone came through the skin."

"Has a physician seen it?"

Fiona grimaced. "Of course. He wanted a surgeon to amputate."

"And?" Henry gave Fiona a strange look that she didn't like one bit.

"I thought we could try—"

"Fiona, you're not a physician! A wound like that might send infection through his whole body. What if he dies? Do you want to be responsible for his death?"

Fiona gaped at him. "What happened to your faith in these medicines? You, of all people—"

"My confidence in the medicines hasn't changed, but that's not the point. My point is, that you're not a physician—homeopathic or otherwise."

"But if the *physician* in question wishes to do something permanently damaging, that could be avoided with the right homeopathic or herbal cure, surely—"

"These remedies are subject to human error in prescribing. Do you know for certain that symphytum is the remedy needed if you haven't done the research on it? If you haven't studied diagnostics?"

"Comfrey is the bone knitting herb, so—"

"Nevertheless, you can't be so sure it will work unless you're trained in diagnostics and prescribing. And it's not the remedy's fault if it doesn't work when an amateur prescribes it, but it's then called useless by those who see that it hasn't worked. Careless prescribing harms the cause of homeopathy in general."

Fiona stared in disbelief. "But symphytum is for bone breaks, is it not?"

"It is, but there may be others—not yet discovered—that would be the better fit in this case."

"In your opinion, Henry, will symphytum work?"

"I've told you before, Fiona, I don't give medical opinions."

"You can relax, Henry. I won't share your opinion with Beau's physician." Fiona didn't bother to hide her exasperation. "Between us, tell me what you think."

"It might work."

"Then it's worth trying, to save a man's leg. To not try would be criminal." Fiona turned to go, tired of Henry's ever-present logic, and anxious to return to Beau. She knew Henry had a point—the remedy might fail—but she also knew that if she gave in to his cold assessment of the situation and didn't try to save Beau's leg, she would never forgive herself.

Henry moved in front of the door, blocking her way. "I must say, I cannot quite understand why you are even here."

"I stumbled into this nightmare while I was bringing herbal tonics to Beau's father, and since *I'm* the one making the decision against the physician's wishes, I think it's only right that I watch this leg nonstop for the next day or so. It would be irresponsible of me not to."

Of course, there was the glaring fact that she loved Beau. That was the most important reason why she was staying. But that admission would come later. She didn't have the heart to break her engagement with Henry right after he had obligingly brought the remedy she'd asked for.

Henry departed, taking his ponderous disapproval with him, making Fiona clearly see that she *needed* Beau's passion and joie de vivre. Without it, she might become as dry and scientific as Henry—never trusting her intuition, never loving passionately. She shivered at how close she had come to such a fate.

But now wasn't the time to think of all that. Now she had a bone to mend, a wound to medicate, and a confession of love to repeat.

***

A loud clap of thunder rattled Beau's bedroom windows, and his dark lashes twitched. He spoke a few incoherent words and Fiona held her breath, wondering if he was waking up. He had been asleep for an hour and a half.

"Wake up, Beau," she whispered. "I need to talk to you."

But he was sleeping the deep, drug-induced sleep that only the acutely traumatized are capable of.

Fiona stood to stretch. She had been so focused on Beau, even watching him as he slept, that she had not really noticed her surroundings.

Beau's bedroom: A place infused with his personality and preferences, Fiona thought with interest. She glanced around.

The large four-poster bed stood against the wall opposite the fireplace. The jutting mantel, like the bed, was made of dark walnut. The dark furniture was nicely offset by curtains, rugs, cushions and slipcovers in varying combinations of midnight blue trimmed in coral. It was masculine but cheerful, Fiona thought as she circled the room, looking and touching. She didn't quite dare open drawers, but nothing on top surfaces was left unexplored.

There was the usual comb and mirror, this time silver inlaid with copper and gold; matching shaving necessities near the wash basin; a London Times and a book of poems—Donne, she saw with a smile—were on a table in the sitting area. A vial of oil sat on the dresser. Fiona opened it and sniffed, immediately recognizing sandalwood laced with a touch of cedar. She smiled again, thinking of how Beau's natural essence mixed with the oils to create a unique scent whose magic drew her. Also on the dresser were three snuffboxes. One was ivory with gold piping and it was filled with a sweet-smelling snuff. Fiona thought of cherries when she smelled it. Another, in an ebony box with a B monogram made of inlaid diamonds, smelled earthy, like dirt after it has been well-tilled and watered. A third one smelled like pepper and made Fiona's eyes water. She snapped it closed and examined the box, a small wooden one with a mahogany MP monogram starkly contrasting with the lighter cherry wood of the box itself.

"MP," she said aloud. "A maternal grandfather, perhaps?" She replaced the box and returned to Beau's bedside. Sighing, she sat down to continue her watch over him.

***

Beau opened his eyes to see Fiona dozing. She sat in a chair, her head cradled on her arms that rested on the side of his bed. He twined his fingers into her mussed hair, tumbling it more completely out of its hairpins so that it spread over his midnight-blue coverlet. He stared in drugged fascination at the color contrast as he absentmindedly pulled at a tangle.

"Uh-uh," Fiona complained in her sleep.

Beau quit tugging at the tangle and rubbed Fiona's scalp instead, his fingers gently exploring every inch.

The day was mostly a blur, with memories being distant and unreal. He remembered the confrontation, the shooting, the injury, the regret regarding this beautiful woman whose head lay on his bed. After that, pain and weakness—and very probably laudanum, although he didn't remember taking it—had muddled events in his mind.

His left leg throbbed dully and seemed to be resting against something hard. He lifted his head off the pillow and a ringing sound filled his ears, so he let it drop heavily back.

"I have to know," he muttered.

Gathering strength, he lifted his head again, this time focusing his blurry eyes on the place where his feet should be. He saw *two* feet poking up under the covers so was reassured that the word "amputate" had either been his imagination or an option discarded. "Thank God." He let out a long breath as his head fell back onto the pillow. He wished that the ringing in his ears would stop. Now that his head was flat, the ringing came in pulsating bursts, seemingly in tandem with his heart.

Another memory from the day emerged, this one delicious as honey, and he fervently hoped it hadn't sprung from his imagination. Glancing down at Fiona's sleeping form, he resumed his massage of her scalp. A smile tugged at the corners of her lips and her breathing deepened.

After a few minutes, he stopped. "Fiona," he whispered, patting now, trying to wake her.

"Don't stop."

"Wake up, my dearest love."

Her green eyes opened but were sightless because she was still watching her dreams.

"What are you dreaming?"

Fiona gave a slight shake of her head and closed her eyes again. "Lilac needs sunlight," she muttered. But in the next instant, her eyes flew open and she sat up straight, one hand flying to her hair. "Beau! You're awake! How do you feel?" she said in a rush, blinking the sleep out of her eyes.

He laughed, loving the intimacy of seeing her emerge from sleep.

"What's so funny?" Fiona demanded, self-consciously smoothing her hair with one hand while she gathered hairpins with the other.

He shook his head, still smiling widely, "Nothing. I'm laughing with joy. You give me joy, Fiona." But suddenly his smile disappeared as his heart clenched tightly in fear that she hadn't really said those tenderly whispered words. Had the poignant memory been nothing but a laudanum-induced hallucination?

Fiona's lovely eyes filled with worry. "What's the matter? Do you need more laudanum?"

"Not now," Beau lied. He'd be damned if he'd go back to sleep before he got to the bottom of his memory. He thought he remembered her soft breath tickling his ear and neck as he heard the words that would be more medicinal than any potion or remedy that anyone could offer him. *Were they real?*

"Can I get you anything?" She was kneading his hand gently as she spoke, and the massage sent shivers of pleasure through him.

"Your company is all I need," he said, closing his eyes. Should he simply ask her? *Fiona, do you love me?*

"Beau, your leg—" Fiona said, but stopped, frowning and biting her lip.

Since he'd already looked to verify that it was still there, her words didn't freeze his heart.

"Dr. Rufus wanted to call in a surgeon to take it and I wouldn't let him," Fiona said, adding, "With your mother's permission, of course."

Beau smiled at her adorable concern. "Thank God you were here, then."

"You may not say that if the wound gets infected. Beau, Matthews and I are medicating it 'round the clock. Dr. Rufus thinks we're fools. I pray he's wrong." She let his hand go and circled the bottom of the bed to get a better look at Beau's leg.

Pulling the covers back, she worriedly eyed the wound. Beau tried to lift himself onto his elbows to look, too, but the effort brought back the ringing and sent a stab of pain into his leg. He grunted, falling heavily back onto his pillows.

"Let me," Fiona said, coming to his side to ease an arm behind him. "You must keep this leg perfectly still. That means no muscles pulling on it from your hips, which means when you want to change position you'll have to ask for help."

Her tantalizing nearness effectively numbed his pain, but he struggled to focus on it so that one of the bumps under the covers wouldn't start looking like a tent pole.

Fiona propped Beau up enough to see his leg. A nasty gash was held together with sticking plaster, and three strips of cloth held two boards flat against either side of his leg. He nodded, which sent his head into a dizzying spin, and Fiona slowly lowered him back to a reclined position.

"Beau, what happened?" she asked, pulling the covers back over his leg.

He let out a large breath and passed a hand over his brow. The truth, connected as it was to an ex-mistress, was too risky. The love that he dared to have confirmed this very day was too new, too delicate to stand the onslaught of a seedy revenge story.

"I ran into a group of poachers at daybreak ... on my way to Castlewood," he finally said.

"That's strange. I haven't heard news of any poachers in the area." Fiona ran a finger along his rope burn. "How did you get this mark?"

"What? Oh ... they pulled me off Merlin with a rope—that's how I broke my leg. I assume they wanted to stall me, so they'd have time to get away."

Fiona's brow furrowed prettily. "How dreadfully unlucky! Have you ever had problems with poachers before at Castlewood?"

"Not in my memory. It *was* stupid, bad luck," Beau said, averting his eyes from her penetrating gaze. He hated to lie.

"Why were you out so early?"

"I ... I had a dream about my father. Silly, really, to rush out on such a whim, but—"

"Oh, no! I'd have done the very same thing." Fiona gave him an approving smile.

It made him feel dreadfully guilty, so he decided to change the subject.

"As horrible as this leg business is, I'm grateful for it as well."

Fiona sat on the edge of the bed next to him, clearly surprised. "What is there to be grateful about?"

"As I lay on the ground, wondering if I was going to die, I realized that I hadn't yet told you that I love you. That's my greatest crime to date—that I never said those three very important words: I love you," Beau's thumb traced circles on her leg. He felt her shiver.

Tears rimmed her eyes, one spilling over onto her cheek. "I love you, too, Beau. So much," she whispered, swallowing hard. "But you're not the criminal here. You might have neglected the words but I denied their very existence. When I finally acknowledged them, my heart almost floated away, it felt so light."

Beau opened his arms and Fiona placed her head on his chest. He reveled in the feel of her petite body and the glorious feel of her silky hair cascading over him, for she hadn't bothered to pin it back up. She smelled delicious today, like orange blossoms with a hint of cloves.

He hadn't been wrong. She loved him.

"Kiss me." His hands on her shoulders guided her upward. Fiona tilted up her head and kissed him gently on the lips. Joyfulness turned into something earthier when she opened her mouth and ran her tongue over his lips.

"Bliss…" he groaned.

But the next moment Fiona silenced him by dipping her tongue into his mouth, running it along the back of his teeth, drinking him in as if her life depended on it.

She pulled away from the kiss to look at him and her eyes were filled with a tenderness that made his breath catch.

"Marry me, Fiona," he said. "We belong together."

Fiona smiled. "Yes, we do."

"Featherstone will understand," Beau insisted, feeling a surge of anger at the thought of his rival.

Fiona's eyes lit with reluctant amusement. "He may not understand but he'll have to accept."

And Beau had nothing more to say because Fiona was kissing him again.

***

"Henry, please explain it to me again. I do *not* understand it," Lady Richland said. They were playing gin rummy in the Hasseltons' drawing room, after a delicious dinner of mushroom-stuffed pheasant.

Henry discarded a king of clubs. "What?"

"Why Fiona is nursing Lord Albert this evening. She's engaged to *you*. It seems quite inappropriate to me," Lady

Richland huffed. She picked up her nephew's discard and rearranged her cards.

"She considers herself a healer first, a debutante—or engaged woman—second," Henry explained grouchily. "But you needn't worry about appearances. He's on a sickbed. Possibly his deathbed."

"But they're barely acquainted." Lady Richland put down a two of diamonds and Henry took a new card, considering it carefully before he spoke.

"Doesn't matter. She'd want to heal a perfect stranger with her herbs—or my remedies. I'll cure her of that when we're married." He discarded.

"Sooner than that! People might talk, otherwise, and we don't want our family names besmirched with scandal." Lady Richland threw down a card more forcefully than necessary, the rings on her pudgy fingers glinting furiously in the firelight.

Henry coolly picked it up and placed his discard face down. He fanned out his cards for her to see. "Gin."

She ignored his cards. "Did you hear what I said, Henry?"

"Yes. Shall I deal?" Henry gathered the cards.

"Oh, go ahead! But, Henry, you're not going to get immersed in your laboratory and forget, are you? This is very important. You need to get her back here by tomorrow."

Henry shook his head as he expertly shuffled the cards. "Stop worrying or you'll lose again."

***

Fiona sighed, grateful to see Castlewood in the distance. It already felt like home to her, and she needed its soothing presence to calm her nerves after her meeting with Henry.

He had heard her explanation of why she was breaking their engagement, and had given her a skeptical smirk in return. "Mark my words, Fiona, you'll come to regret your decision. But I can see that there's no changing your mind.

Lord Albert has managed to bewitch you as thoroughly as he does every other woman. I thought *you* knew better."

"No, Henry, we love each other. I'll be getting back to him now," she had said, leaving Henry's cloud of disapproval and ridicule as quickly as she could.

Patterson let her in, and she hurried upstairs to see how Beau had fared in her absence.

She was about to open the door when she heard him complain, loudly, "I feel like a damn pig on a spit."

Pushing open the door, she saw that Matthews was in the process of turning Beau onto his side. "Ya don't wan' no bed sores formin,'" Matthews lectured, grunting as he attempted to tuck a pillow under Beau's injured leg.

"Let me help, Matthews." Fiona hurried over and tucked the pillow under Beau's leg after Matthews carefully held it up.

Beau sighed in exasperation. "Fiona, tell Matthews that I don't need turning, like some slow-cooking pork roast."

"Matthews is right to do it, Beau." She placed a hand on his head, feeling for fever since his hair was clammy with sweat. Thankfully, it seemed to be coming from the exertion and pain, not infection. "Do you need more laudanum?"

Beau shook his head and snorted. "I couldn't tell you my own birthday right now, I'm so foggy-brained. That stuff is poison."

"How about some valerian? It's an herb; not as strong as laudanum, but it might help," she said, stroking the damp hair off his face. "And I can try to wash your hair in the basin."

Beau nodded in response to Matthews' gruff goodbye, then switched his gaze to Fiona. "I'm sorry. I'm not being a very good patient."

His voice sounded parched, so Fiona poured him a tumbler of water from the pitcher on the washstand, and he gulped it gratefully.

Fiona reached for the bell pull. "I'll ring for your tea."

Beau hastily wiped his mouth with the back of his hand. "Don't."

She paused and turned toward him, half-worried, half-puzzled, and he smiled, patting the bed.

"If I'm hungry for anything it's another one of your kisses. Come here."

Fiona smiled now, thrilled that the prospect of her kiss could so easily take the pain from his face. She would kiss him a million times each day if that's what it took to get him well.

She sat on the bed and leaned forward to kiss him, but he pulled away. "No. Lie down next to me," he urged.

She did, and he put his arm around her and drew her close until there was less than an inch separating their lips. "I love you so much," he whispered, just before bringing his lips to hers.

His kiss deepened quickly and Fiona kissed back without reserve, no longer perplexed at the sensations his nearness provoked in her. Instead, there was a desire to explore them further, to understand them better.

She stroked a hand down his back, dipping it below the sheet and resting it on his well-muscled buttock. She felt his muscles tighten and heard a slight intake of breath, but his tongue did not stop its slow, tantalizing exploration of her mouth.

She slid her hand forward, over his hipbone, until her palm encountered crinkly hair and the sharp angle of his leg where it met his torso.

Beau tore his lips away from their kiss. "Fiona, you have no idea what havoc you're wreaking." He took in a jagged breath and stopped her exploration with his free hand.

Fiona allowed him to pull her hand up. "Did I hurt you?" She searched his face for signs of increased pain.

"No. You've obliterated all thoughts of my leg," Beau said wryly.

"Then why stop me?" Fiona said, beginning to understand his meaning. "We can consider this part of your healing."

She pulled her hand free and slid it down Beau's chest, loving that her touch made him moan and close his eyes, delighted that he didn't try to stop her again. When she closed her hand around his erection she heard his sharp intake of breath.

"I know what happens between a man and woman," Fiona murmured, gently rubbing. "I've watched our stable cats." She trailed her fingers slowly up Beau's shaft. "I never understood why our tabby finally allowed the male to … to mount her until recently. She must have had the same ache I do."

She gasped when Beau drew his fingers down the line of her throat, dipping one between her breasts. "I think men and women take a little more pleasure in lovemaking than cats," he said lazily, pulling his finger to the side to gently stroke a nipple. Fiona moaned, arching against his finger, her nipple puckering in pleasure.

"That … that makes me want—" Fiona stopped, not sure what exactly it was she wanted.

Beau slipped his hand out of her bodice and stroked down her stomach. His hand traveled lower and she moaned again. *"There."*

"I know." Beau gently pushed her onto her back. He inched up her skirt, at the same time exerting a delicious pressure on that oh-so-sensitive place with the weight of his arm. "I'll show you—" he paused to kiss her earlobe. "—Something tomcats never do." He suckled her earlobe now, but after a few seconds he gave it a soft nip.

Fiona cried out, but a moment later, when Beau's fingers reached her skin, she shuddered in anticipation. He stroked the velvety cushions of flesh at the tops at her thighs, at the same time teasing what lay above.

When he slipped two fingers into her wetness Fiona whimpered. He gently rocked his hand until she was groaning, and then he slowly slid his fingers upward to her pulsing, swollen nub, rolling it gently between his fingers. Delicious warmth spread through Fiona's body and she gasped as a jolt of pleasure caused an uncontrollable shudder. A few moments later, she felt limp, exhilarated.

Like she did after completing a lengthy, brisk walk—only far better.

She turned her head to gaze into Beau's eyes. "That was ... truly ... the most incredible thing," she confessed.

"It gets better," he returned, stroking softly down her thigh.

Fiona considered his words carefully, then smiled.

"Now it's your turn," she said, almost laughing when he gaped at her.

"My turn?" he asked, his eyes telling her that he knew exactly what she meant.

"Yes," Fiona said, running a finger down Beau's torso, her eyes never leaving his. When she reached his erection she encircled it, gently stroking, and he closed his eyes, breathing hard.

"Our relationship will be famous for its equality ... among other things," she whispered, using both hands now.

"I see," was all he managed before losing his ability to speak.

13.

Two months later

Daphne set her breakfast tray aside and pulled her newspaper closer, flipping it open to scan the headlines. She yawned, turning past the news of peers who had died or been injured in the latest Napoleonic battles, looking for more local gossip. At page five she stopped, sinking into her pillows, stomach-wrenching hatred washing over her.

He was back in London, with his fiancée, to finalize wedding plans.

"No!" she screeched, pushing the paper so that it fell to the floor, scattering halfway across her bedroom floor. "He doesn't deserve this happiness!"

Her new lover sat bolt upright in the bed, his hair sticking straight up. "What is it? What? What?"

"It's nothing, Landers. But while you're up, you might as well be on your way." She hated to see him so mussed and smelly. It was bad enough that he was a merchant, but now the stench of unscrubbed teeth was assaulting her nostrils.

***

At that very minute, Beau was taking advantage of the unexpectedly balmy weather to ride in Hyde Park with Fiona.

"Do you have any desire to see the new exhibit at the British Museum? There'll be time after my final fitting, and I've heard it's excellent," Fiona said.

Beau tightened the reins to avoid two squirrels that had chased in front of his team. "I'll go wherever you lead me, my love."

Hyde Park was glorious. Mother Nature had bestowed a gift of seventy-degree weather in early September, and Beau hadn't thought twice about taking advantage of it. Ever since Dr. Rufus had released him from his tedious recovery, he'd taken in more fresh air and exercise than he had in the previous five years combined. He simply couldn't get enough.

"You're in such a good mood, you'd probably agree to go to one of Henry's homeopathic lectures," Fiona teased.

"It's good that he's sharing his passion with a broader audience. I think Lady Clarissa is a good influence on him. Not that you were a bad influence, but true love inspires."

"Yes, Henry is much better off without me. Thank goodness you came along and set us all straight."

"Thank goodness you listened. Although I sometimes wonder what would've happened if I hadn't broken my leg."

Fiona smiled. "It's true that your leg expedited things, but sometimes I like to indulge a fantasy: You're bursting into St. John's to snatch me away from Henry, just before the minister pronounces us man and wife."

Beau laughed, but was serious a minute later when he said, "I like to think my accident brought us together. That way it's not a wholly black event."

"That man—whom you shot. Who did he turn out to be?"

"He was doorkeeper at a pub in St. Giles for a bit, then worked as a hired thug for a moneylender, but he obviously had other unsavory ways of making money." Beau paused, thinking, *Tell her. Tell her the truth.* The lie he had told had gained weight as time had passed. The ugly thing pressed directly on his heart, heavy and unrelenting.

"Beau, I invited Henry and Lady Clarissa to the wedding party. You don't mind, do you?"

Fiona had a way of tilting her eyebrows asymmetrically when she was worried that Beau had grown to cherish, and he smiled, deciding not to mar the beauty of the moment. His confession could come later, perhaps at the museum that night.

Beau pulled his horses to a stop and turned to face her. Shifting the reins to one hand, he placed the other on Fiona's knee. "Satan himself could be at the wedding party, but it wouldn't matter. I'll have eyes only for you. Do you know how much I adore you?"

"Yes," Fiona breathed, the adorable worry replaced by a marvelously innocent sensuality that didn't lessen one jot when she changed the subject.

"I hope Felicity didn't annoy you too much at lunch today. She's practically beside herself that you're to be her brother-in-law. You'll make her the happiest girl in London if you'll dance with her at the party."

Beau took the reins back up and nudged his superb gray pair, Merlin and Maelstrom, forward. "Of course I'll dance with her."

Fiona watched as he deftly turned his phaeton around the fountain. "Any regrets, Beau? If you could change one thing, what would it be?"

"I do have a regret! A huge one!"

"What?" Fiona urged.

"I'm out a thousand pounds and Smithers won't be telling me who his love interest is. I made him a wager, just before I met you, that I wouldn't be getting married this year. Who would've known that an angel would appear before me at the Aldwinkles' garden party? Smithers was apparently the only one, although my parents hoped it was so."

"Do you think things would have been different if we'd met at that ball in London? Lady Stanton's ball?"

"Yes. I wouldn't have found you attractive at all in that setting," Beau teased, pulling off the main thoroughfare and stopping his team again.

"Seriously, Beau," Fiona admonished.

He turned toward her and took her hand. "We were meant to be together, and it would have happened no matter where we'd met. You are my one and only love." Beau brought her hand to his lips, then leaned down and kissed her upturned face, on her nose. He tilted her chin and kissed her lips.

"I suppose we *should* stop, but I don't want to," Fiona murmured.

"Since this outing will be plastered in the papers just as assuredly as our arrival in town was, we might as well give them something of substance to write about."

Fiona hummed her agreement as he kissed her again.

***

Reeves, the Fairmonts' butler, delivered a tea tray to Lady Clarissa Cowper. "Lady Cowper, Miss Fairmont is not yet home. If you wish to wait, I've brought this tea tray."

Lady Clarissa's eyes lit up when she saw a box of chocolates on the tray. "I'll wait."

Twenty minutes later, Lady Clarissa looked up from a half-empty box of chocolates when Fiona entered the Fairmonts' drawing room. Cherry cordial dripped onto her chin as she bit into the chocolate she was holding. "Goodness! That one dripped!" she exclaimed, wiping her chin with a napkin.

"Lady Clarissa, it's good to see you. Congratulations on your engagement," Fiona said, sitting across from her. "And congratulations on getting Henry out of his laboratory. If I wasn't so busy with wedding preparations, I'd attend one of his lectures."

"Truly? Oh, I almost forgot! You share his hobby, don't you? Henry knows better than to ask me to attend!"

Fiona hoped that Lady Clarissa would get to the point of her visit. She knew better than to think it was strictly a social call. Lady Clarissa's reputation for loving gossip was too well established for that. "Will you be in London long?"

"No, we leave tonight. By the way, please don't be offended that Henry isn't here too, but our day completely wore him out. I left him in a rather bad mood, but hopefully his new book will placate him. If that doesn't, our ride home will soothe his temper." She smiled mischievously, exposing her ready dimples.

Fiona thought she understood the smile but pretended not to. "I know he's looking forward to getting back to his provings. Tea?" She indicated the as-yet-untouched pot of tea with a nod.

Lady Clarissa nodded, picking up a cup and saucer and holding them out to Fiona. "Those provings have got to stop! Last month his experiments gave him a dreadful rash across his chest that took days to clear. And all he could say was 'Be grateful I wasn't one of the mercury provers because my teeth would likely have fallen out.'"

Fiona tutted sympathetically, grateful Henry's provings were Lady Clarissa's problem and not hers.

"Miss Fairmont, the reason I'm here isn't to discuss Henry." Before continuing, Lady Clarissa added three lumps of sugar to her tea. Her face held a strange combination of sadness laced with fascination, if such a thing was possible.

Here it comes. The explanation for this visit. "Oh? What then?" If she had been asked to guess Lady Clarissa's next statement she would have failed miserably, given a thousand tries.

"Daphne Tarkington invited us to tea yesterday, and she wanted us to pass on a warning to you."

"Daphne Tarkington?" Fiona was puzzled. "I don't know her. Why would she—?"

"You don't know her, but Beau does. They were involved just before he met you. Don't you remember the scandal? He broke with her publicly and it socially ruined her! Granted, anything she has to say about him is probably rubbish, since she hates him so much."

"She hates him?"

Lady Clarissa looked at Fiona in astonishment. "Yes, don't you remember? He humiliated her in public! Not that she didn't deserve it—she's really a horrible woman. You must not read the gossip papers."

Fiona set down her teacup. "What warning does she wish to give?"

"First of all, she claims that Beau's poacher story is nonsense. He was attacked because of gaming debt. It appears that he is a member of a highly secret club that holds their gaming sessions at a place called Morgan's Pier. He supposedly has already lost vast sums to this establishment—to the point of pinching his estate's coffers. Apparently, he was late in his repayments and was sent a message—the broken leg. But I'm sure the poachers have been caught, haven't they? Showing her explanation to be what it is—vicious rumor mongering?" Lady Clarissa looked at Fiona expectantly.

"No, but that's not unusual." Fiona sounded more sure than she felt. A chill of doubt had encircled her heart because she had just remembered something: a snuffbox she had seen on Beau's dresser with the monogram MP. She had meant to ask him what MP stood for, but never had. And something else occurred to her. Beau himself had, just that morning, told her that the man who was killed had worked for moneylenders.

Lady Clarissa finished washing down a lemon tart with a huge sip of tea, continuing after a noisy swallow. "The second thing she told us was that Beau recently visited an old friend—Lady Wolfrey. If you remember, he was engaged to her—Miss Elliot—six years ago. Yesterday's visit never made the papers, but Daphne Tarkington's maid is the sister of one of Lady Wolfrey's footmen, or some such thing. I assured her that it was just a visit between old friends but, of course, she thinks the worst of Beau and said so. She insinuated that Lady Wolfrey, perhaps unhappy in her marriage, is now seeking Beau's comforting shoulder." Lady Clarissa examined the few chocolates left in the box.

"Yes, a visit between friends is all," Fiona said—softly, because she felt like the wind had been knocked out of her. Beau hadn't told her about such a visit. If he wasn't hiding something, then why wasn't it mentioned?

"I'm sure that was all it was. By the way, Daphne also said that you should protect your dowry—some women tie them up in trusts for future children. If you don't, she is sure that it will be gone within days after your marriage." Lady Clarissa popped the next-to-last chocolate in her mouth.

Fiona stood. "I hope I'm not being rude, but I'm due to meet Beau at the museum in a short while. Will you excuse me?"

"Of course," Lady Clarissa said through cream-filled chocolate. After swallowing she said, "I have to get back to Henry now, anyway. He'll be wanting to go home."

After Lady Clarissa left Fiona sank onto the sofa, her heart heavy, her mind racing.

Could it all be true? This new explanation about his broken leg made more sense than the "poacher gang." That story had always seemed odd to her, especially since news of other attacks in the vicinity hadn't been reported.

But he's sincere in his love! Isn't he? Fiona thought, desperate to return to the haze of happiness she had been living in before hearing Lady Clarissa's words. *Of course you'd think so! Beau's an expert at making women fall in love with him. And doesn't every woman that feels the warmth of his attention desperately hope that they have the power to capture his heart once and for all, to keep that heart forever? And yet none have before you, so why have you fooled yourself into believing that you're the one who did? You should have trusted your first instinct!*

Fiona sunk her face into her hands and sat that way for several long minutes, trying to think what to do. Finally she went upstairs to write a note pleading a migraine headache, excusing herself from the museum outing. She couldn't face Beau right now. The only thing she felt capable of was lying in bed with a cool cloth over her eyes, escaping painful doubt with sleep. Perhaps she'd take a dose of laudanum ...

14.

Beau frowned when he saw the clock in the Wolfreys' hallway. He hastily gathered his hat and coat from the butler and left, taking the stairs quicker than his newly healed leg liked. A breezy wind threatened to send his beaver hat flying. He pulled it firmly onto his head and turned in the direction of the British Museum.

The ten-block walk had *seemed* a good idea when he'd sent his carriage home, but now—between the wind and the lateness of the hour—he cursed his earlier decision. He tried to walk briskly, but his leg—still unused to exercise—had him limping by the third block.

Damn! Lady Wolfrey, beautiful but demanding as ever, had been more than willing to grant him his favor, but her price had been steep. At his first visit, yesterday, to make his request, he had had to listen to her travelogue of Paris, where she and her husband had recently vacationed. But she had also insisted that he return, today, to retrieve his heirloom bracelet in person—instead of simply sending it to his house. She had wanted him to have tea with her and her husband, Lord Wolfrey. The visit had been amiable; Lord Wolfrey was an articulate and entertaining host, but now he was running late. Or limping late, to be exact.

You might want to use a cane the first few weeks, his physician had advised. But Beau had scoffed at the idea of a cane and had promised his physician that he'd be careful. He hadn't realized exactly how painful overtaxed muscles could be.

He blew out a large sigh of relief as the museum came into sight and slowed a bit. He could see people coming and going, and if he saw Fiona leaving—he wouldn't blame her, he was thirty minutes late—he could shout out to stop her.

He finally reached the door and pulled it open, momentarily forgetting his pain in anticipation of seeing Fiona. He stepped inside and scanned the crowd for her red-gold hair, then frowned and looked toward those people who were entering behind him. Not seeing her there, he moved toward the ancient, stone benches that sat back to back in the middle of the main hall, wondering if she was sitting out of sight on the other side of one.

Before he'd taken three steps, he heard his name, but it wasn't Fiona's voice so he felt a pang of annoyance. Turning, he saw one of the Fairmonts' footmen.

"Lord Albert, sir?" the man repeated.

"Yes?"

"Miss Fairmont said to give you this." He handed Beau a letter and turned to go.

"Wait. Do I need to send a message back?" Beau asked, thumbing open the seal.

"Miss Fairmont didn't say to wait. If you wish me to, I will, my lord." He clasped his hands in front of him and stood, his gaze averted.

Beau read his letter:

Dear Beau,

I can't meet you after all. The fitting gave me a migraine. I've gone to bed and will send word tomorrow when I'm better.

F

It was the first letter he had ever gotten from Fiona, he realized with interest. There was something quite jarring about it—its brevity and lack of warmth, to be precise. He assumed it was her usual style and made a mental note to tease her about it tomorrow, when she felt better.

"Tell her I'll call on her tomorrow after I hear from her," Beau said to the footman, who nodded and left.

Beau limped the rest of the way to the stone benches and sat with a grunt, stretching his hurting leg out in front of him. "Something's wrong," he muttered.

He watched people coming and going for a moment, trying to analyze his apprehension. The note was still in his hand and he shook it open to reread it. No apology. No 'with love' at the end. It felt angry.

She's found out about the lie. God, I'm an idiot! he berated himself. But a second later, rational thought took over: *How would she have heard? That's ridiculous.*

He shook his head and heaved a disappointed sigh. As he tucked the note away in his coat pocket, he felt the soft velvet sack that held the hard-won bracelet. He rubbed the soft material between his fingers for a moment, lost in thought, then pulled it out and undid the drawstring that held it closed.

Curious to see it again, he wondered if the sapphires were as beautiful as he remembered. He pulled the bracelet out to examine it. The deep blue stones caught the light from the wall sconces, causing a fire to dance within them; the gold settings were so delicate that the gems appeared suspended in air. Beau envisioned it on Fiona's wrist and smiled, knowing that she would love its timeless beauty.

He slipped it back into the gray velvet bag and pulled the drawstring tight when, from somewhere behind him, a small hand appeared and snatched it from him. He whirled around and caught sight of a boy making a wide circle around him, headed for the exit. The black-toothed grin was the only thing that gave away his lowly status. Upscale clothes had been a perfect ruse, allowing him to gain entry into the museum.

Beau ran after him, and a stab of pain ripped through his sorely taxed leg. He ignored it, determined to reach the door before the boy did, but lost faith in his ability with each step.

"Stop that thief," he yelled, pointing to the boy.

His words caught everyone's attention, but no one reacted quickly enough. The boy slipped through the door a few crucial seconds before Beau did.

"Stop! I'll give you money instead," he shouted, watching as the boy took the steps in two neat leaps. "Stop!" he shouted again, limping pathetically down the steps as fast as his bum leg would let him. One gentleman made a feeble attempt to clutch the boy's coat as he ran by, and was rewarded for his efforts with a violent push. He fell backward, crushing a woman's toe as he attempted to right himself. The woman gave a quite unladylike howl and hit the man over the head with her reticule, then tried to hit Beau as he limped by.

Beau dodged her and chased as fast as he could after the boy, but it was no good. The thief quickly increased the distance between them, finally leaping onto the back of a moving carriage, his coattails flapping in the wind. He looked back at Beau and waved, the audacious punk.

Beau shook his fist in return. He groaned in disgust—mostly at himself for being so foolish as to take the bracelet out of the safety of his pocket—and leaned a hand against the brick building he'd ended up next to. He bent his throbbing leg at the knee to take pressure off it and leaned down to rub it.

"May I help you, Lord Albert?" a man's voice asked concernedly.

Beau turned and saw a constable.

"Not unless you can tell me the whereabouts of that thief that just made off with my property. Did you see him? I tried to catch him, but this blasted leg—"

"I saw him wave, but I can't say as if I've ever seen that one 'round here. They use different disguises all the time, which keeps us guessing. I'll send papers 'round to your residence, my lord, so you can fill out a report."

"Do you really think that'll help?" Beau asked tiredly.

A small crowd had gathered, and he realized that he had created a scene. Wonderful! Yet another story for the papers, this one worthy of a satirical cartoon of a crippled peer buffoonishly trying to chase a thief. He turned away, walking slowly to minimize his limp. After twenty paces, the weight of the dozen pairs of eyes on his back became too great and he hailed a carriage, enclosing himself in its welcoming darkness after giving his address to the bleary-eyed driver.

"I'm a bloody fool," he moaned, disappointment clogging his throat. He'd be amazed if he ever saw the

Beaumont bracelet again. It was gone. He had endured long hours in Lady Wolfrey's company for naught.

The hired hack pulled to a stop and Beau got out, wincing as his sore leg touched the ground. He didn't feel like being alone and he knew sleep would evade him in his present mood—but what was the alternative? White's? No, he didn't feel like cards or gossip. There was that invitation to Lady Rennington's ball, but he didn't want to go without Fiona.

Fiona. He craved her presence and was tempted to act the lovesick fiancé that he was and visit her regardless of her note. A hand-delivered bouquet of healing lavender sprigs could be his excuse for ignoring her wishes.

But the more he thought about it, the less confident he felt about intruding on her privacy. If her note had hinted at a need for pampering, he would have been there already, but it hadn't. In all probability Fiona was sound asleep and wouldn't appreciate being disturbed.

Beau handed his hat and coat to Smithers.

"Will you be going out again this evening, my lord?" Smithers asked.

"No. Send up a bath and find those salts that Fiona gave me."

"Is anything amiss, my lord?"

Beau exhaled tiredly. "The heirloom bracelet is gone, Smithers. Stolen. And it's my own stupid fault."

***

Fiona awoke at five in the morning in a laudanum haze, wishing she hadn't taken the loathsome stuff. Yes, she had escaped a sleepless night, but now she had to sort out some of the darkest worries she'd ever had with a fuzzy brain. Maybe after some coffee she'd be better equipped to think. She'd developed a habit of drinking tea in the morning, ever since Henry had lectured her about the evils of coffee (it weakened homeopathic remedies and slowly destroyed a person's good health), but at the moment she didn't care.

While she waited for Anna to respond to the bell, she picked up the new book she'd shyly bought at the bookseller's the day before, thinking that she might need it within the next year: *Herbs for Ladies With Child*. Opening it, she saw a line drawing of red raspberry, but as she read and reread the sentence, 'it strengthens the womb for an easier delivery with less bleeding,' her mind wandered to Beau. His face, his laugh, his hands ... his declarations of love.

Tossing the book aside, Fiona pulled on her thickest wrapper and sat before the cold fireplace with arms wrapped around her and feet tucked under her. The weather had cooled overnight, chilling the air just enough to warrant a fire.

Anna found her that way a minute later. "You're up bright and early!" she chirped, setting down a tea tray and heading for the fireplace.

"Anna, I desperately need coffee. Would you mind?"

Anna smiled. "Of course not. I guess since you're not engaged to Lord Featherstone anymore you can go back to coffee without feeling guilt."

Anna left with the tea tray and was back in three minutes with coffee. "We drink it downstairs, so it was ready," she said.

Fiona picked up the steaming cup and savored her first sip. The dark, bitter liquid almost made her groan with delight. She had missed her morning coffee. "Anna, who do you think will make the better husband, Henry or Beau?"

Anna stopped tending the fire to look over her shoulder at her mistress. "They'll both be good in their own ways. For you, Lord Albert is better."

"What makes you so sure?"

"You love him. He loves you."

Fiona knew without a doubt that she loved Beau, but the insidious thought that his love was transitory made her shiver.

"Thank you, Anna," she murmured, stretching cold toes toward the blazing fire.

Anna glanced at Fiona worriedly. "Can I get you anything else, miss?"

"No, thank you. The coffee is perfect."

Anna left and Fiona's morose thoughts came flooding back. Would Beau deny Lady Clarissa's allegations? Or would he rationalize them? Or, worse, would he admit to them and expect her to marry him anyway? Would she be able to believe a denial?

The warmth of the fire—or maybe it was the barrage of tortuous doubts—made Fiona fall asleep again with her head drooping on her chest.

***

At one in the afternoon, Beau knocked on the Fairmonts' door. Fiona had written another note—this one as terse as the first—giving him permission to call on her that afternoon. This time he wondered if her note's curtness had to do with the morning paper, which had snidely insinuated that he and Lady Wolfrey were far more than old friends. The article had ended with an infuriating question: *Will Miss Fairmont's dazzling happiness begin to fade?*

Another lie to explain, Beau thought, shaking his head. He had wanted the bracelet to be a surprise, but now his secrecy about it seemed foolish.

The fact that yesterday's visit made the papers at all had made him almost choke on a strip of bacon that morning. Hopefully the expected cartoon of him limping after the thief would help him to explain everything.

Beau found his fiancée in a well-stuffed armchair by the fire in the drawing room—reading—with her legs tucked up under her skirt.

He stood watching her for a moment, relishing the beauty of her firelit hair at the same time that he cursed the uncomfortable certainty that something was wrong between them. He knew women too well not to recognize the vague forebodings of trouble. She must know that he was standing there, but she remained buried in her book, refusing to acknowledge him.

"Fiona," he finally said, from the doorway. When she looked up, his last hope that all was well between them was dashed. If anything, her tired expression intensified at the sight of him.

"Beau. I woke up with a stiff neck this morning. Headache's gone, but now this—" She winced and rubbed the back of her neck.

"Let me," Beau said, coming to stand behind her. He slid his hands under silky tresses tied back with a thin black ribbon, and gently rubbed her delicate neck. Her hair smelled wonderful, like lemony lilac.

She felt tense under his hands, unable to relax even when he softened his touch to mere feather strokes, and after a minute she pulled away to stand and face him.

"Thanks for trying, but it's too sore right now. Beau, you're limping more than usual. Would you like to sit down?" Fiona indicated the chair that faced hers.

Beau paused. He'd like to sit, but only if he could pull Fiona into his lap, bury his face in her hair, and caress her until she lost every ounce of her prickliness. "Never mind my leg. You saw the paper this morning," he said gently, staying where he was.

"What? No! Why?" Fiona said, puzzled.

"You didn't?" Beau yelped, mirroring her puzzlement.

"What's in it?"

Beau circled the chair that stood between them and took Fiona's hands in his. "That I visited Lady Wolfrey yesterday, instead of going to White's. I assumed you had read it, since you seem angry this morning."

"So it's true?" Fiona disentangled her hands and folded her arms in front of her.

"Yes, but if you didn't read the paper, then how did you know? Look, I know it seems strange that I didn't mention it, that I said I was going to White's, but there is a perfectly good explanation. I visited her for your sake. May I explain?" Beau took Fiona's elbow and guided her back to her chair. He dropped on one knee beside her, so that their faces were level and he'd be able to see a smile if one began to form.

But Fiona's accusing eyes stabbed his heart as sharply as a knife would have. "Yes, you said you were going to White's. Why the lie?"

"Please accept my apology for lying, Fiona. My intentions were right-minded, and if you'll hear my explanation it will erase your hurt," he pleaded, taking one of her hands.

She pulled it away from him and tucked it into the folds of her skirt. "I'm not hurt! I simply asked a question. It seems a reasonable one to ask in the face of a newly perceived deception."

Beau wished for passionate anger rather than this coldness. Passion he could handle; the coldness felt impenetrable.

"I didn't try to deceive you, Fiona. I told you I was going to White's so that my retrieval of an heirloom bracelet from Lady Wolfrey could be a surprise. I wanted you to have my grandmother's bracelet, that I had stupidly given away before I had any sense about such things, and I wanted it to be a surprise. It was as simple as that."

"You, of all people, should know that you cannot take one step in London without it being splashed in the newspapers. You cannot be so dense that you thought a visit to your first fiancée would go unnoticed?"

"Call me dense if you will, but I actually did." The conversation wasn't progressing at all as Beau had hoped, but suddenly he remembered something. "You didn't read the newspaper. How did you know?"

Fiona's eyes narrowed. "Never mind yesterday's news. What about your visit to Lady Wolfrey a few days ago? You haven't yet mentioned that visit. Perhaps there was an heirloom necklace, or—or some earrings to gain from that visit?" Fiona said, her sarcasm causing Beau more pain than tears would have.

"I—"

"Lady Clarissa sat just there, in that chair that you refuse to take—I wish you'd get off your knee, Beau, your leg must be throbbing by now—and told me all sorts of things!" Fiona's voice sounded brittle, but Beau saw her lip tremble before she bit it still.

Beau remained on his knee. "Lady Clarissa? Why would she *do* that?"

"She had warnings to give me from Daphne Tarkington, your supposed archenemy."

That name—Daphne Tarkington—spoken from his beloved's lips caused a visceral reaction. Beau felt as if he'd been punched, and he finally understood the accuracy of the phrase 'seeing red.' He pushed himself to a standing position and paced slowly to the window, trying to make sense of this new information. He could feel Fiona's eyes on him, and he finally turned to face her.

"What else did she say?"

"That you're a member of Morgan's Pier and in debt, and that's why your leg was broken. That I should secure my inheritance in trusts for my ... our—" Fiona looked away and gave a small shake of her head. "And that Lady Wolfrey was regretting her decision to end her engagement to you." She looked up and took a deep, shaky breath.

Beau was beside her again in three long strides, stifling a grunt as he knelt again. "Dearest, it's all a pack of lies, and I'm to blame for this—your pain—since I told my own lie. I was a bloody fool to keep this from you, but I feared you would—you hadn't yet told me you loved me. Fiona, Daphne hired Jack Whitehead to hurt me because she's hated me ever since I publicly broke with her, causing her social downfall. Now she's trying to cover her crime by manufacturing this story about debt, but I assure you I'm not in debt and never have been. I'll have you meet with my banker, if you don't believe me."

"She *hired* him to hurt you? How do you know this?"

"I don't know for sure. I'm basing my assumption on something one of Jack's men said."

"Why haven't you confronted her with it?"

"That's complicated. I don't have proof and I feared she'd set her evil sights on *you*. Of course, she did anyway," Beau reflected tiredly.

"So the poacher story was a lie as well? How many other lies have you told me?"

Beau groaned. "That's the end of them, I swear to you. Please, Fiona, don't do this. Please forgive me and I'll never lie to you again, ever. I was a fool to lie in the first place." Beau had never pleaded with a woman in his life, but he'd grovel on the ground before her if it took away her disillusionment.

Fiona took another deep breath. She smoothed her skirt absentmindedly, frowning, as he willed her to believe him. *Please, God, don't let Daphne get her revenge this way.* He would rather have lost his leg than this.

"I don't know," she finally said, refusing to meet his eyes.

Beau awkwardly got to his feet and sat heavily in the chair opposite Fiona, stunned and disbelieving. This was far worse than hired footpads. Daphne had successfully stained a love that, before now, had been magical in its purity. What hurt most was that his lies had caused the damage. Why had he been such an idiot?

"Your visits to Lady Wolfrey; why not write her a letter and achieve the same thing?" Fiona said, chewing on her bottom lip. "Here's an opportunity for you to tell me the truth, Beau. Are we to have a marriage like my parents after all?"

"Fiona, it's not like that! How can I make you see? You are the only woman I have ever loved or will ever love. That's not a lie."

Fiona stood and moved to the window and he followed her, barely feeling the twinges in his leg as he stood. His very soul hurt, erasing all other pain.

"I desperately want to believe you, but why is my heart aching so?" Beau barely heard her since she spoke quietly, with her back to him.

He noticed that it was still blustery outside, and watched as the wind took an unlucky gentleman's hat into a nearby tree. He realized, with a sinking heart, that he had to give her one more piece of information that would not help his cause at all. But it must be said now. He had learned his lesson and would not put it off. There would be no more lies or secrets between them.

"Fiona, the bracelet was stolen from me at the museum last night. I stupidly advertised its presence to a thief by pulling it out to look at it. It was snatched, and you'll probably never see it now. I'll show you the article about it in the newspaper, if you like."

He lifted his hands to caress her shoulders, but something in her stance made him stop and drop them to his sides. "I love you so much. Please, tell me what I can do to make you believe me."

"I wish we'd never come to London. Mother and Felicity could have finished the preparations. I loved being at Castlewood so much," Fiona said, almost to herself.

"Then let's return there. Tonight, if that would suit," Beau said urgently.

"It would feel different now. Doubt is a horrible thing." Fiona was still turned away from him, still gazing out the window.

"You are the love of my life, Fiona. How can I make you see?" Desperation made his voice break.

Fiona wistfully shook her head, and Beau took a step back and rubbed a hand over his face, trying to ease the grief he felt. Finally he said, "I can see that words aren't going to suffice. My reputation haunts me once again. God! That I had lived differently!"

Fiona turned and put a hand on his arm. Her sad reticence felt hopeless. "Beau, I love you. I do."

Her declaration, as welcome as it was, had an implicit "but" attached and Beau's heart clenched.

"I'm going to make you believe in me again—if it's the last thing I do," he said, covering her hand with his own, grateful for that small physical contact.

He reluctantly released her hand and strode to the door. "I love you, Fiona."

"I know, Beau." But her eyes said that love wasn't enough.

Beau gave her a choked smile and left, determined to do anything to make her trust him again.

15.

Beau knocked on the recently painted black door. It had ornate gold hinges that glinted brightly in the sunlight, making him squint.

The hour was too early to be calling on this particular person, but Beau wasn't worried about such niceties at the moment. Fiona's sad distrust still fresh in his mind, he didn't care if he had to drag his nemesis off her chamber pot—he would see her now and he would make her listen.

A new, more fashionable butler let him in and he wondered what she had done with poor Ridley. In fact, she not only had a new butler and a new residence in a nouveau riche neighborhood, but she also had completely new furnishings. Beau's eyes narrowed at the realization that she was far too comfortable at present. Her merchant lover might have lowered her standing in the eyes of society, but discomfort from that fall was well-cushioned by wealth. Beau would prefer to see her languishing in a gaol cell, or mired in the filth of a prisoner's ship as she was transported to some faraway destination.

He waited ten minutes in a painstakingly designed Egyptian drawing room before she entered, and in that time he reviewed all the possible revenges he could inflict on her. He wasn't used to thinking in such terms, so he finally decided that revealing the truth to his acquaintance at *The Palaver* would be his best defense. Perhaps a scathing caricature in that newspaper would seal society's disapproval once and for all, for Beau didn't imagine for one moment that Daphne Tarkington accepted her current standing. She was a lady waiting to make a comeback. The décor of the room said it all.

He heard the door open and turned away from a window draped in shiny gold material with a blocky, black border. The level of hatred he felt at the sight of her took him by surprise; it clogged his throat and made him want to retch.

"So, you found a new lover who is rich as Midas. I congratulate you," he said, watching in satisfaction as her smug expression disappeared. He snorted, wondering at her audacity. Had she really expected him to play nice and kiss her hand?

Daphne regarded him coldly for a moment, but finally sat, indicating to Beau with a haughty nod that he should sit in the chair next to hers. "Yes, Mr. Landers is highly successful at whatever it is he does. And generous."

"He's a water closet merchant, and I prefer to stand," Beau rejoined, and her wince, though small, brought a grim smile to his face. "Can you guess why I'm here?"

"Because it's not enough that you humiliated me in public? You now wish to humiliate me privately?"

Her eyes, so full of venom, told the story of deep hatred, and Beau shuddered. The thought that its unwarranted depth signaled insanity crossed his mind and pulled him up short. If he was dealing with a madwoman there would be no reasoning with her.

Swallowing hard, he tried to make his next statement less angry-sounding than it was.

"I'm here to issue a warning: leave Miss Fairmont alone or I'll give *The Palaver* all the sordid details of your depraved preferences. You'll never regain your standing in society if I do."

"It's your word against mine. Besides, two can play that game. I'll let it be known that you were the worst lover I ever had—never available and selfish beyond belief," she spat, her voice full of fury.

Beau knew better than to take up that gauntlet. He struggled to maintain an even tone of voice. "And what do you think London will think about the fact that you hired Jack Whitehead to hurt me? That's more than sordid. It's illegal."

Daphne's pale cheeks sprouted red spots. "I don't know what you're talking about."

"Your denial is boringly predictable, but you were outed. Jack's men told on you after he died. They thought I was going to die, too, and didn't care what I heard." It wasn't quite the truth, but it might force a confession.

"No one would believe you!" Daphne snarled, her lips disappearing in their distortion. She stood and gestured toward the door. "I want you to go. Now!"

"Heed my warning, Daphne," Beau said, one hand clenched tightly on the back of the hieroglyph-covered chair that stood between them. He pushed away from the chair and stepped around it, noting the alarm on her face. Good, let her be afraid. "You are never to approach my future wife again—not through letters, not through gossip-mongers, not in person. Do I make myself clear?"

"I haven't—"

"Do I make myself clear?" Beau stepped closer to make his point.

"Don't touch me!"

"I won't touch you," Beau said, and the underlying disgust in his words wasn't lost on her. He saw a spasm of pain cross her face in the split second before she managed to control her features.

"Leave!"

He ignored her command. "You were quite busy this week, telling Lady Clarissa and God knows who else lies that you knew would find their way straight to my fiancée."

Daphne lifted her chin defiantly. "I only told the truth. You *did* visit Lady Wolfrey and you *do* belong to Morgan's Pier. And when you were with me you were indebted to them. You're a liar if you say otherwise."

"I lost a few bets, never to the point of indebtedness, but that's not the point. Here it is and I'll repeat it as many times as needed for clear understanding: you are not to involve my fiancée in your abhorrent schemes ever again. *Do I make myself clear?*"

Daphne met his gaze squarely, her blue eyes coldly calculating. Beau's stomach lurched from their close proximity, but he stood his ground, waiting for her answer. Each second felt like a minute, but he wouldn't give her the satisfaction of looking away.

"I see that my words have already inflicted a degree of damage to your precious relationship. I see the pain of it in your eyes," she finally said.

A fresh surge of hatred made Beau say, "After I've told everything I know about you to my friend at *The Palaver,* I'll tell your new lover a thing or two. Or maybe he was in favor of your suggested ménage-à-trois with Mr. Glendale? Perhaps he *likes* your sadistic tendencies?"

Daphne's eyes narrowed. She took a deep breath and in the next instant a loud scream issued from her throat as she methodically ripped the bodice of her dress and camisole. They dangled raggedly, exposing one meager breast.

"You're insane. I—" Beau got no further because two male servants made an appearance, one much too small to matter but the other quite sizeable.

"He attacked me!" Daphne screamed, pointing. "Subdue him, tie him up!"

To stop them from mauling him, Beau deftly pulled his pistol out from under the coat he had never removed. The larger footman stopped short, but the small one lunged for the pistol, showing that he had brains to match his size—or perhaps it was raw courage he had, Beau wasn't sure which. The pistol went off in the struggle, shattering a vase across the room and startling the man into dropping Beau's hand. Beau backed quickly toward the door, putting as much distance as he could between himself and the pipsqueak hero.

"Stay where you are. I'll use this thing as a bludgeon if I have to," he warned the footmen, indicating the spent pistol with a nod. To Daphne he said, "You've been warned. It's the only warning you'll get."

"You'll learn that you can't threaten me," she said.

Before Beau left he felt compelled to set the record straight, even if it was only for the benefit of the two footmen. "Your mistress ripped her own dress. If I'd attacked her she wouldn't have been able to call for help." He backed out the door and slammed it behind him.

He hadn't gotten what he'd come for—resolution; Daphne's word that she would never bother him or Fiona again—and he'd been a fool to think he could get it. Daphne was far too venomous and insane to allow such peace of mind. If anything, he'd stirred her to seek more revenge.

Taking the steps in one leap, Beau strode toward his waiting carriage. His plan had been impetuous and foolish, driven by his anguish over Fiona's attitude, and he swore to himself that he'd never allow his usual good judgment to become so clouded again. If Fiona wished to break with him, he'd have to face the hideous fact that he could not control the situation, much less her.

"White's," he said tersely, stepping into his carriage. He tucked his pistol into the pocket of his greatcoat as the carriage rolled forward, not caring that the smell of gunpowder from the discharged weapon would be in his clothes for days.

"Bloody hell!" he shouted, slamming his fist into the plush seat and startling his footman.

"Are you well, my lord?" the footman called from the driver's seat.

"As well as can be expected after encountering a mad she-wolf," Beau muttered, before yelling back, "Fine! Keep driving."

***

Fiona's heart skittered nervously, but she forced her hands to stop fidgeting with her skirt so that she'd at least have an appearance of calm. The plan to visit Beau's first fiancée had *seemed* good even half an hour ago, but now she felt foolish. She forced herself to take a deep breath, determined to make the most of the situation now that she was here.

Lady Wolfrey entered, bringing with her a cloud of expensive lilac scent. "What a nice surprise!" she said, bypassing formal modes of greeting in favor of a genuine smile and a quick squeeze of Fiona's hand.

Her beauty was remarkable: Red-gold hair was expertly piled on top of her head and her large blue eyes were clear and intelligent. Her perfect complexion was the color of fresh cream, and her full lips were rouge-free yet rosebud pink. She sat next to Fiona on a comfortably upholstered blue and red striped sofa.

"Thank you for seeing me on such short notice, Lady Wolfrey."

"Please, call me Lucinda and I'll call you Fiona. I hate formalities." Her voice was so melodic it would soothe a rabid dog.

"Lucinda, then." In any other person, Fiona might have been repelled by the physical closeness and quick familiarity, but Lady Lucinda Wolfrey had a charisma that defied any such reaction. No wonder Beau had been compelled to visit rather than write. Fiona couldn't fault anyone for being attracted to Lady Wolfrey's supernatural appeal.

But Fiona was unsure of what to say next. *Are you my future husband's mistress*? was not an option.

Lady Wolfrey came to her rescue. "Fiona, while I'd love to think that you're visiting simply to make a new acquaintance, I know better. You're here because of today's newspapers, aren't you?"

"I—" Fiona began, but as the question had been rhetorical, Lady Wolfrey continued without waiting for the answer.

"Beau is very much in love with you and the newspapers' insinuations are completely false. There! Do you feel better?"

"I—"

"Beau had a perfectly valid reason to contact me, and I suppose he could have written, but he knows better. He remembered that I require more than my fair share of attention and he dutifully listened to my travelogue of Paris before disclosing his reasons for visiting. And the reason had nothing to do with me and everything to do with you, my dear." She smiled, her cornflower blue eyes sparkling with laughter. "I can't reveal anything more, but know this: A wonderful surprise will soon be yours."

"I already know about the bracelet. Did you read that it was stolen?"

"No! How?" Lady Wolfrey's consternation was just as pretty as her happiness.

"It was in the paper—"

"But I don't read the paper. I only know of the other article because it upset my husband rather badly."

"It was stolen at the museum. Beau took it out of his pocket to look at it—"

"Why would he do something so addle-brained?"

"It *was* a bit addle-brained, but it's my fault really. I was supposed to meet him—"

"Something delayed you and he took the bracelet out to imagine it on your wrist. That is so like him! Oh, my dear, he loves you so much. Whatever you might think, never doubt his love for you. During our visit he told me how he met you at a country ball. I've never seen such a smitten look as when he described seeing you for the first time. You are his true love, my dear, and count yourself lucky. He's an extraordinarily generous and warm-hearted man."

"Yes, we met at a ball—" Fiona repeated vaguely. She was distracted by an uncomfortable realization: After all that she and Beau had been through, she had allowed one nasty piece of gossip to weaken their bond. And Beau's charisma meant that gossip—both good and bad—was a fact of his life. Was she going to allow each nasty tidbit to whittle away her love, or was she going to love him based on what she knew to be true?

"You're the envy of many, you know, some of whom will try to mar your happiness because they're horrible, jealous people who think they have nothing better to do. You'll learn to ignore them. Do you think Beau will ever stop limping?"

"If he faithfully does the exercises prescribed by our physician. Lately he's been distracted by our wedding preparations."

"And poachers attacked him! How dreadful," Lady Wolfrey said, puzzled.

Beau had stuck to that story for society's sake as well, but suddenly Fiona gasped. Beau had told her that he would make her believe him, but what did that mean? Had she pushed him to contact Daphne Tarkington? If so—if Beau had confronted the woman who had hired a man to hurt him—well, no good could come from such a meeting.

She tried to explain her gasp as she stood and faced Lady Wolfrey. "You've been so kind. Thank you for talking with me, and please don't think me rude, but I must go now. I fear that my doubts have placed Beau in harm's way. Will you excuse my haste?"

"Of course! Harm's way? How so, and may I help?" Lady Wolfrey stood and tucked a beautifully manicured hand around Fiona's elbow to walk her to the door.

"Thank you for the offer, but I don't think so." With a final wave she left, almost running to her waiting carriage.

She closed her eyes and leaned her head against the plush backrest, allowing remorseful tears to fall unchecked. "Why am I such a suspicious witch? Beau would never have doubted me, if the tables had been turned," she whispered, ashamed.

She craved Beau's arms around her, his warm breath fanning the top of her head, his kiss ...

Drying her face impatiently, she determined to give Beau an apology that he'd remember for the rest of his life. She'd kiss him insensible—for starters—and she would *never* give him reason to doubt her love again. The memory of their last meeting made her throat constrict tightly. She had never before seen such disappointment on his face, even when she and Henry had announced their engagement.

The carriage stopped and Fiona stepped out, already planning the note she would write Beau. It would be the beginning of her lengthy and memorable apology, and would begin, *Dearest Beau, I'm a jealous fool. Come back immediately so that I can tell you so in person—*

She was surprised when her mother pulled the front door open so forcefully that the knob was snatched out of the footman's hand.

"Fiona, come with me." Lady Winifred said, pulling her daughter into the foyer and hustling her down the hallway toward her father's study.

Fiona knew from her mother's face that something dreadful had happened. Her pallor showed up more wrinkles than Fiona had ever noticed before, and her hair was askew—something that never happened. "Mother, what is it?"

"Wait. You'll know soon enough," Lady Winifred said, ushering her into her father's study. A stranger was there with her father, and when the two ladies entered he stood and bowed.

"Mr. Shaw, my daughter, Miss Fairmont. Fiona, Mr. Shaw is an attorney. Beau's attorney," Lord Fairmont said heavily. He motioned that they all sit down.

Fiona had noticed the dossier that Mr. Shaw held tightly under his arm and had guessed that he was a lawyer. That he was *Beau's* lawyer tripled her anxiety. *Please let him be all right. Please, God.*

Mr. Shaw cleared his throat. "Lord Albert is at this very moment in jail—with charges of murdering Daphne Tarkington against him."

"No," Fiona groaned.

"He claims innocence and has given no confession, but there was evidence enough against him for the arrest, which took place at White's. The worst of it: a discharged pistol in his coat and his admission that he'd visited her. We're still waiting for the report that will tell us whether or not the ball removed from the victim might match his pistol," Mr. Shaw clarified.

This was all her fault. Fiona could barely breathe, but she managed, "May I see him?"

Mr. Shaw turned beet red. "Newgate isn't a place for ladies, Miss Fairmont."

"May I see him?" Fiona repeated firmly.

Disbelief puckered Mr. Shaw's strawy eyebrows, stemming more from her family's permission than from Fiona's desire, his look at Lord Fairmont clearly said. "It can be arranged."

"When?" Fiona urged.

"I—I'll make inquiries as soon as I leave here," Mr. Shaw spluttered. "Which will be now." He picked up his hat and bowed in the general direction of the two ladies before turning to leave.

Lord Fairmont stood, giving Fiona's shoulder a fatherly pat, and walked Mr. Shaw to the door. Fiona heard him whisper, "What are his chances?" as they left.

Fiona sank her face into her hands. Her heavy burden of guilt and self-loathing dried tears that might have relieved her anguish. She felt her mother's consoling hand on her shoulder and shrugged it off. She didn't deserve pity.

"Fiona, dearest, what is it? You're acting as if he's been condemned. Surely his lawyer will find a way to acquit him. We must have hope, for Beau's sake."

"This is my fault. All my fault," she said through her fingers.

"Of course it isn't—"

"It is!" Fiona hissed, finally meeting her mother's eyes. Before her startled mother could respond, she continued, "I drove him to her with my doubts and insinuations and stupidity! Why couldn't I have believed him?"

"Believed him? Fiona, what do you mean?"

Lord Fairmont popped his head in the doorway and started to say something, but his wife shooed him away with a wave of her hand. He left, eyes wide and worried.

"This all started yesterday. Lady Clarissa visited, full of gossip that she had acquired from—oh, Mother, this is where I made my first mistake. I allowed *gossip* to make me doubt Beau's love. Daphne Tarkington—who has hated Beau ever since he rejected her last spring—put it about that Beau is marrying me for my money. She's also insinuating that he has established Lady Wolfrey as his mistress."

Lady Winifred blinked in amazement. "This is absurd. First of all, if Beau had been looking for money he could have found someone far richer than you."

"She said he was in debt through Morgan's Pier and that money-lenders broke his leg."

"What's Morgan's Pier? Poachers—"

"Morgan's Pier is an exclusive gambling club, and since I'd seen a snuff box on Beau's dresser with 'MP' on it I knew the connection was real. The debt part was a blatant lie—Beau told me so himself—and I think I would have dropped the matter if he hadn't visited Lady Wolfrey. I didn't believe his explanation that he had visited her only to retrieve an heirloom bracelet, but when I paid Lady Wolfrey a visit today I realized how suspicious and foolish I'd been."

Lady Winifred gaped. "Goodness! You visited Lady Wolfrey?"

"Mother, I had to know! It was unceremonious of me to visit without an introduction, but the doubts were torturing me. She's actually very nice."

"Has Beau ever given you any reason to doubt him?"

"No. But I did anyway because I'm a suspicious, cold witch. I don't *deserve* him. He never would have doubted me, if the tables were turned. But I told him I doubted him and—oh, Mother—because of me he left vowing to make me believe in him again. I think he visited Daphne Tarkington and … and maybe he really shot her. I'll die if he's ruined his life because of my suspicions." Fiona's tears were falling swiftly now, freed by her confession.

Her mother handed her a handkerchief. "He's saying he is innocent, so we can hope he'll be acquitted. I'll pray very hard for such an outcome."

Fiona dabbed at her eyes. "Do, Mother! For if there's any other outcome I'll never forgive myself."

Lady Winifred patted her leg consolingly. "Let's not think another thought about it. Everything will be all right. Beau *will* be acquitted."

"How, Mother? I have no faith that our justice system sets innocent people free. And what if he really did it? Could he be driven to do such a thing?"

"I don't think so. Come, dearest." Lady Winifred stood and helped Fiona to her feet. "Go rest."

Fiona allowed her mother to lead her into the foyer and upstairs. After her mother left her, she laid face down on her bed, allowing thoughts and pictures to course in and out of her head unchecked. Beau, asleep in the sunflower garden, one beautifully masculine hand resting on his rising chest, his eyelashes making deep shadows on his cheeks. The rolled-up poem on cream-colored parchment, tied with green ribbon, which was on her breakfast tray the day that Beau got hurt. (She had dug the poem out of the dustbin later that morning and had read it three times, rubbing the soft parchment between her fingers and bringing it to her nose to see if it smelled like Beau—it disappointingly hadn't.) Beau's face on his pillow, its pain and pallor from the broken leg making her breath catch. Beau's uproarious laugh at one of Lady Boswell's risqué jokes. Beau's head framed in sunshine as he gave her their first kiss in the lilac garden. God, she loved him. He had to get through this. He had to be acquitted.

She finally fell into a troubled sleep, her face half mashed into her pillows, her arms thrown over her head.

.

16.

Beau awoke, groaning with the realization that no, it hadn't all been a bad dream. He had been dragged from White's with a stinky pistol in his pocket. Well, not really dragged, he went willingly to avoid a scene—but it was probably the most humiliating moment of his life.

He sat up quickly; the itchy straw mattress did not invite lolling. His banker might have greased the sheriff's hand for a private cell, but it was still not the least bit comfortable. God willing, he'd be acquitted as soon as Daphne Tarkington's footmen were interviewed and the truth, that his pistol had shattered a vase, was common knowledge. And the minute he set foot in his townhouse he'd order a hot bath, and steep himself for two hours in a mixture that Fiona had given him of citrus oils and lavender. It would take that long to get the stench and feel of this bloody cell out of his pores.

Beau sighed loudly as he eyed the splintery bucket that held his water, then resignedly dipped his hands in and splashed his face. He took another handful and wet his hair; he didn't need a mirror to tell him that it was sticking up in places.

"If this is the state area I'd hate to see the common one," he muttered, drying his face on his shirttails; the limp, gray towel wasn't something he cared to touch.

He peered out of the barred window in the door and could see a corner of blue sky above the brick wall on the other side of the quadrangle where the male felons were kept. Direct sunlight filtered down into his cell for only half an hour per day, he'd discovered. The rest of the time his cell was a gloomy, dank hole.

He peered into the dark corner behind his cot at the sound of scurrying feet—the four-legged kind. "Not so sure it's private, at that."

"At least you have a window. The prisoners on the next level down barely have any light with which to see." Beau turned and saw his lawyer standing outside his cell door. The loud snores coming from the prisoner next door had prevented his hearing anyone approach.

Beau's mood lightened at the sight of him. "Any news?"

"Just a moment, my lord. I thought that turnkey was right behind me." Mr. Shaw looked to his left in irritation, down the gloomy stone hallway. "Their position gives them a little power and it turns them surly. Ah! Here he comes."

His lawyer stepped aside to make room for the turnkey, and Beau saw the coldly dispassionate face that he had quickly grown to loathe framed in the barred window. The large man completely ignored Beau, but that rudeness was preferable to the aggressiveness with which he spoke whenever talking was a necessity.

"Good morning, Brown," Beau said, refusing to play the role this turnkey had assigned to him: a man whose life would soon end at the end of a rope; a man who no longer had the power to demand civilities.

Mr. Brown ignored him, saying to Mr. Shaw, "How long?" His voice was bored and asthmatic.

"Give me half an hour."

"Right," he grunted. And after allowing Mr. Shaw to slip in, he relocked the door and left.

Beau gestured for Mr. Shaw to take the wobbly stool while he sat on his cot. He didn't like the worried frown he saw on his lawyer's face. In fact, Beau had never seen him looking so distraught.

"The news is bad?"

"It's not good. The footmen left on a family emergency. They're cousins, apparently, and they told Daphne Tarkington's butler that they had to go north to attend a dying grandfather's funeral. No one remembers where exactly in the north they went, and no one remembers when they said they'd be back. I suppose the shock of the murder has made everyone forgetful. Also, did you say the vase was on the table nearest the window? There is an intact vase standing there as we speak, and no broken shards to be found. Also, no bullet lodged in the wall; it must have continued out the window."

Beau stood, too restless to sit, and paced to the door. "So someone cleaned up the broken one and replaced it. That's disappointing but shouldn't be suspicious. Back to the footmen—isn't their quick departure, in and of itself, odd?"

"Possibly, but what motive do they have? Not one thing has been stolen. The housekeeper took a thorough inventory." When Beau shook his head in disgust, Mr. Shaw added, "Anyway, that's the constables' understanding of it. Mind, they haven't ruled them out; they've put a man on finding them. But that's not the worst of it, my lord."

"Why doesn't that surprise me?" He folded his arms across his chest, waiting for the bad news with narrowed eyes.

"They've removed the ball from Daphne Tarkington's eye, and determined that it could, indeed, have come from your pistol. I reminded the constables how ridiculous that piece of 'evidence' is, since every man in London buys lead balls at Rogers and Banks," Mr. Shaw said, giving his head an impatient shake and leaning forward to hand the report to Beau.

"I didn't even know she was shot in the eye, yet here I am." He didn't bother to take the report, and his lawyer quit offering it after a moment.

"Any good news?" His question lacked hope; was, in fact, cynical, which deepened his lawyer's frown.

Mr. Shaw looked up from the task of tucking away the ballistic report with a forced smile. "I've made arrangements for Miss Fairmont to visit you this afternoon."

"You have?" Beau asked, stunned. "Did she ask to come? Or was it arranged for publicity's sake?"

"She insisted, if you must know," Mr. Shaw said sourly.

Beau smiled wanly. "She's a determined soul. It's one of the things I—" He stopped, and the smile dropped from his lips as a horrible thought occurred to him. Was she planning to break their engagement? Was that the reason for her insistence? After their last meeting it was a very real possibility, but he didn't have the stomach to voice it so he changed the subject.

"What about the lover? Is he a suspect?"

Mr. Shaw grimaced. "Her lover has an airtight excuse, since he was at the docks literally all day, with witnesses to back up that fact. His new shipment of water closet makings saved him, it seems."

"He could've hired someone to kill her, and if he did I wouldn't blame him. Has Bow Street cleared him based solely on his alibi?"

"I believe they have. I gathered that he came across surprised and grief-stricken enough to convince them."

"I wouldn't trust that! People can act, can't they?" Beau ran a hand through his still damp hair. "Did they interview Ridley yet? What's the story behind his dismissal?"

"He wasn't dismissed at all. The lover gave him a nice pension and he retired."

Beau kicked his water bucket and it fell onto its side, water darkening the stone floor in an arc. "Shaw, I have to get the hell out of here. I'm bloody trapped like a bloody animal, waiting for the bloody hangman to come along and bloody well finish me off."

"Try to remain calm, my lord. I'm doing the best I can." Realizing that his voice sounded whiny, Mr. Shaw cleared his throat before continuing. "I'm making careful inquiries into Jack Whitehead's world and discovering that there's an entire underworld there that Jack was only one small part of. He worked independently—up to a point—but had some seriously shady connections as well."

Beau slumped onto his cot and rubbed his face tiredly. "Maybe she still owed him money. There was probably a balance due after the job was finished, but since he died ...

You'd think, though, that a broken hand—or some such injury—would come before murder."

"The authorities *did* find an anonymous dun in her desk for a rather large sum of money—to be brought to a pub in St. Giles. The same one that Leila Hemmings, Jack's common-law wife owns, to be exact. If that's a coincidence, I'll eat my hat," Mr. Shaw said dryly.

"Of course it's not! Is there a date on it?" Beau felt a glimmer of hope. This was the best lead he'd heard so far.

"Now that you mention it, it was dated a few weeks after your injury, so perhaps money *was* owed on delivery and Jack's wife tried to collect it for him. It makes sense."

"Did she pay it?"

"The constables are looking into that."

"This is it, Shaw. It has to be. She didn't pay and those two footmen got themselves hired—probably at Leila's bidding—in order to either steal from her or find a way to blackmail her. They must be involved; their disappearance is too much of a coincidence. But then I came along and Leila saw an opportunity to avenge Jack's death completely. Revenge was sweeter than the money."

"That's a bit far-fetched. First of all, your visit wasn't planned so someone would have had to act mighty quickly."

Beau raised his hand to halt Mr. Shaw's flow of doubtful words. "Wait. Wait. Let's think this through." He rubbed the back of his neck and winced. "Let's assume that the footmen were looking for ways to blackmail her. I come calling and they know I'm not her lover, so they listened to our conversation, hoping to get blackmail fodder. They heard that I was the man she targeted through Jack and they passed that information along to Leila, who saw her chance to get rid of both of us. Now we simply need to implicate her in the plotting of it. And who knows? Maybe she also pulled the trigger."

Mr. Shaw shook his head. "But how do we *do* that? Go to her pub and ask for a confession?"

Beau exhaled loudly, thinking. "Did none of the servants see their mistress alive again after my pistol discharged? Talk about unlikely—"

"As you know her townhouse backs up to the grounds of a private hunting club. Her staff has become immune to hearing shots fired. When questioned, they all claimed to have heard multiple shots that day."

Beau snorted. "That's convenient."

"My lord, your theory is certainly possible. I'll try to find out more." Mr. Shaw gave Beau an encouraging smile.

"Goddamn it! It's not that I don't think you're doing all you can for me, Shaw—I do—but if I could just get out of here for one day. Will any amount of money buy me that?" Beau already knew the answer, and Mr. Shaw's troubled headshake confirmed it. Taking a deep breath, he asked, "What do my parents know?"

"Your father doesn't know about it. Your mother feared it would be the death of him and hopes for the best possible outcome—that you will be cleared in time for the wedding. Which reminds me that I need to write her. I've put it off since—" Shaw stopped and pursed his lips.

"Since news isn't leading to that best possible outcome at present. I know. You never bargained on this mess when you followed your father into law, did you, Shaw?"

"I have never regretted our connection, my lord. Even now, in these difficult times," Mr. Shaw said, emotion warbling his voice.

Beau leaned his back against the rough stone wall and regarded his lawyer a moment. The worry lines on Shaw's brow foreshadowed the deeply lined face to come—the one that would mirror elderly Mr. Shaw's face.

"Thank you, Shaw," he finally said. "What time will Miss Fairmont be here?"

Mr. Shaw looked relieved at the subject change. "Between two and three."

"And we felons can't have razors, so she'll see me looking like this," Beau said, rubbing the shadowy whiskers on his chin.

"She's in love with you. It won't matter."

"Is she? I wonder," Beau said, more to himself than to Mr. Shaw. His mood was spiraling downward. News of the reappearing vase, the matching ammunition, and the conveniently disappearing footmen had doused his soul with a chilly, dank depression. His hopes of being quickly released had been reduced to a mere glimmer. His one hope, in fact, lay in his theory, and—as Shaw had pointed out—Leila wasn't going to confess.

"Don't despair, my lord. The doors have not all closed. Not by any stretch of the imagination."

"Any word on a trial date?" Beau asked, not wishing to be mired in sympathetic words. Pity threatened to make his depression worse.

"Not yet, and we don't want to rush that. We need time."

Beau nodded, his throat too tight to speak. This was real. He was charged with murder and might be hanged. He was stuck in this hellish place until his trial, which was going to occur sometime in the distant future. Daphne Tarkington was probably, even from the depths of hell, laughing at him. He barely heard the rest of what his lawyer had to say. After Mr. Shaw left, he lay face down on his mildewed straw mat, glad for the physical discomfort since it distracted him from the mental picture of himself—hanged—in the public square just outside Newgate Prison. Worse was the vision of Fiona's beautiful face, doubt etched on it whenever memories of him emerged in her mind.

***

Fiona stepped from the carriage and stared at the massive structure that was Newgate Prison. The idea of seeing Beau in this gloomy place filled her with apprehension. Was he being well treated? How would she find the words to tell him how sorry she was?

Mr. Shaw pointed the way, toward one of three entryways into the place. "We'll go this way, Miss Fairmont. They're expecting you."

Fiona nodded distractedly, turning toward the carriage. "Wait here, Anna. Mr. Shaw will accompany me inside."

"Yes, I'll wait right here," Anna said thankfully.

Fiona turned to follow Mr. Shaw. Their first destination was a small room made smaller by the large desk and multiple file drawers crammed into it.

"And this lovely young lady must be Miss Fairmont," the portly man behind the desk said, delivering his pen back to its inkwell as he stood and bowed. "Mr. Shaw, you're a lucky man to have such a fine companion today."

"Miss Fairmont, may I present the keeper of this jail, Mr. Oxley? He arranged this meeting," Mr. Shaw said.

"Thank you, Mr. Oxley," Fiona responded, without much effusion. She knew that he had been well paid for his pains.

"You're very welcome, and let me add that I'm quite happy to oblige your visits any time. May I request your company for tea after the visit? My cook just made her specialty—plum tarts." Mr. Oxley said, clasping his hands to his breast and eyeing Fiona as if she was one of the cooling pastries.

"Miss Fairmont has to leave directly after her visit. She has an appointment with a florist," Mr. Shaw said, adding hopefully, "I'd very much like a cup of tea and a tart while I wait for her."

Mr. Oxley obviously had no interest in entertaining a lowly lawyer. "Ah. I have another meeting in five minutes, but I'll ask my servant to bring a pot of tea to the turnkeys' quarters while you wait. It's just through here." Opening a door, he gestured for them to pass through.

Fiona opened her mouth to ask Mr. Oxley how much time she had with Beau but never formed the question—since his eyes were firmly fixed on her décolletage. She hurried past him as fast as she could, into a sitting room that was stuffy from pipe smoke. It had a patched but comfortable-looking sofa, a dilapidated table that housed a pile of newspapers four inches deep, and two mismatched wingback chairs. The first chair had a set of manacles in it;

the other one contained the smoker. When he heard the door open he pulled his newspaper down from his face just long enough to see who was entering, then continued to read without giving any sort of greeting.

Mr. Shaw frowned at him disapprovingly. "Excuse me, are you our escort to Lord Albert's cell?"

The frown was wasted. Without moving the newspaper the man said, "Nope. He'll be along."

Mr. Shaw pulled out his handkerchief and snapped it against the seat of the sofa until he'd cleaned it to his satisfaction. He gestured for Fiona to sit down, whispering, "I warned you that they're rough sorts. And Oxley isn't much better. I'm sorry you had to suffer his impertinence."

"No need to apologize, Mr. Shaw. You did, indeed, warn me. I just hope they don't make us wait too long." She perched on the edge of the sofa. She didn't really feel like sitting, but since Mr. Shaw had gone to the trouble of cleaning it for her, she did.

Ten minutes later, her eyes burning from the tobacco smoke, Fiona was relieved to see the door opposite from Mr. Oxley's office open.

"You're back with the young lady, then," a very large man said. His coal-black eyes were almost obscured in the fleshiness of his cheeks. He plucked the newspaper from his colleague's hands as he passed, rolling it in one deft movement and thwacking him on the head with it.

"'Ey!" the man complained, coughing out a cloud of pipe smoke.

The newspaper was tossed back to him as Mr. Shaw made introductions.

"Miss Fairmont, Mr. Brown, the lead turnkey. I assume you'll be leading Miss Fairmont to Lord Albert?"

"Yup. Follow me."

"I'd come if I could. They only let one visitor back at a time," Mr. Shaw apologized.

"No worries, Mr. Shaw. I'll be fine."

Fiona followed Mr. Brown through the door he had just entered, shuddering slightly when he slammed it shut.

"The male felons are kept in the back," Mr. Brown informed her over one powerful shoulder as they walked.

Fiona winced but didn't miss a step. They made their way down a damp stone corridor to another doorway, this one blocked by a heavy door that was locked in three places.

Mr. Brown easily found the keys needed, out of the mass of keys on his keychain. "He's got it good, your fiancé. He's got a private cell—thanks to the right greased-up palm of the Lord Mayor. Your visit greased it, too. Poundage talks around here, it does." He sounded more cheerful than cynical.

They were walking past a cell that had several women prisoners in it, one of them moaning loudly, but Fiona managed to say, "'Good' can't possibly describe his situation, Mr. Brown."

His response was a coarse snort of laughter. "You'd think so if you could see the whole place, miss."

After a few minutes of walking they rounded a corner and came to a sudden stop in front of the first of six massive wooden doors with barred windows, just past a stairwell.

"Here it is," Mr. Brown wheezed.

Fiona peered into the poorly lit cell but couldn't see Beau. Mr. Brown turned the necessary keys, opening the large door without effort, and stood aside to let her enter.

"Fiona."

"*Beau.*"

He emerged from the dark corner and she stepped quickly to meet him. In the next minute the squalor of the hideous cell was forgotten because she was pressed against his warm chest, allowing his beating heart to soothe her ragged nerves. She wished to stay just so, listening to the steady beat forever, because she dreaded what she might hear once they started talking.

"I'll be sitting outside this door, miss. You have fifteen minutes."

Fiona nodded, still not letting Beau go. He was in no hurry to release her, either.

Mr. Brown addressed Beau sharply: "Step outta line and I'll cut the visit short. Money won't buy you grace from refractory time, if it's what you deserve, and know this: I'd love an excuse to drag your arse outta this hoity toity cell."

Fiona hated the turnkey then, more fiercely than she'd ever hated anybody. Worse, Beau hadn't even flinched; he was obviously accustomed to the verbal abuse, even in the short span of time he'd been here. But she held her tongue because she didn't dare stir up this beast of a man. He'd cut the visit short just for spite, if it pleased him to do so.

She closed her eyes to shut out Mr. Brown's mean face. She had glimpsed its puffy lips and tiny eyes glaring at Beau through the bars as he relocked the cell, and she tightened her grip on Beau, willing him to know how sorry she was.

Mr. Brown's heavy body creaked the chair outside the cell door, indicating that they had as much privacy as they were going to get. Beau led Fiona to the solitary stool next to the cot and stood behind her, gently caressing her shoulders. His hands were warm despite the dankness.

"I hate seeing you in this horrid place but selfishly wouldn't have it any other way," he murmured.

"Beau, what happened?" she whispered, looking up into his face.

A crease appeared between his eyebrows. Coming around to sit on the cot facing her, he took her hands, rubbing his thumbs across the backs of them, visibly trying to work out what to say first.

"Beau, I'm so sorry," she said, before he could speak. Using his hands to pull herself toward him, she settled next to him on the cot and slid her arms around his waist.

"Why?" He encircled her shoulders with his arms and kissed the top of her head. When she looked up, the tenderness in his expression made her breath catch. Why had she messed everything up so badly?

"Don't you realize? I'm responsible," Fiona confessed. Tears trickled down her face, but she didn't bother to wipe them away.

Beau did it for her. He also kissed the tip of her nose, before saying with a half-smile, "You killed Daphne Tarkington? I didn't realize you were such an excellent shot."

They both spoke softly, so that Mr. Brown couldn't eavesdrop.

Fiona reached up and traced Beau's upturned lips. "I'm grateful to see even that tiny smile. Beau, I love you unreservedly. I fear I left you with a different impression at our last meeting. That's why you went to Daphne Tarkington's, isn't it? That's why it's my fault."

Beau hugged her close and shook his head. "You mustn't blame yourself. It was bad judgment on my part, thinking I could threaten her into behaving. I didn't murder her, though."

"Tell me what happened."

Beau dropped a lingering kiss on her forehead. His warm lips eased the tension in her head better than a draught of St. John's Wort would have. "I'm either being framed or I have hideous luck, and I tend to lean toward the first option." He went on to explain what had happened, and to share his theory about Jack's wife.

"But how *will* you get her to confess?"

"The constables are looking into it," Beau said dispiritedly.

"The constables? What can they do, truly? Jack and Leila's group seem as if they'd have ready alibis and plenty of support." This was worse than she had feared. Beau's one real chance to be acquitted depended on a hardened criminal's confession? Her scalp prickled in horror as she fully realized that Beau might not be getting out of this mess at all.

"Beau, if I hadn't doubted you, you wouldn't be here. Because of me, you—you might ... Oh, what have I done?" she gasped, standing to face him.

"Don't, Fiona. We have to hope." But his eyes belied hope. He reached out a hand to pull her against him again, saying quietly, "Holding you feels good."

Fiona knew that her remorseful words weren't helping Beau's mood. She bit her lip and willed herself to calm down, ashamed of her hysterical outburst. No more of that! From now on, she would exhibit nothing but faith in his acquittal. Maybe blind faith would manifest Beau's freedom from this wretched place. Nothing else seemed to be working.

Beau nuzzled the top of her head. "I'd feel more hopeful if I could get out of this hell-hole, even if it was just for a day. Shaw's doing the best he can, but—"

"Let me help, Beau. I can go to Leila Whitehead and—ouch!"

Beau was squeezing her shoulders tightly. He took her chin between his fingers and turned her face toward his. "Promise me, Fiona. Promise me you won't contact any of those people. They're dangerous and you could be killed. Do you understand? Promise me."

"But, Beau—"

"No! Promise me!" he rasped.

Fiona nodded.

"Say it!"

Fiona crossed fingers that were hidden behind Beau's back. "I promise." She hated to deceive him but if his life was at stake she'd be damned if she'd sit about and do nothing, especially since she was responsible for his incarceration.

Beau distractedly kissed her again, but stopped to say, "If anything happened to you because of this I'd go insane. We have to trust the constables to find the answers. What I need from you is prayer and daily visits."

"Fervent prayers and twice daily visits if you wish them." She reached up for another tantalizing kiss.

It might have gone on indefinitely if they hadn't heard Mr. Brown's chair scrape as he got to his feet.

"I can't bear letting you go," Fiona whispered.

Beau gave her one final kiss before reluctantly standing and pulling her to her feet. "When I'm released I'm going to hold you for days and days and not let go."

"When you're released." Fiona repeated his words back to him, willing him to believe them, wishing that the smile she got in return wasn't so indulgent.

As she left, she glanced back to give Beau one final smile, but he didn't return it.

"Remember your promise," he said, stepping forward and grabbing the bars for emphasis.

She nodded and kissed the tips of her fingers, pushing the kisses through the bars to Beau's lips. "I'll see you tomorrow." His response was a worried frown that almost broke her heart.

A few minutes later, when they were in the carriage and moving away from Newgate, Fiona asked Mr. Shaw what he knew of Leila Hemmings Whitehead.

"Nothing much. She and her brother, Lester Hemmings, run a public house on St. Giles Street."

"But isn't she a suspect? If Daphne Tarkington owed her money, isn't she the most likely suspect? I don't understand why she isn't behind bars as well."

Mr. Shaw grimaced. "A dun is not as incriminating as a pistol."

"But the constables think it's a valid theory, correct? You're positive they're following that lead?" Fiona pressed.

"They are," Mr. Shaw confirmed. "They're looking for the footmen who've disappeared, as well. They may have had a grudge against their mistress and taken the opportunity to kill her, when they saw that they could blame Lord Albert."

"That doesn't feel right," Fiona said bluntly, and Mr. Shaw didn't argue with her. A minute later she asked, "What's the name of Leila's public house?"

"Why do you ask?" he asked, amusement distilling his chronic worry.

Fiona shrugged. "Just wondered."

"Seven Dials Public House because it's in Seven Dials. Very original," Mr. Shaw said sardonically.

"I see."

Anna gave her a questioning look, but she ignored it.

17.

Leila Hemmings Whitehead's hair was her best feature. It was as black and shiny as a raven's wing and waved perfectly around her face. Few people noticed her too-thick nose and close-set hazel eyes next to her gorgeous hair and alluring smile.

Her brother, Lester, was not so blessed. His dark hair was badly receded and his deep-set brown eyes were hidden under thick eyebrows.

He sat at their bar and watched his sister rinsing out tankards in preparation for the evening's crowd. After a few minutes, he spat into the sawdust on the floor. "Any news?"

"'E 'asn't been released, 'as 'e?" Leila said glibly.

"No, but a thief-taker was askin' about Niven and Broderick's whereabouts earlier. They're wantin' 'em for questionin'."

"Whatcher tell 'im?"

"Nothin'. Justa get the 'ell outta 'ere."

"Who was it?" Leila asked, more curious than worried.

Lester's lip curled in dislike. "That one-eyed bloke, Witchell."

"Maybe you shoulda passed on the rumor o' them goin' north to the funeral. They're regulars. It wouldn't 'ave seemed strange you knowin' it," Leila said, shrugging.

Lester dismissed her suggestion with a wave. "Nah."

"Well, I don't know why you 'ave to be like that. It would 'ave sent bloody Witchell away from 'ere. Now our two best 'ave to stay 'idden."

"Not long. Witchell'll get the squat from someone else," Lester said, motioning for his sister to fill one of the tankards for him. Laughing unpleasantly, he added, "They'll be at runnin' booze agin next week. No one'll find 'em then. The swell will swing, I'm sure of it."

Leila plopped a full tankard of ale in front of Lester, not caring that it slopped on his sleeve. "We can 'ope. Charlie repaired the 'ole in the wall, an' the bullet matches. I made sure o' that."

He grunted. "It's a common match."

Three men entered noisily, one clapping another on the back, all of them laughing raucously. The evening's festivities had begun so Leila and Lester said no more.

"'Ey, mate. Want to join us?" one of the men called out to Lester.

"Not now," he growled. He drained his tankard dry and left.

"Whatsa matter with 'im?" another of the three asked Leila, pointing a thumb at Lester's retreating back.

"Bellyache. Usual, Frank?" Leila said, giving the man a smile. It was no coincidence that her bar was the most popular in Seven Dials. That smile was famous.

"Aye, beautiful. Can it include a kiss, just this once?" Frank begged, placing his arms on the bar and leaning forward.

"When daisies grow outta the sawdust, love," Leila quipped, lessening the sting with another smile, this one teasing.

"Give a bloke a break," Frank moaned. But he recovered quickly, saying, "'Ey love, 'ave you seen my brother?"

"Nope," Leila lied. The truth was that Frank's brother, "Tiny" Broderick, was hiding out in her brother's lodgings with Charlie Niven. The two men she'd hired to worm their way into Daphne Tarkington's servant pool were lying low until Captain Hackett's ship was refitted for his next trip to Normandy, to get another shipment of illicit French brandy and wine. They planned to be on that ship.

The door to the bar was hesitantly opened, drawing the attention of the group at the bar. A boy entered with a young woman, both of them strangers, but the fact that the boy was the most beautiful creature Leila had ever seen stopped her from asking Frank to boot them out. She didn't have patience for peddlers, but these two—especially the visually favorable boy—stoked her curiosity.

Eyeing the basket that hung on the girl's arm, she said, "I usually kick tha likes of you right out, but I'm in a good mood today. Wha' are you sellin'?"

The girl stopped just inside the door, but the boy grabbed her by the sleeve and took a few more steps into the bar.

"Please, ma'am. My mum just moved here 'cause my father was killed in the war. We're desperate for someone to give us a chance. No one seems to want to—" the boy said, his voice breaking.

"Wha' are you sellin'?" Leila repeated, shushing Frank, who had mimicked the boy's last sentence perfectly and was now feigning loud bawling on one of his chum's shoulders.

The boy came a step closer. "Herbal potions, to cure all kinds of ailments. My mum makes them." He pulled one of the bottles from the basket and started to say something more, but Leila interrupted him, more interested in their history than their merchandise.

"Is that yer sis? You don't look much alike," she asked, scanning the two faces for any hint of a resemblance.

"She's my cousin. Her parents are dead."

"Hmmmmm." Leila gestured toward the basket. "Do you 'ave anythin' for dry skin?"

The boy put the bottle back and fished out a jar. "This cream might work." He opened it and offered Leila a closer look.

"Might? Lad, yer not a salesman usin' words like that!" she chided him.

"Try it, then." He stepped forward so that she could dip her fingers in it.

Leila obliged him and brought the cream to her nose. "It smells all right. Tell you what, I'll rub it in—" she rubbed it into her hands, then put the excess on her elbows, "—and if it's 'elped me dry 'ands by night's end I'll buy some tomorrow. In the meantime, I just 'ad a wild thought. You seem rather desperate, and I just lost a bar boy. You'd earn a lot more money from me if you did more than collect for this cream." Leila gave the boy her most winning smile. If only parents could pick their children. If she'd been guaranteed a boy like this, she'd have had that baby that Jack had been so keen about.

"I think she'd let me. I'd have to ask me mum."

"O' course, dear. Run tell yer mummy that you stand to make a good wage. Much more, I'm sure, than you take in 'awking that stuff. Run along now, but be back tomorrow or I'll give the job to someone else." She made shooing motions with her hands.

"What about my cousin?"

"I'm full up on barmaids at present. Sorry, dear," Leila said, giving the girl a perfunctory smile. "Be 'ere tomorrow at four thirty sharp if your mum allows it," she continued to the boy, turning away to tap ales for another group of customers who had entered.

As the pair turned to go, one of the men with Frank whistled loudly, leering at the girl. "I've got a job for ye, miss. Come sit on me lap and I'll teach ye a thing or two about pump handling."

The girl ignored him and practically fell over the boy in her haste to get out the door, causing the man to laugh. "Ooo, a sweet one! Untouched but just as ripe as a juicy pear, ready for pickin'," he yelled after her.

The boy and girl quickly headed out of Seven Dials and toward gentility. They didn't say a word to each other until they turned down St. James Street, and then the girl stopped, placing a hand over her heart and turning toward the boy.

"You're not going back there tomorrow without me," Anna said, glaring fiercely at Fiona. "I'll tell your 'mum' if you *dare*."

"Anna, be reasonable. This is for Beau. He needs our help," Fiona admonished her.

"I bet he'd go gray if he knew what we'd done already, and we're not talking 'we' anymore, miss. It would be you, all by your lonesome tomorrow. I'd deserve to be drawn and quartered if I didn't try to stop you."

"Just one more time, Anna. I'm confident I can find *something* out in one night. Please."

"Don't beg, miss. 'Tisn't right! And I doubt you'll get anything from her. She's wily and tough as nails, that one."

"I'll tell Beau about it tomorrow morning when I see him. If he thinks it's a good plan will you *please* not tell my mother?" Fiona begged.

"He won't think it's good at all," was all Anna would offer.

They entered Fiona's house through the servant's quarters and Fiona slipped into Anna's room. She changed into the day dress waiting for her there, before heading upstairs to her own room, making certain to take the boy's clothes with her. She didn't trust Anna not to give them back to her brother before she could wear them again.

***

This time the turnkey was less fat, more muscular and taller than Mr. Brown. But he was only slightly less hostile toward Beau, who had paid—through Mr. Shaw—the outrageous sum of five hundred pounds to get an hour's visit with his beloved.

"When you're acquitted I hope you'll give the turnkeys a good dressing down. They're horrid—every single one of them," Fiona said, once they were alone.

Beau pulled her onto his lap and buried his face in her neck, deeply breathing in her scent. "And if I'm not acquitted?" He pulled back to look into her eyes.

Fiona froze, not even taking a breath as she stared back. She had never seen Beau look so defeated. His eyes were dark pools of desolation. "Don't say that," she entreated.

Beau looked away and ran a hand through his untidy hair. "Shaw's news gets bleaker and bleaker. It seems they have no evidence to pin on anyone else. Those footmen can't be found, and the constables don't believe that Daphne hired Jack in the first place. They think the dun had to do with an illegal liquor purchase, which is typical from places like that." He shook his head, continuing, "Is this how my life is to end, Fiona? Hanging for a crime I didn't commit? Daphne Tarkington, in death, will have the ultimate revenge."

"No! It cannot be. I won't let it be. I won't let you hang," Fiona said determinedly.

Beau's answer was a tired, disbelieving smile.

"Oh, Beau. Please—" Fiona broke off and framed Beau's chin with her hands. She brought her lips to his and he responded, closing his eyes and tightening his grip around her waist, kissing her with an intensity that burned into her soul. She kissed him deeply, shivering when his hands caressed her back and hips, and relishing the feel of his hard thighs under her bottom and his scratchy beard beneath her fingers. She remembered his acute anxiety, when he had forced her promise yesterday, and she let go of the confession she had formulated on the ride over. She couldn't bring him down further with tales of yesterday afternoon's doings.

Beau stopped kissing her and she sighed. "Again," she insisted.

He kissed her chin. "My love, my dearest love. This hour is almost a quarter gone. These kisses, delicious as they are, make me yearn to have you in my bed, as my wife. That you may never be there fills me with despair."

"You *must* remain optimistic. Dark thoughts will do you no good."

His response surprised her. "Fiona, do you remember when you shared your book of poetry with me?"

"Of course. I was determined to flirt with you that night, not quite realizing that I was madly in love with you even then," she chattered, trying to pull a smile from him. She won a quick upturn of his lips, but then it was gone.

"I had a dream that night that I now think might have been a premonition."

Fiona smoothed a dark lock out of his eyes. "What was your dream?"

"I dreamt that Henry framed me for murder, so that I wouldn't be a threat to him anymore. He certainly has nothing to do with this, but isn't it odd that I'm now in prison, framed—in my opinion—for a murder I didn't commit?"

"How did the dream end?" Fiona asked, fearful of the answer.

"I hung. In my dream I didn't die, of course, but I was being led to the gallows when it ended. You were in the crowd, and I could tell from your face that you believed I was a murderer. *Do* you think I killed her, Fiona? My worst nightmare is that I'll hang and you'll forever wonder if I didn't really do it." Beau lifted Fiona off his lap and onto the cot so that he could stand.

He turned to face her and she reached out to take his hand. "Beau, I know you didn't kill her. I believe you."

"But if I die for this, if no other evidence comes forward to disprove my guilt, you may—over time—wonder. That's what hurts the most."

Fiona sighed and stood too. "You needn't worry about that. Beau, I've never seen you like this and it worries me. I'm going to do everything I can—"

"What do you mean? What can you do?" he said harshly.

"Not that," Fiona said, laying a calming hand on his arm. "Don't worry. Please. I didn't mean anything by that. I only meant that I'll be praying very hard and getting my parents to call in every favor owed to them."

Beau shook his head. "There's nothing more anyone can do. The evidence is too hard and fast against me. The fired gun in my pocket. The type of bullet in her head. Not one shard from the shattered vase found, and no bullet lodged in the wall. Motive? An old, unresolved lover's spat, they're saying. My one regret, if I hang for this, is that I *didn't* kill her."

"You'll be released. I know you will."

Her hand was still on his arm and he looked at it now, as if noticing it for the first time. He took her hand in his and pulled her into his arms for a tight, breath-stealing hug.

"My one regret will be that I might never make love to you, my dearest love," he whispered into her hair.

"Don't," she murmured, and they kissed again, Beau's mouth devouring and relentless. He drank of her essence as if it was the last time, and salty tears fell from both their eyes.

***

Anna still wasn't budging about letting Fiona go by herself, so they finally agreed that Anna would peddle herbs across the street from the pub while Fiona worked inside. The plan didn't make Anna happy, though, and she swore to Fiona that this one night was absolutely the only one she'd agree to. For additional protection from the drunken thugs bound to veer her way, they had bribed Anna's mother into coming along by offering a gift of the same cream that Leila had tried. The cream almost convinced her, but it was Fiona's tears and dire predictions about Beau's future that finally did.

"There, there, deary. Stop crying. We won't let nothing happen to Lord Albert if we can help it," Mrs. Stiles had said, patting Fiona's shoulder.

Fiona sniffed loudly. "Thank you, Mrs. Stiles. And you needn't worry. You'll see me through the windows. How's this? If I walk past and pull on my hat brim it means I'm in trouble and you need to bring the constable. Does that suit?"

It was agreed upon.

***

Fiona sauntered into the bar at the appointed time and was surprised to see someone else behind the bar—a man with deep-set eyes and a scowl.

Fiona adopted what she thought was a boyish pose: elbows on a chair back and one foot on the chair rung. She remembered to deepen her voice. "Excuse me, sir. The lady yesterday told me to come back today and she'd put me to work. Is she here?"

The man eyed her skeptically. "She's in the back."

Fiona turned to go through the designated door, but the man stopped her with a grunt. "'Old up. Wait 'ere."

"Yes, sir, but she wanted me to be on time. What if she thinks I'm late?" Fiona tried to make her voice a little whiny. She must have succeeded because the man scowled and answered her with a jabbing finger, indicating that she should wait on one of the stools and keep her mouth shut.

Fiona sat, wondering how she'd get any information if she wasn't allowed free access to the place. Was this man going to be watching her all night? She nervously bit on a thumbnail, which might have looked the part but wasn't an act. After five long minutes, Leila emerged.

"So yer mum approved, did she? Well, let's see 'ow good you are. You're going to 'ave to work 'ard if you're goin' to last 'ere. Start by scattering a fresh layer of sawdust on the floor. The bin of sawdust is in the back, on the left," she said, pointing the way.

Fiona slid off her stool. "Yes, ma'am."

The man glared coldly at her as she passed him. "If you want to collect your wages, you'd best step lively," he growled. "If I see you slackin' off I'll throw you out the door meself."

"Yes, sir."

Fiona made a quick exit into the back room. She glanced around hopefully, but felt an immediate sense of disappointment. There was the large bin of sawdust, with a dusty ladle and bucket on top of it. On the opposite side of the room were barrels and barrels of what she assumed must be ale. Shelves covered an entire wall; one shelf held dusty wine bottles; three shelves were crammed with gin bottles; the rest of the shelves contained an odd assortment of cleansing powder, tools, rat poison, holiday decorations, a broken dartboard with a cluster of rusty darts stuck in it, two battered serving pans, exiled from the kitchen, and an array of old newspapers. Nothing to take note of; everything fit the description of what a typical pub might have in its storeroom.

Fiona ladled sawdust into the bucket and carried it back to the main room. She grabbed a handful at a time and scattered it over the floor, making sure to cover the areas that were still damp from last night's spilled ale. She didn't look too closely at a puddle that looked like sick, but quickly covered it with averted eyes.

Fortunately, the grouchy man was too busy talking to Leila to notice Fiona. She inched closer to them, hoping to hear their conversation, and was surprised to find that she was the topic.

"Let it go, Lester. I've needed 'elp ever since tha' rotter Ollie left. Besides, 'e 'as the face of an angel," Leila was saying.

"Riiiiight. 'E's a real angel, 'e is," Lester scoffed, adding sarcastically, "I've an idea. Next time you need 'elp, 'ow about I go to Bow Street and ask for a recommendation? At least then we'd *know* we 'ad a snitch on our 'ands. Do you even know 'is name?"

"'E's too sweet-faced to be a snitch. Look, if you're so worrit, you 'ave my permission to put the fear o' God in 'im—after 'is mum's gotten used to the steady pay and won't let 'im quit."

"I don't want that 'assle, Leila. 'E's yer problem. I've got me own problems to worry abou'."

"Witchell still pesterin' you?"

"'E left town."

"The boys'll be 'appy to 'ear that. They can 'ave a bit o' fun tonight."

Before responding, Lester glanced at Fiona. Unfortunately, he caught her staring.

"What're you gawkin' at?" he snarled, standing and taking a step toward her.

"I'm sorry, sir. I heard you talking about me," Fiona answered honestly. She reached into her bucket and scattered another handful of sawdust, willing Lester to resume ignoring her.

He glared, but sat back down—much to her relief.

After another trip to the back to refill the bucket and another few minutes scattering sawdust, Fiona was finished. Luckily, Lester had left.

"Ma'am, what do you want me to do now?" she asked Leila.

"'Ave a seat for a minute, deary," Leila said, pointing to one of the wooden stools that lined the bar.

Fiona did as she was told, puzzled.

"You might well be wonderin' because it won't be often I ask you to sit, if ever. We 'aven't been properly introduced. You can call me Mrs. Whitehead and I'll call you—?"

"Tom, ma'am."

"Tom. Yer last name?"

"Stiles, ma'am." Fiona said a silent prayer that Anna's mother wouldn't hear how her son's name was being used.

"Well, Tom, a few rules. They're easy so I'm sure a smart lad such as yerself will remember 'em. First off, you answer to both me and Mr. 'Emmings. That's the gent I was talking to a few minutes ago. As long as you do what we tell you, you'll 'ave a job; otherwise, yer out. It's that simple, love."

Fiona nodded, but Leila wasn't finished.

"Yer also not to go tellin' tales about anythin' you 'ear in 'ere. Whatever you 'ear stays in 'ere, got it? If yer mum or cousin asks 'ow yer day went, yer ta simply say 'fine' or 'bad'—or whatever single word you want to give—and let it go at that. Understand?" For the first time, Fiona didn't hear an undercurrent of amusement in Leila's voice.

She nodded.

"Good. 'Cause if it ever gets back to us that yer a blabbermouth, Mr. 'Emmings will kick yer arse to the end of St. Giles Street and back, and you won't 'ave a job no more."

Fiona nodded again, but when it seemed that Leila was expecting more she said quickly, "Yes, ma'am."

"I'm glad we understand each other." Leila tossed her a grubby, damp rag from under the bar. "Now take this and wipe down them tables. We open whenever the first drunk walks through that door."

Three hours later Fiona was sure that she'd discovered Hell. Her bottom had been pinched twice by a tipsy old lady with no teeth and badly thinning hair, a mean-faced young man had thrown a dart at her back, and she'd been grabbed by her jacket and dangled an inch off the ground by a large man with onion breath, who'd claimed she had bumped him with her elbow to be cheeky. Luckily, Leila had witnessed the whole thing and rescued her handily.

The torture would have been worth it if she had learned something—*anything*—worth remembering. The only glimmer of a clue was a name—Witchell. Who was he, and why did he give Lester a hard time?

"Stiles!"

Fiona recognized Lester's voice and, with a sinking heart, she turned from her job of mopping up a spilled tankard of ale. She was surprised to see two men sitting at the bar in front of Lester, avidly staring at her. As she started to walk closer to hear what it was Lester wanted he waved her away and leaned over the bar to talk to the smallest of the two men.

A few minutes later she heard her name again, this time at close range. Hating that she visibly started, she turned and saw one of Lester's cronies standing at her elbow, practically eye to eye with her since he was so short. He regarded her insolently, a cruel smile twisting his thin lips, and Fiona wondered if something was wrong.

"Yer awful pretty for a lad," he finally said.

Fiona didn't answer. She was suddenly grateful for the pinching hag, the dart thrower, the man with bad breath, and all the rest of the teeming crowd. This was one man she would not want to find herself alone with.

"Lester wants you to fetch him some gin from the back," the short man said.

Fiona glanced around at Lester. He caught her eye and jerked a thumb in the direction of the back room, scowling.

"Yes, sir." She wished she wasn't so far away from the windows. This might be a good time to pull on her hat brim. Of course, she had nothing that would help to acquit Beau yet.

She had to hope that her worry stemmed from nerves, so she made a beeline for the storeroom, breathing a sigh of relief when Shorty didn't follow her. When she got there she practically ran to the gin shelves. She was determined to get back out into the crowded main room in under a minute. Her hands were both enclosed around the necks of gin bottles when she heard a sound that froze her movements. The storeroom door had closed, and in that second of realization Fiona wondered if she had made a fatal mistake.

The next second she didn't have the ability to think anything because she was surrounded. One man removed the gin bottles from her hands, another knocked her hat off her head, and a third wheeled her around. His handling of her was so fast and rough that her auburn locks swirled around her face before settling in a mussed cloud on her shoulders.

The man who'd spun her was Lester. The one putting the gin bottles away was the taller of Lester's two friends, and the one who had knocked off her hat was Shorty. Heart beating almost out of her chest, Fiona met Lester's narrow-eyed glare. "I can see n-now that this was absolute folly on my part. You see, it was a dare and I stupidly accepted it," she said, trying to laugh. It came out as a warbled squeak. If they would only take a few steps back, so that she could breathe properly, she might be able to think her way out of this frightful mess.

"You expect me to believe this was a dare, *Miss Fairmont*?" When Fiona gasped Lester gave an ugly laugh and continued, "We may not 'old titles 'ere in Seven Dials, but that don't mean we're stupid. Why're you 'ere?"

Fiona took a step backward and bumped into shelves. Gin bottles rattled and danced. "I told you. I *am* here on a dare."

"She's 'ere on a dare." Lester's mocking tone boded ill.

Regardless, his attack took her by surprise. Faster than she would have believed possible for such a stocky man, his hand shot out and slapped her hard, knocking her into the serving pans. They clattered noisily as they fell to the floor.

Fiona steadied herself against a barrel of ale, one hand held to her stinging cheek. The slap might have forced tears into her eyes, but she wasn't going to give Lester the satisfaction of seeing her cry outright. She took a shaky breath, wondering if she could force enough air into her lungs for a respectable scream. Would Anna and her mother hear a scream from here?

"Why're you 'ere?" Lester repeated grimly.

It was time to tell the truth. "I hoped to discover something that would help to acquit Beau—Lord Albert," Fiona said, folding her arms protectively in front of her stomach when she saw Lester's fists clench. "He wondered if Leila was trying to avenge Jack, since he was the one who killed him."

Lester considered her a moment, his eyes narrowing. One of the other men—the short one—started to speak, but Lester held up his hand warningly. Finally he spoke, and his words were stated matter-of-factly, belying their nastiness.

"You'll tell 'im that 'e's barkin' up the wrong tree. We know 'e killed Jack in self-defense or 'e'd of been dead months ago—not that Leila will mind seein' 'im swing for this other murder. Another thing: I'd think twice, if I was you, before riskin' that pretty neck agin. Another man might not be so nice as me and, besides, what're you riskin' it for? A bloke who's guilty? Think on it, love, and don't let yer lovey-dovey feelin's blind you from the truth. Yer fiancé was still up Daphne Tarkington's skirt, prob'ly right up 'til 'e killed her."

Fiona didn't answer. Silence seemed the safest option at the moment.

"To show you exactly 'ow nice I am, I'm goin' to let you walk outta 'ere in one piece. To return tha favor, you'll give yer intended a message: that me and Leila will see 'im outside Newgate on 'anging day. Got it, love?" Lester gestured for Fiona to walk past him to the door.

He was letting her go? Fiona blinked back tears of relief. She took a few steps toward the door but Shorty blocked her way, roughly grabbing her shoulder. "You were asked a question. Answer it," he ordered.

She stepped back, pulling away from his grasp. "I'll give Lord Albert Mr. Hemmings' message," she said neutrally.

But he continued to stand between her and the door, an ugly smile drifting over his face. "Count yerself lucky it's not me callin' the shots. I would'na let you go so easy."

Fiona focused her gaze on the door and stepped around the short bully. She half expected him to stop her again but he didn't, and she unlocked the door with shaking hands.

Leila gasped in surprise as Fiona walked by the noisy bar with her hair trailing down her back. "'Ey now! What's this?" she yelled, but Fiona didn't stop to answer. If anything, the question made her break into a run.

Darting outside, hair flying, she dodged an inebriated man as he crossed the street on his way to Leila's establishment. She flagged Anna and her mother, indicating that they should follow her quickly. Mrs. Stiles snatched a bottle of willow bark tincture back from an old man, just as he was sniffing it, and tossed it into the basket that Anna held open after hastily corking it.

Once out of sight of the pub, Fiona leaned against a storefront, gasping for breath.

"What happened, miss?" Anna exclaimed, catching up to her.

Fiona shook her head. "Later, Anna. Let's get home first." She pressed her lips together, determined not to cry.

"Oh, dear. Oh, dear. What's happened?" Mrs. Stiles asked.

Fiona took Anna's hand and pulled her in the direction of home. "Let's go. Quickly." They passed another pub three blocks from St. Giles and the light from inside illuminated Fiona's face.

Anna gasped. "Your face, miss!"

But Fiona was unwilling to give explanations on the streets of Seven Dials so they continued on in silence. Except for Anna's mother, who muttered, "Dear me," every few steps.

***

A few hours later, fresh out of a bath and tucked in bed with a book, Fiona heard Anna's familiar three-raps knock.

"Come in," she called.

Anna put a tray of steaming hot chocolate on Fiona's bedside table before speaking. "Lord Albert will see that bruise and wonder," she said worriedly, staring at the purplish marks on Fiona's cheek. There were four distinct lines representing each of Lester Hemmings' fingers.

Fiona blew on her chocolate and took a small sip before answering. "I know. The leopard's bane poultice didn't work very well. I needed Henry's arnica remedy," she said dully. "I could lie and tell Beau I fell, but it's rather obviously a handprint. Besides, we've promised to always tell each other the truth." She took another sip. "I'll make a full confession, but I wish it contained something valuable. I wish I'd heard something that could help him. The name 'Witchell' and ..." her voice trailed off and she frowned. While she'd bathed, she'd had the uncomfortable feeling that there was something important she had missed. But what was it? Nothing was coming to mind.

"He'll insist on my dismissal, but may I ask you for a reference, miss?" Anna asked tearfully, distracting Fiona from her thoughts.

She brought her cup crashing down on its saucer, her frown deepening. "You *won't* be dismissed, Anna. This was all my doing. You were the forced accomplice. Please don't say another word about it."

"I deserve dismissal. I should have stopped you," Anna insisted, her brimming eyes overflowing.

"Anna, you're not my mother. I was going to follow through with my plan, with or without you. Short of locking me up, no one could have stopped me." Fiona pulled a handkerchief out from under her pillow and pushed it into Anna's hand. "It's clean."

"But Tom's clothes—"

"I would've gotten clothes elsewhere if you hadn't helped. I was determined to do this, Anna. I was sure—" Fiona broke off, making an impatient noise. "Your position is safe, Anna. Now shoo and get some sleep."

Fiona downed the rest of her chocolate in one gulp and put it on her bedside table, then primed her pillows with a few determined fluffs and settled her head in the perfect spot she'd made, giving Anna a look as if to say, *you're still here?*

Anna took the hint and left, taking the tray with her. The second the door closed, Fiona sighed loudly. "What am I missing? Something—" she murmured, worrying the coverlet with restless hands. She stared at the ceiling for a long while before a light sleep finally claimed her.

At five fifteen in the morning, Fiona sat bolt upright in bed and muttered, "The short one." She kicked off her covers and rang for Anna on the way to her writing desk.

Anna appeared within minutes, sure that Fiona had revisited the St. Giles incident in a nightmare. Instead she found Fiona at the writing desk, calmly folding and sealing a slip of parchment.

"Anna, have Morton take this to Mr. Shaw immediately, and tell him to wait for an answer. Then come back and help me dress. I'm hoping Mr. Shaw can see me first thing." She handed Anna the letter.

Round-eyed, Anna took it. "What is it, miss?"

"I put a few bits of information together, and I'm hoping they'll lead to Beau's acquittal. Say a prayer that this will be the answer, Anna. Pray very hard." Fiona said her own silent prayer that this would be the last day she'd have to go anywhere near Newgate Prison.

18.

Beau slept soundly, exhausted. The forced idleness and malnutrition of Newgate had sapped his strength worse than a match at Jackson's did. He awoke now only because the turnkey was roughly shaking his shoulder.

"Wake up. You've been acquitted," the man growled.

Beau sat up so quickly that the room spun. He dropped his head into his hands, willing the room to stop moving.

"Acquitted?" The word got caught in the phlegm that coated his throat. He cleared his throat loudly and got to his feet, face to face now with the impassive turnkey.

"Acquitted?" This time it was a question that demanded an answer.

"That's right. I'm here to lead you out."

It didn't matter that there was no congratulatory slap on the back, no handshake, not even a glimmer of a smile. Beau's exultation was enough for them both.

He pulled on his boots and grabbed his overcoat from the bottom of the bed, then followed the turnkey out, the grin on his face immutable at that particular moment. He didn't ask the turnkey a single question, knowing that the answers would be unsatisfactory. Men who made their living by keeping criminals locked in cages had generally lost the capacity for empathy. Now that he was free, Beau felt more pity than anger toward them.

Beau cleared his throat again, spitting the last of the sticky saliva from his mouth, sure that he'd never take Castlewood's well of deliciously cold water for granted again. Clean water. Amazing how a few days in prison, with the threat of hanging looming over one's head, changes one's perspective. This ordeal had the potential to leave scars but Beau told himself that he wouldn't let that happen.

Instead, he'd doubly appreciate all the wonders in his life, starting with beautiful Fiona. Was she here at Newgate, waiting for him to be released?

The turnkey stopped where the hall dead-ended in front of a door that had two locked bolts. He searched his ring of keys, finding one and fitting it—only to discover it was the wrong key. He was one of the newer turnkeys, and his keys were not yet the familiar objects they would become to him. He force-fitted another to no avail.

Beau wanted to shout, *Hurry*. He felt the sort of impatience he remembered feeling on Christmas morning as a boy, when his father insisted on gathering the family for a prayer before stockings could be ransacked. Clenching his jaw, he watched as the turnkey found one match, then repeated his laborious search for the second key.

The knowledge that he would—in a matter of minutes—be riding away from this place and breathing fresh air again sustained Beau as he waited for the turnkey to finish his clumsy search for keys. Now that he was free he realized exactly how much hope he had given up; how close to certain he had been that he would be put to a hideous and wrongful death.

Through the door there was another short hallway, this one leading to another door with a standard doorknob. They stopped at it and the turnkey knocked.

"Come in," a cheery voice boomed from the inside. The turnkey turned the knob and pushed the door open, but then stepped out of the way and signaled for Beau to go in without him.

As Beau stepped into a tastefully decorated drawing room he heard a gasp, and in the next second Fiona flung herself into his arms, her breath catching on a sob.

"Beau. Oh, Beau. Beau," she said, her voice quavering.

He was still dazed from sleep and this new turn of events. He held her tightly and kissed the top of her head, clearing a throat that was now clogged with emotion. "What precipitated my release?" he finally asked, looking up to see his lawyer and Mr. Oxley, the man who'd taken his belongings when he'd first been brought to Newgate.

"Lord Albert, I'll let your beautiful fiancée fill you in on all the details. Your possessions are in that sack—minus the pistol. That was sent to another location and will be returned to you by tomorrow," Mr. Oxley said, pointing to a burlap sack that lay conspicuously on the red wool armchair.

Mr. Shaw motioned them toward the door. "Thank you, Mr. Oxley. My lord, your carriage awaits you outside."

Beau grabbed his belongings and led Fiona forward. "Goodbye, Mr. Oxley. Think of me—next time you arrest someone who says they're innocent."

Oxley's answer was a snort of laughter.

Beau didn't want to spend one more second than he had to at Newgate Prison but he paused in the doorway. "No, I'm dead serious."

Seeing that Beau expected an answer, Mr. Oxley gave a small bow. "I'll take your advice under consideration, Lord Albert."

Beau closed the door but didn't follow Fiona and Mr. Shaw down the steps. He stood, breathing in several deep breaths of air. "It might be a bit sooty, but this is the best air I've ever smelled. I'll never take fresh air for granted again."

He joined Fiona and Mr. Shaw next to his carriage, stroking the silky noses of his matched grays.

"I'll never take *life* for granted again."

"My lord, we're so grateful," Mr. Shaw said. "And just about now your parents should be getting my note. They'll be so relieved."

"What did it, Shaw? Did they find the footmen?" Beau asked.

"That's a story I'll let Miss Fairmont relay to you. If you'll excuse me, my lord, I have business in the next block over."

Beau looked from his lawyer to Fiona in amusement, but the smile dropped off his face when he noticed that Fiona was shivering in the unseasonably cool September air. He bundled her into his carriage after a quick farewell to Mr.

Shaw and stepped in after her, pulling her into the crook of his arm after cracking open the carriage window.

"I have a need for fresh air that cannot be denied, but I'll keep you warm."

"I won't be cold next to you." Fiona snuggled closer and looked up into his unshaven face and sleep-ridden eyes, apparently not caring that he smelled of sweat, unwashed clothes and dirty hair.

"I didn't even take the time to wash my face," he said apologetically, running his free hand over his eyes to clear them of sleep. "First thing I'm going to do is wash the stench of Newgate off me. And the second thing—" He tilted her chin up so that he could look into her eyes, but they dropped to her cheek and he frowned. "Is that a bruise?" he asked, gently rubbing a finger over it.

"Yes."

Beau waited, eyebrows raised, for her to continue. When she didn't, he prompted, "And you got it—?"

Fiona took a deep breath and gave Beau a tight smile. "First, I must remind you that I love you dearly, and it was my love for you that prompted me to break my promise."

"You contacted Jack's friends."

The knowledge that one of them had given Fiona a bruise made his stomach churn in anger. "Is that why I've been released?" he asked, cutting to the heart of the matter.

"Yes, and it's quite a tale, which is why Mr. Shaw and Mr. Oxley left it for me to tell. They both insist that you'll be angry, but I hope not. Beau, prove to me that you are far more broad-minded than either one of them," Fiona said, gazing anxiously into his eyes.

He reassured her with a smile, but it wasn't convincing. Not with that loathsome bruise staring him in the face. "Let's hear it."

"I dressed as a boy and peddled my potions—with Anna—at the Hemmings' public house and, as luck would have it, Leila Whitehead Hemmings needed a bar boy and hired me on the spot. I think I made a rather lovable lad because she seemed quite taken with me."

Beau stroked back a piece of her hair. "You're lovable in any form. Go on."

"Her brother, on the other hand, was suspicious of me from the start. At first because I was an unknown, but later he—or one of his cronies—figured out who I was. He got me alone by asking me to bring gin from the storeroom in the back. Wait, Beau! Don't look like that; hear me out," Fiona urged.

Beau gritted his teeth, unbearable possibilities parading across his imagination. "Go on," he said grimly.

She continued, squeezing his hand as she spoke. "He asked me why I was there, and when I told him it was on a dare he slapped me."

"I'll see him hang! I'll taunt him even as the noose is being placed," Beau growled.

"Wait, Beau. He didn't touch me again after that because then I told the truth, that I was there for any sort of information, and that you wondered if they had framed you because you'd killed Jack. Of course, I didn't get anything at all from Lester Hemmings except assurances that he'd gladly see *you* hang, and that you were guilty."

Beau's eyes narrowed, but he nodded for Fiona to continue.

"He let me leave then, with instructions to give you that very message, but I didn't *want* to leave. I still had *nothing* of substance to help you, or so I thought. At the same time, I had a horrible feeling that I was missing something vital. Can you guess what that something was, Beau?"

"This happened last night?" When Fiona nodded, he asked, "You left that pub without proof of my innocence?" She nodded again.

After a moment's thought, Beau said, "Just tell me, dearest. I'll never guess."

"Early the next morning I woke up remembering something! I remembered your story about the short footman at Daphne Tarkington's. Beau, one of the men with Lester *was the shortest man I've ever seen.*"

Beau scowled. "*With* Lester? What do you mean?"

"In the back room, when he confronted me."

"Exactly how many men were there?" Beau ground out.

"Two, other than Lester. I think it was one of them that recognized me and let on to Lester that I wasn't a boy. Until they came along, Lester was more unfriendly than suspicious. He—"

"Let me see if I understand this correctly. You were in the back room of a bar on St. Giles street with three hostile men?" Beau's anger was palpable.

"They let me go! Yes, I got slapped but it was nothing. Just a little bruise," Fiona snapped, pushing away from Beau and turning so that she could face him.

"Do you understand now why I asked for your promise? Things could have gone much worse. *Much worse.*" Beau emphasized the last words with a pointed finger, getting angrier by the moment since Fiona showed no contrition.

"Anna was outside the bar with her mother and would have heard me scream."

"Do you really believe that?" Beau shouted.

"I—don't shout at me! If it weren't for me, you'd still be in Newgate." She was every bit as angry as he was now.

"And if it weren't that you have some sort of transcendent guardian angel, you'd be raped and beaten—perhaps dead. And I'd be in Newgate, bearing the dreadful news as I awaited my hanging!"

"Oh, please," Fiona scoffed.

"You might have been killed, goddammit. At the very least acknowledge that you know that." Beau put his hand to his forehead and wasn't surprised by its clamminess. This story had almost undone him. The reckless stupidity of what she had done was frightful.

"Oh course, I know it. Do you think I'm an idiot? I was terrified, but I did it anyway because I love you. I wanted to see you freed from prison. But if you're going to be unforgiving and ungrateful then I want you to take me home." Her words started out angry but ended on a half sob.

They also served to deflate Beau's anger. He exhaled deeply and watched as Fiona pulled her handkerchief out of her pelisse pocket and twisted it without mercy, while her beautiful throat convulsively swallowed the tears back. She stared out the open window, her eyes filled with hurt, and Beau's heart melted.

He gently pulled her chin around so that he could look into those luminous green pools that had so effectively captured him, heart and soul. "Where will I take you if I'm grateful?" he asked softly, his dark eyes no longer angry, his lips relaxed and upturned.

Fiona stared, her eyes growing darker as her pupils expanded. Her lips parted and one eyebrow shifted upward, as if she was going to speak, but then she slowly shook her head. Finally, she said, "To *our* home."

Beau's groin clenched. She was so beautiful and—amazingly—she had freed him from Newgate Prison and a hideous fate. Reaching out a finger to stroke her cheek, he whispered, "You're my Joan of Arc ... my heroine ... my Fiona."

She smiled then, a smile full of promises—good promises worth keeping. "I don't want to let you out of my sight."

"Perfect," he said, lowering his head to give her a kiss. He pulled her back into his arms, deepening the kiss in response to her sigh of satisfaction. He tasted the salt from her tears and the remnants of tea taken with Shaw and Oxley. The feel of her delicate frame against his body made him ache with joy. He was free. Unfettered from the claustrophobic stone walls and the prying ears of the turnkeys, he was free to kiss his future wife with abandon; to make love to her, if not now, then in eight days' time after their wedding. Eight days ...

Beau pulled away and took a deep, steadying breath. "Fiona, in eight days you'll be mine. Eight *long* days," he repeated, closing his eyes and leaning his head on the carriage seat. "Each one will feel like a year, I want you that desperately."

Fiona leaned forward to gently kiss his eyelids. "I've never been a stickler for traditions," she whispered. Beau opened his eyes and gave her a puzzled smile as she continued, "In my heart I'm yours already; in eight days time society can catch up to us."

The carriage rolled to a stop and Beau heard his footman's approaching steps. He took Fiona's hand and brought it to his lips. "And I'm yours," he said, pressing another kiss on top of the first.

***

Beau grunted with pleasure as Fiona scrubbed his scalp. "I'm pleasantly surprised that I didn't get lice." He leaned forward so that she could pour a pitcher of fresh water over his head to rinse it, tossing back clean hair a minute later.

"You soaked me!" Fiona laughed, reaching into Beau's tub to splash him back.

He deftly grabbed her wrist. "That's not soaked, my love." With his free hand he showed her what soaked really meant.

"You fiend!" Fiona shrieked, boldly splashing back. In two minutes' time the bath water was mostly on the floor or on Fiona, who had fared worse than Beau since she had clothes on. Not that it mattered. They had ordered a new bath, one they could share.

"Truce?" Beau suggested, laughing as Fiona wrung out her skirt over his naked chest.

"Never!" she threatened playfully.

Smithers chose that moment to knock. He entered, followed by two footmen who each carried a large vat of hot water.

Beau climbed out of the tub, wrapping a towel around his waist. He guided Fiona behind his dressing screen and helped her peel out of her wet dress while the footmen made quick work with the fresh tub. Down to her pantalettes and camisole, the wet fabrics clinging to every curve, she took his breath away.

"Do you want me to fetch a mop, sir?" he heard Smithers ask. Glancing around the edge of the screen, he saw that Smithers was eyeing the sodden floor disparagingly and attempting to sop up the mess with a towel.

"No. Just leave the towel over it."

"Will there be anything else, sir?"

"No, Smithers."

He watched the footmen follow Smithers out, one of them shutting his door quietly, and then he turned back to the prized task of helping Fiona out of her wet clothes.

But she had already removed them. In fact, she was already halfway to the steaming water, the delectable curves of her trim waist and bare bottom making him groan out loud.

She leaned down to stir in lavender oil with her fingers. "It's too hot," she murmured.

"It's perfect," Beau whispered appreciatively. He stepped behind her and wrapped her in his arms, one hand gently cupping a breast, the other hand splayed on her stomach as he nuzzled her neck. He could feel her arch into his hands as she took a deep breath.

She whispered his name, her breath growing ragged as he gently pinched her nipple. Breaking free and turning to face him, she stood on tiptoes and brought her lips up to meet his, her hands pushing his towel down to the floor.

They kissed, sweetly at first, but then with bruising intensity. Beau was keenly aware that his stiff member was pressed between them, impassioned and nudging.

Fiona pulled away from the kiss and turned her head to whisper in his ear. "Beau?"

"Mmmm?" he answered, almost insensate from her delicious taste and the agony in his loins.

In response, she stepped into the tub and pulled him in after her. She gently pushed on his shoulders, to make him sit down in the warm water—it had cooled to the perfect temperature—and settled herself on top of him. Her knees straddled his thighs and her perfectly shaped bottom fit into the cradle of his hands. He slid one hand across the top of her thigh, and felt the involuntary clench of her buttock when his hand settled on top of her silky mound of hair. He held her there, lightly squeezed between his hands, until the pressure had her writhing with desire.

But then she shifted and was pressing against him, rubbing herself slowly up and down his shaft until he groaned in pleasure.

His hands slid along her tiny waist and cupped her breasts, providing friction on each of her up and down movements until her breath came in gasps and her grip on his shoulders marked him.

"*Oh, Beau.*"

He understood. His hands moved again to her bottom and he held her poised over him for a moment, before settling her ravishing femininity onto him, her sweet tightness surrounding the top of his shaft. Slowly, he thrust his hips upward, pushing into her a little more, stopping only because he felt her legs stiffen.

But before he could express concern she sank down, enveloping him completely in her softness. She felt wonderful. He cried out at the rightness of it.

"Let's stay like this, still for a moment," she whispered, out of breath. He could feel little jolts of energy shooting through her that triggered similar jolts in him.

They kissed, gently, sweetly, as if they were back in the lilac garden exploring each other's mouths for the first time. But then Fiona began to move rhythmically up and down, slowly at first. Beau rounded his back with the third downward stroke, deepening the penetration and making Fiona cry out in pleasure, and then Fiona moved fast and hard, meeting each of his small upward thrusts with a groan.

She arched her back so that one nipple brushed Beau's lips. He licked the hard nub, then pulled it into his mouth to suckle it, relishing her scream of completion, groaning as he pumped his pleasure deep within her.

***

Fiona woke up with her arm thrown over Beau's chest and her cheek against his shoulder. They were in his massive four-poster bed, their damp towels in a heap on the floor. Beau was still asleep, lying peacefully on his back, and Fiona inventoried every inch of his sleeping face. Long lashes dusted his cheekbones; his sensual lips, slightly parted, called up memories from the night before that warmed her deep inside.

She wanted to make love again—even after they had made love once more in front of the fire and twice more in bed—and her unquenchable desire caused an unexpected memory to pop up, making her smile. In it, she was telling Felicity that the man she married would have to accept that her plants came first. Well, her priorities had certainly shifted. Her green darlings would always have a place in her heart, but not first place. In fact, at that very moment her plants were at the mercy of Felicity's nonchalance—if her sister was even bothering to follow the hastily scribbled instructions she had sent over with the note to her mother.

Beau took a deep breath, obviously sound asleep, and Fiona decided it was time to wake him up. She slid her hand down his chest and across his stomach, smiling when he made one of those sounds that cannot be mistaken for anything other than unmitigated pleasure. His lips smiled, and he slowly opened eyes that were happy and desirous at the same time.

He turned to face her. "I'm going to send word 'round to your family not to expect you home today. I cannot let you go until tomorrow. This day is for us, and no one will be allowed to intrude."

"I imagine my mother is already shocked about yesterday's note. One more won't trouble her too much." Beau's fingers were drawing light circles on her lower back, making her shiver with pleasure.

He momentarily stopped the massage to reach the bell cord. "I'm ordering another bath and a huge breakfast. Even after last night's feast, I'm starving after all that prison food." He rolled on top of her and cradled her between his arms. His hair—a wild, black mop due to its recent washing—fell into his face, giving him the appearance of a satyr and causing Fiona to laugh.

"What?" he asked, looking lovably perplexed.

"Your hair is an untamed, glorious mane. I love it and hope our children inherit it," she replied, reaching up to plant a soft kiss on his stubbly chin. He still hadn't shaved, but the hair had grown so long that it wasn't prickly.

"Let's have ten children—five of each. They can all have *your* hair, as far as I'm concerned," Beau teased, nuzzling her neck with his lips and downy jaw.

His lips were magical. They sent thrills down her spine even when they were focused on her toes. She'd found out that interesting fact last night. His abilities were truly remarkable.

Smithers chose that moment to knock, and Beau looked up from Fiona's neck long enough to shout, "Come in." He told Smithers the morning plans, adding, "You'll be happy to hear that I plan to let you shave me as well." Yesterday's disappointment at not being able to accomplish that task had not been well hidden on Smithers' part.

"Very well, sir."

The door had almost closed when Beau called him back. "Smithers? Bring the bath and breakfast in an hour." After Smithers had left, he reflected, "That should give me just enough time to kiss every inch of you." And he set out to do just that.

***

Seven days later

"With this ring, I thee wed," Beau repeated, slipping the ring onto Fiona's finger. Following the minister's instructions, he lifted her veil and gave her their first kiss as man and wife.

It was a chaste kiss that ended in applause, and Fiona and Beau turned, smiling into the exhilarated faces of their family and closest friends.

"Bravo, son," old Lord Beaumont wheezed. Lady Margaret, sitting beside him, concurred with nods and brimming eyes, dabbing her eyes frequently with her handkerchief.

Fiona's mother was busy wiping a sopping wet face, for her eyes had overflowed. Her husband, in an attempt to hold his own tears at bay, took up teasing Felicity.

"You'll have a hard time topping your sister's wedding," he whispered "She not only snagged the biggest catch of the decade, but she's already seen him through two nearly fatal experiences. You'll have to marry an exiled French nobleman who escaped Napoleon's prison and survived a shipwreck to beat it."

"I have my work cut out for me," Felicity giggled back. They were headed toward the dining hall, where André had prepared a wedding day feast.

Although the actual ceremony had been small, tomorrow's wedding party promised to be a much larger event, with many invited guests making a two-hour trip from London to attend. All of Castlewood's guest rooms would be full, and both the Aldwinkles and the Hasseltons were accommodating large numbers of guests for tomorrow night, as well. It promised to be the event of the year, since the Prince Regent himself was rumored to be making an appearance.

Felicity watched Beau lean toward her sister and whisper something that lit Fiona's face better than any book had ever done. They were perfect. There was no other word to describe them.

Epilogue

Beau released Anna from her duties with a nod and turned to tie Fiona's sash himself, kissing her neck in the process. "I have a surprise for you."

Fiona's heart drummed double-time at the feel of Beau's lips on her neck. "Is it another bottle of amber oil? I loved the other one so much that I've used it all up."

"Consider it bought, but no. Close your eyes."

Fiona complied as he turned her to face him, then felt a bracelet encircling her wrist.

"Open," Beau instructed.

She did, and saw a delicate sapphire and gold filigree bracelet whose beauty made her breath catch. "Is it your grandmother's? Where did you find it?"

"Yes, the heirloom bracelet has found its way back into the Beaumont family. Witchell found it for me in a pawn shop near the docks." He held her arm up so that candlelight played on the gems, showing off their inner fire.

"Witchell? The thief-taker who arrested Tiny Broderick?"

Beau sat and pulled Fiona onto his lap. "Yes, I find I've befriended Witchell. He's quite a decent man, with many *quite* interesting stories. I told him about the bracelet and gave him a description of the thief, and three weeks later he sent me a letter that he had instructed one Mr. Lodge—a pawn shop owner—to hold the bracelet until I could retrieve it. That was the main reason I traveled to London last week, although I also got my quarterly meeting with Brimley over with early."

Fiona circled her arms around Beau's neck. "I'm forever indebted to wonderful Witchell. He's truly an angel, even though he reminds me of a pirate with his eye patch and his gravelly voice, like he's been shouting orders at sea for decades. Would your mother mind if we invite him to dinner?"

"Not at all! She'll welcome the opportunity to introduce him to my father. They both know that, next to you, he's the one most responsible for my acquittal. I'll invite him."

"But not for next weekend. You remember that we have Henry and Clarissa's wedding to attend." Beau smelled wonderful, as always. Fiona leaned in close and nipped his earlobe, inhaling deeply.

She had a piece of news herself and was trying to work out how best to tell him, but for the moment all she could think about was how much she wanted to kiss him.

So she did, and for several long, delicious moments they both forgot that they had a dinner engagement at the Hassletons. Rupert and his wife were back from their tour of Europe, and Fiona was finally going to meet them.

Beau spoke through their kiss, his voice heavy with desire. "I'll cancel our dinner plans. We can try to see them tomorrow for lunch before they leave for London."

Fiona gave the proposition more consideration than it deserved, but finally pulled away. "No, Lady Amelia deserves better than that." She sighed and tried to stand up, but Beau had her around the waist and wouldn't let go.

"Then we'll be fashionably late," he said, reaching down to slip one hand under her skirt.

It was an excellent compromise.

In the carriage, forty minutes later, Fiona remembered her piece of news. She had thought of presenting it in some unique way, but decided that now was as good a time as any. "Beau, I had a visitor while you were away. Can you guess who?" In the dim light of the carriage she could just make out Beau's eyebrows, furrowing in puzzlement.

"Felicity?"

It was a good guess because he knew how much Fiona had missed her. "No. Care to guess again?"

Beau laughed. "This is quite mysterious. Let's see. Who would make your eyes sparkle with such happiness? Did Donne's ghost give you a personal reading of 'The Flea'?"

Now it was Fiona's turn to laugh. "Clever guess, but no." After pausing a beat, she said, "Dr. Rufus came to visit."

"Your old nemesis? What, has he been converted? Was he asking for advice on herbal potions and homeopathy?"

Fiona smiled. "No, dearest. It's standard practice for a physician to visit a woman who suspects a new life is growing."

For the beat of two seconds Beau pondered her words, but then his jaw dropped open. "Fiona, you're expecting?"

She nodded and laughed. "Your mother guessed it when she ran into Dr. Rufus and hadn't asked for him herself. We've had the hardest time keeping quiet until I could tell you. I haven't even told my mother yet."

Beau placed a hand on Fiona's abdomen with infinite care. "So tiny still. You can't see a trace."

"In another few months you'll see plenty. And I plan to use a midwife. Dr. Rufus and I still do not see eye to eye. He told me to stay away from all herbs, for fear of harming the infant, if you can imagine."

"I can, from him," Beau said, leaning over to plant a kiss on her stomach. "God, I love you."

When he sat back up, Fiona was astounded to see tears in his eyes. She placed a hand along his jaw and turned his face toward hers. "Beau, you're crying?"

"Because I'm so happy, and I don't deserve such happiness. The life I led before I met you was shallow and hedonistic. You've made me a better person, Fiona. Without you I'd be nothing." He took her hand and brought it to his lips.

Fiona turned his hand over so that she could kiss his palm. "And without you I'd be a crusty cynic, old before my time, trying to find satisfaction in plants and research while my heart slowly withered. You made me believe in love, Beau."

They rode the rest of the way in silence, nestled in each other's arms, comfortable in their shared understanding of perfect love.

***

Seven months later Fiona delivered twin boys, the spitting image of their father—or so Lady Margaret said. Sadly, Lord Beaumont died two days after the birth. It was as if the sight of his two grandsons allowed him to finally let go and find peace.

Fiona and Beau named the oldest baby James, after his grandfather. Michael came up with the younger baby's name: Jeremy.

"Why Jeremy?" Beau asked his brother.

"'Cause it sounds good with James," was the response.

And no one argued.

Check www.secondwindpublishing.com for additional titles from Lucy Balch as well as other Romance novels including:

Loving Lydia
Amy De Trempe

A sweet, inspirationally touched romance, set during the regency era. When Lady Lydia, a moral, naive young woman enters society, she is confounded by Lord Alex, a known reprobate rumored to have a dark side. Yet he captures her heart. When Lydia is sucked into his dark world, can he save her and their love?

Hand-Me-Down Bride
Juliet Waldron

Based upon the story of the author's great grandmother, who was a real life mail-order bride. Sophie agrees to marry a wealthy man she's never met--but life has other plans.

A Love Out of Time
Mairead Walpole

Soul-mates, twin flames, "split-aparts"
...philosophers, poets, and priests have pondered their existence and their nature.
Such a love can transcend death, stand the test of time, and make all things possible. Some know the truth, while others hope and dream.

Indian Summer
Dellani Oakes

A unique regency novel of a girl's coming-of-age. The Spanish call it "quinceanera," a girl's 15th birthday. Gabriella Deza, innocent daughter of a nobleman in 1739 St. Augustine, Florida, finds herself caught up in international intrigue and romance far beyond her years.

Love is on The Wind
Valentine's Anthology

The first anthology from Second Wind Authors, and a few new comers. Full of the romantic side of life.

Made in the USA
Charleston, SC
06 February 2010